PRAISE FOR CAR(

'Heart-thumping moments that left me desperate to read more.'

—The Book Review Café

'The very definition of a page-turner.'

—John Marrs

'The tension built up and up . . . I devoured every page.'

—Mel Sherratt

'With her police officer experience, Caroline Mitchell is a thriller writer who knows how to deliver on plot, character, and, most importantly, emotion in any book she writes. I can't wait to read more.'

—My Weekly magazine

THE FAMILY AT NO. 1

ALSO BY CAROLINE MITCHELL

Detective Jennifer Knight Series

Don't Turn Around

Time to Die

The Silent Twin

Detective Ruby Preston Series

Love You to Death

Sleep Tight

Murder Game

Slayton Thrillers

The Midnight Man

The Night Whispers

The Bone House

THE FAMILY AT NO. 1

CAROLINE
MITCHELL

THOMAS & MERCER

Text copyright © 2025 by Caroline Mitchell
All rights reserved.

Published by Thomas & Mercer, Seattle
www.apub.com

Amazon, the Amazon logo, and Thomas & Mercer are trademarks of Amazon.com, Inc., or its affiliates.

EU Product Safety Contact:
Amazon Media EU S. à r.l.
38, avenue John F. Kennedy, L-1855 Luxembourg
amazonpublishing-gpsr@amazon.com

ISBN-13: 9781662524608
eISBN: 9781662524615

Cover design by The Brewster Project
© Richard Nixon / ArcAngel Images; © Volodymyr TVERDOKHLIB / Shutterstock

Printed in the United States of America

*To my family, who remind me
there's a world beyond my laptop.*

What terrors lurk inside the maze of a heart,
that they turn love to spite?

—Unknown

PROLOGUE

ALI

Time passed normally at No. 1 Aspen Hollow. The metal gears of the wall clock in the master bedroom moved at their usual pace. Its batteries were fresh, each beat accurate. But during the last moments of Ali Wilding's life, each second was stretched taut, like an elastic band ready to snap. The faster her heart pumped, the slower the world moved around her.

That morning she had sighed as she slid the cardboard inner of a toilet roll from the stainless-steel ring. With a well-practised hand, she'd dropped it into the silver bathroom bin and replaced it with a fresh roll. Then she'd walked the long corridor of her home, passing the framed monochrome photographs. The Lowry in Salford, the Gherkin in London, the Glasshouse International Centre for Music in Gateshead. All beautiful structures that her husband Bruce had admired enough to hang on their walls. With bemusement she'd wondered how someone with a master's degree in architecture couldn't change a toilet roll or straighten a bathroom hand towel.

Now, as her world was shattered into fragments, every final moment was magnified and stretched. Her senses hyper-aware, she felt every pound of weight of the body pressing her on to the memory foam mattress. Felt every tiny bead of sweat breaking out on her brow. Each strand of hair as it stuck to her face. She even felt the cold shooting sensation of adrenaline flooding her veins. It was not enough to help fight off her attacker. She opened her mouth to scream but her protests were smeared by the feather pillow that she had plumped that morning and placed on the bed. The crash of the bedside lamp echoed long after the shards settled, as time continued to stretch thin.

Their home in Aspen Hollow was picture-perfect. Ali had never been as happy as the day they moved in. But as each day passed, a dark undercurrent had crept closer. She felt it now, closing in upon her as her body gave up its fight. Her consciousness blurred around the edges, her limbs finally becoming still. Such a beautiful place . . . and she'd been proud to be part of it, once. But the community of people she had so desperately tried to impress had known where this was heading all along.

OCTOBER 2025

**For Sale: Five Double-Bedroomed Detached
Family Home
REDUCED**

Luxury Awaits at Aspen Hollow
Discover the epitome of modern luxury in one
of the most coveted plots at Aspen Hollow. This
five-bedroom residence, just a short walk from
the stunning Burton Waters Marina and a seven-
minute drive to the nearby city of Lincoln, offers unparalleled elegance and sophistication.
Surrounded by meticulously landscaped gardens
and framed by a serene woodland backdrop, this
property stands as one of only four exclusive
homes in the area.

Architectural Masterpiece
This architectural gem boasts versatile accommo-
dation spread across two expansive floors. The
ground floor welcomes you with a grand entrance

leading to a spectacular open-plan kitchen and dining area, fitted with the latest high-tech appliances and premium finishes. Bifold doors seamlessly extend the kitchen space into the beautifully manicured garden, creating a perfect blend of indoor and outdoor living. A cosy snug area, a large utility space and a walk-in pantry enhance the functionality and luxury of the home. A generous living room, complete with a large open fire, completes the perfect family space.

Exquisite Bedrooms and Bathrooms
Double stairs ascend to a generous first-floor landing, opening up to five opulent double bedrooms. Three of these bedrooms feature luxurious en-suite facilities, providing ultimate comfort and privacy. The master suite boasts a lavish en-suite with a roll-top bath and integrated Bluetooth speakers, perfect for unwinding in style. At the rear of the property, a unique secondary staircase offers an additional layer of privacy, leading to a secluded en-suite bedroom and a spacious boot room with secondary exit downstairs.

Premium Features and Amenities
- Designer Kitchen: State-of-the-art appliances, custom cabinetry and elegant countertops.
- Smart Home Technology: Integrated systems for lighting and climate control.
- Eco-Friendly Design: Energy-efficient features and sustainable materials throughout.
- Exclusive Location: Just a short stroll from the

vibrant Burton Waters Marina, with its array of shops, restaurants and pubs.

Experience a lifestyle of unparalleled luxury and sophistication in this extraordinary property. Whether you're entertaining guests in the expansive living spaces or enjoying a quiet evening in the serene garden, this home offers the perfect sanctuary for the discerning homeowner. Buy now, and celebrate Christmas in your new home.

CHAPTER 1

If Laura Bradley knew what awaited her, she never would have taken the listing on. But she was too invested in her future to listen to any passing concerns. Selling houses was in her blood. As her father used to say, in his thick Yorkshire accent: 'Look, love, you're not just shifting bricks and mortar, you're selling a dream.' So when the opportunity arose, she never questioned her transfer to the Lincoln branch of Ridgeway Residential. But they had plenty of willing estate agents who would happily take on the big commission. Why bring her in to handle the sale?

The old but comfortable single bed creaked in protest as she leaned back against the headboard and drew up her knees. The pages of her worn journal were dense with scribbles and annotations, and she bowed her head and stared at her own form of hieroglyphics. Dyslexia did her no favours. Her writing was so bad, it was like a language only she could understand. Her wide-framed glasses slid down her nose. She needed a new fitting. She'd lost weight from the stress of the last year, and these days everything seemed too big. Her bedroom lamp cast a shadow over a fresh page as she continued making plans for her new listing. At the top of the page, she wrote: *every house has a story.*

It was her job to find it. She wasn't interested in rehashing the impersonal sales spiel that her colleagues used, or going over old ground. Finding a family their perfect abode felt more like a calling than a job. She would capitalise on the lifestyle that Aspen Hollow had to offer, then matchmake the house with a family who would love every room. She stifled a yawn, blinking as the words blurred. She wrote a little more, her eyelids leaden as she scribbled *waterside leisure activities* and *woodland pursuits*. Sleep laid claim as her chin dipped, her fingers relaxing over her pen. It was not the first time she had dozed off while working in bed. Her ringtone sliced through the silence, making her heart stall.

'Jesus, Cally, you frightened me. I was just dropping off.'

'I'm only Jesus at weekends,' her older sibling laughed. 'Sorry, I didn't mean to wake you.'

'It's OK.' Laura slipped her glasses from her face and rested them on the bedside table. 'What are you up to?'

'The usual,' Cally said cheerfully. 'Watching YouTube. Did you know that when you sleep in a hotel bed, you could be lying where someone died? Happens more often than you'd think – about six hundred people die in English hotels every year.'

'Cally, I'm about to go to sleep. Could you not?'

'It's true!' Her sister chuckled again, clearly in her element. 'They clean it all up, obviously, but you'd never know. That weird stain on the mattress? Probably tea. Or maybe something worse.'

'You're terrible, you know that?'

'Oh, come on. It's fascinating. Imagine the stories these rooms could tell!'

Laura pulled a face. 'I don't know how you watch that stuff. I'd have nightmares for weeks.'

'It's not as scary as moving back in with Mum.'

Laura undid the top two buttons of her cotton pyjamas as a flush rose to her skin. 'It's only temporary. Just a base until I sort myself out.'

'I'm sure she gave you a warm welcome.' Cynicism laced Cally's words. 'How does Shane feel about it?'

Laura grimaced at the mention of her husband's name. 'The same way he feels about everything I do these days – staunch disapproval.'

'It's just a pothole in the road. Things will sort themselves out.'

'It's more than a pothole. It's a ruddy great crater.' Laura glanced around the poky bedroom that she'd grown up in. It still had the same frayed grey curtains, the same discoloured stippled paint on the ceiling. Time had stood still in her old haunt on Burton Road. Gloria, her mother, had made it clear that her stay here was temporary, but now she'd made the break, Laura's pride wouldn't let her return home. What had started out as just another row with her husband had ended with her packing a bag. But Gloria's hospitality didn't extend to her five-year-old grand-daughter, whom she'd deemed 'too noisy' for her liking. Now Laura had to content herself with seeing Esme during evenings and weekends.

'Are you sure about staying there?' Cally's voice was thick with concern. 'She's hardly rolled out the red carpet.'

'She's not that bad.' Laura smiled into the phone. 'And the sale of number one will help us with a deposit for a place of our own.' The generous commission came with the expectation that she sold soon. Even after Ridgeway Residential took their share, she would be left with a tidy sum.

Laura allowed herself a smile. The prospect of so much income from one house was thrilling. She tuned back in to her sister's voice as she replayed a speech that Laura had heard too many times before.

'You should never have accepted that house. I told you at the time. I said, Laura, nothing in life is free. You're better off standing on your own two feet—'

'I know, but it's done now,' Laura interrupted. 'We'll get a place of our own soon.' She wasn't in the mood for another lecture. Shane's parents came from money and had disapproved of . . . no, they'd *hated* Laura from the start. The offer of one of the many properties in their portfolio had seemed like a dream come true. But the house in the Cathedral Quarter had come with a price. Her in-laws had a key and treated the place as their own. Her mother-in-law's interference was the cause of every row Laura and Shane had. It was why Laura had stormed out in the night, vowing not to return until she and Shane could afford a place unconnected to his parents.

She checked the clock on the wall and sighed. So much for having an early night.

'Wait until you see the house.' Laura tactfully changed the subject. 'It's stunning. Buyers won't be able to resist.'

'But didn't you say you're the third or fourth agency to try to flog it? What's that all about?'

'It's just the market, it's been all over the place lately. I'll find it some lovely new owners. Mark my words.' Laura knew little of the previous attempts to sell. Simon Grimshaw, her boss at Ridgeway Residential, had insisted that she approach the listing with 'fresh eyes'.

'You're a grafter,' Cally said, admiration threading her response. 'If anyone can sell it, you can.'

'I will. Look out for me on the 'gram! I'll be posting loads of reels once I get the place looking nice.' The use of social media was another tool in Laura's armoury.

'How's Mum?' Cally's words hung in the air.

'Mum's Mum,' Laura simply said, picking at the frayed bedspread. 'Everything OK with you?' Laura listened as Cally filled her in on her week. Her job in the Louth bank might not be hugely exciting, but she seemed happy enough. As their conversation ended, Laura was unable to hold back another yawn. 'I'm bushed. Speak soon, yeah?'

'Will do. Love you. Take care, OK?'

'Will do. Night. Love you.'

Laura felt the scale of her undertaking. She had promised to sell a house when everyone else had failed. But she'd worked hard over the years to gain her reputation for selling the unsellable. Mr Grimshaw called her a 'miracle worker', which was surprising, given how well he knew her mother-in-law. At Cambridge University, Mrs Taylor-Brown had earned more than a degree. She'd forged lifelong friendships with successful businessmen and women. A quiet investor in various ventures, she wasn't just a doctor with a thriving practice, she was a trusted advisor too. When Laura had first landed her job at the reputable Louth estate agency Ridgeway Residential, she was sure her mother-in-law had been involved. Her interference rarely came as a kindness, but as an effort to get Laura out of the way. The forty-five-minute commute had been extra time away from her family, and at first her boss had inundated her with work. The further Laura was from Lincoln, the happier Mrs Taylor-Brown seemed to be.

It was strange, how the mothers in her life sat at opposite ends of the scale. Mrs Taylor-Brown virtually smothered her son, while Gloria couldn't care less. Laura had never minded her commute to Louth, but at least now her job was back near Lincoln and nearer to Esme. Her mother's terraced house was a twenty-minute walk from where she lived in the Cathedral Quarter and a ten-minute drive to the property that she needed to sell. She only hoped that everything would work out.

Laura's small bedroom reflected her lifelong ambition and hope. Instead of the Adam Ant posters that had once graced Cally's room, her walls displayed aspirational posters, telling her she was capable of anything. The corkboard that held Polaroid photos of her old school friends was also a vision board. Glossy images featured sunlit beaches, huge houses, designer clothes and expensive cars. Books claiming to unlock the secrets of the law of attraction sat on a nearby shelf, their spines creased from frequent use. Her mother hadn't changed a thing since she'd left as a teen. Not that Gloria was keeping it as any kind of shrine; she just couldn't be bothered. She was the least maternal person Laura knew.

Laura thought of her daughter, and the pain of her absence formed a physical ache in her chest. She sold dreams and perfect lifestyles. But what about her own? Why had hers turned to dust? She swiped away a tear, her chin wobbling as the pressure to do better bore down. She'd worked hard to build a stable family unit, but Shane's family would never accept her, no matter how hard she tried. The sooner she sold No.1, the sooner they could start again. Failure wasn't an option this time.

CHAPTER 2

HMP Wakefield, 5 Love Lane. When it came to letters, was there a worse sender's address? Bruce sighed. 5 Love Lane. Talk about a contradiction in terms. The prison was nicknamed 'monster mansion', according to what he had heard. He hated the prison-issue stationery. With its rough texture and thin paper, everything about it felt grim. He'd never imagined he'd get into writing physical letters again. So few people did these days. When he was young his mother had used Belvedere Bond paper to write to her relatives in Ireland. Then there was the Parker pen that she'd treasured, until the day his father ground it into the wooden floor with the heel of his boot. He'd said it was an accident, but even at the age of five Bruce had known enough to catch the triumph in his eyes. George Herbert Wilding – what a father he'd been, with his stubborn ways and lecturing tone. He had a way of taking everything you treasured and reducing it to ash. He wasn't a violent man. He didn't need to be when he was so good at emotional manipulation. Bruce smoothed over the paper, reading his words one more time.

> *Dear sis,*
> *Thanks for your letter. I know that this has been tough for you. I'm going stir crazy in here, and you're the only one I can talk to now. I can't believe my so-called mate*

went to the newspapers. I've known Pete since school. I could understand if what he said was true, but it's all been twisted for the press. I hope the money he got for his betrayal has been worth it.

People still ask me where it all went wrong. I don't mean the internet trolls, or the armchair detectives who obsess about my family while neglecting their own. I mean my fellow inmates. Not the ones who want to beat seven shades of shit out of me. I'm talking about the lifers, the quiet men, the fellas who I've come to respect. They're no angels, but I've learned not to judge. These inmates have been here so long that nothing riles them anymore. Sometimes they ask out of boredom. With others, it's curiosity. Some want to make extra cash by selling their stories about me to journalists. As if there isn't enough crap in the papers about me already. Murder makes big news, and everyone has an opinion. The lifers just happen to want to hear mine. I shrug my shoulders and tell them that I wish I knew. There's no point in banging on about my innocence. Nobody cares. Besides, it's too late for that now. What upsets me the most is that the monster who killed my family is still out there.

I've had plenty of time to reflect. I always return to the root of the problem. It was the 31st of December 2008, when Ali and I first met. I was eighteen when I gate-crashed Becky Lawlor's New Year's Eve party with my mates from school. Becky lived in a big house near the university, and her parents had gone to London for the fireworks. But it was Ali who turned my head. She was wearing these short shorts with gladiator sandals and a yellow baby-doll top. She didn't seem to care about the cold. I can still remember the sight of her auburn hair, hanging loosely from her messy bun. Trouble was, she was snogging Mike Corrigan to 'Sex on Fire' as it blasted out of the speakers in the corner of the room. You know that song, 'Sex on Fire', it still makes me turn cold.

Bruce blinked as the memory of the tune filtered back into his mind. Dammit. Now it would be playing in a loop in his head for days. *Beats the other stuff*, he supposed. He returned his attention to his letter, revisiting his fractured past.

I was so lost back then. An identity crisis of sorts. I'd always felt different to everyone else. I suppose that's why it became a relief to focus everything on Ali. It quietened the voices in my head. They told me I was a loser. That I didn't belong. I didn't like myself very much. I got to know Ali just enough to become infatuated, but not enough to see who she really was. Dad was embarrassingly inappropriate back then, wasn't he? Inappropriate and cruel. I suppose it's why our family is so disjointed now. You couldn't wait to move to Scotland, could you? It was hard after you left. I focused all my attention on Ali just to get through. My dreams were filled with her. I'd wake up sweating and grabbing the pillow for her ghost. I dated a few people in uni, but none of them could live up to the Ali in my head. The second they said something stupid, or turned up late for a date, I'd roll my eyes because my Ali would never do that. To me, Ali had class. She read literature and held her own in a debate. She was strong and protective. She didn't let anyone hold her back. But she was dating Mike too.
Fixation isn't love. Ali was something safe to anchor myself to. It was inevitable, I suppose, that when we

finally got together I believed I wasn't good enough for her. She couldn't see what was so very wrong about me. You tried to tell me that it wouldn't work. I didn't listen. Ten years had passed. Ali and I had both changed. I wish we'd never met. My family would be above the ground, and I wouldn't be sitting here.

Bruce frowned, before adding a few more words to the page.

I hope this isn't too much of a downer. I'm coping, really I am. I spend time in the gym when I can, and as I said, there's a few guys that I get to talk to. The house is going up for sale again. They have some shit-hot estate agent, apparently. I've tried to tell the cops that the place isn't safe for her. As far as they're concerned, they've got their murderer. But whoever killed my family is still on the loose. Maybe one day they'll find him and I can be free to grieve for my family in peace. Thanks for letting me vent.
It would be great to hear from you. I miss the outside world.

Take care of yourself,
Much love,
Bruce

CHAPTER 3

Bruce had been hopeful when he'd received the letter, presuming his sister had responded at last. It wasn't so much for himself, although any contact with Mags cheered him up. It was out of concern for her. Mags had always found the world a battle. Routine was everything. She had one or two good friends in the neighbourhood where she lived in Stirling, and rarely went further than the local library where she worked. Had pressure from the media made her retreat into herself? He just needed to know if she was OK. But as soon as he saw the dreaded Comic Sans font, he knew the letter wasn't from his sister. It was his stalker. She wrote every second day without fail. He opened the envelope, his bottom bunk bed creaking as he sat to read.

To:
HMP Wakefield
5 Love Lane
Wakefield
WF2 9AG
5th October 2025

Hello sausage,

How's my favourite misunderstood soul holding up? I've been devouring every scrap of information about you from those ridiculous tabloids. TV? A joke, really. It's all lies and distortions. I'm beyond heartbroken to see you wasting away in that dreadful place. Such a tragedy – your beautiful family, torn apart. It kills me, honestly it does. Does your sister come to visit? I didn't see her during the trial. But I was there, every day. You didn't acknowledge me amongst the crowd, but I didn't take it personally. You had enough to contend with. And now, the bank is trying to sell your house! I cried oceans when I found out. It's an abomination.

Bruce scratched his unshaven face. She was so emotionally involved. Why? What was she lacking in her life that made her cling to the charred remains of his? Did she write to other prisoners? Why didn't she sign her name or even give an address? He shifted on the hard bed and focused on her words.

Please don't laugh, but I've spent this week's allowance on lottery tickets. I promised myself that if I hit the jackpot, I'd buy No. 1 Aspen Hollow. I'd also hire the best London barrister to free you. This isn't just lip service. I won't rest until you're out, not while there's breath in my body. Because I know you're innocent. I feel it deep in my bones. No, not feel. I know. Remember, I'll always be here for you, Bruce. Always.
I've been dreaming about you. We're connected, you and me. In my dreams, we're walking through your house – our house. The sun streams through the vast

windows, casting colour over the marble kitchen counters, and everything is just as it should be. But I know that's not how it really is, and it tears me apart. One day, when the time is right, you'll be ready to start again.

I've lost the only friend I had, trying to defend you. I've told you about Imogen, haven't I? I'm not sure. I've written so many letters that it's hard to keep up. She works in my local Lidl. She thinks she's the bee's knees because she manages the place. But she doesn't lift a finger, and she gobbles down their leftover pastries at the end of the day. You don't get to that size by keeping busy. She said that I'm in denial, and won't accept the truth. She called you some terrible names. I do my shopping at Tesco now. I reported her to Lidl HQ for stealing leftover food. People who cross me usually end up very sorry indeed.

I'm like your guardian angel, watching over your house, keeping it safe. I can't let them take it from you. I won't. There's no need to thank me. That's what friends are for.

She's not right, Bruce thought. *This . . .* He sighed. *This isn't healthy. I should throw it in the bin. The last thing I need is to brood.* But yet, he found himself reading on.

Maybe you're wondering why I haven't given you my address. I've waited for good reason. I want you to know that I'm not another vulture out to sell your letters. You've had enough betrayals already. So patience, my love. One day, when I'm ready, I'll send you a picture too. Then you can write back, and who knows where destiny will lead us?

19

Just know that I'm out here. I won't let them take your house. The longer it stays unsold, the more time it gives us to get it back. Trust me. I'll do whatever it takes. I've been visiting it, checking everything's in order. I'll find the money somewhere. In the meantime, I'll make sure nobody else snaps it up. I'll keep it warm for you.
Stay strong. We'll laugh about this one day. The world will see that you're innocent, and everything will be right again. Think of me, and know that I'm with you, every minute of every day.

Yours, now and always.

Bruce folded over the letter and placed it beneath his pillow with the others he'd received. She'd been in the house, fantasising about their dream life. Should he tell someone? Would anyone care? He checked his watch as a buzzer sounded. It was time for the exercise yard. He had bigger things to worry about, like getting through the next hour in one piece.

CHAPTER 4

Laura stood in the kitchen of the Cathedral Quarter house, carefully slicing a banana while glancing at the clock. She had left her mother's early, driving the short distance home so she could pick up her daughter. Laura hadn't told her mother where she was going and Gloria didn't care enough to ask. That was the way their relationship had always been. Gloria was a vacant parent. Laura did what she could to help. At six o'clock this morning, she had awoken to her mum coughing her lungs out. A lifetime of chain-smoking had afforded Gloria a myriad of health problems that she refused to accept help for. There was stubborn, and then there was Gloria, who'd written the book on it.

'I'll be alright once I've had me morning ciggy,' she'd said between rasped breaths.

After making her mother a pot of tea and setting up her oxygen tank, Laura had left to take Esme to school. She'd dressed the part, wearing her best navy skirt suit teamed with a crisp white shirt, her long auburn hair pinned back from her face. Her black leather kitten heels were good enough to look smart, but not high enough to hurt her feet.

She protected Esme as much as she could. Soon they would have a place of their own. At least Shane's mother was busy at work today. But this evening she would be back, allowing herself inside to check on Laura's parenting and give subsequent advice. She'd probably be thrilled to find Laura gone, until she realised Laura was doubling down on her efforts to save for a new home.

Laura sighed. Why couldn't they all just get along? She quickly checked the time. Her tailored jacket was draped over the back of a chair, and she'd already stepped out of her kitten heels, one of which Esme was currently attempting to balance on.

'Esme, sweetheart, you'll break your neck in those!' Laura said, half laughing, half exasperated. She reached down, plucked the shoe off Esme's foot, and set it back by the chair.

'But I walk just like you, Mummy! Look!' Esme stretched up on her tiptoes and wobbled dramatically, holding an imaginary handbag.

'You do,' Laura agreed with a smile, crouching to adjust Esme's grey pinafore. 'Except I don't usually look like I'm about to fall over, do I?'

Esme giggled, throwing her arms around Laura's neck as she lost her balance.

Laura hugged her tight, breathing in the scent of the peanut butter on toast she'd eaten minutes before. 'We'd better hurry up.' She smoothed over her daughter's hair and brushed toast crumbs from her face. 'Perfect, and . . .' She held up a rainbow-striped scarf. 'This, because it's freezing out there today.'

Esme groaned but let Laura wind the scarf around her neck. Laura allowed Esme to put her coat on by herself, Esme's tongue sticking out of the corner of her mouth as she fiddled with the zip.

'Now,' Laura said, turning back to the counter, 'I've put something extra in your lunchbox today.' She tucked the banana halves into a small container. 'This is for Nataliya, OK? And I've popped in some extra cheese strings and a second carton of juice. Her mummy and daddy don't have as much money right now, so we're going to make sure she has a little treat.'

Esme hopped on to the chair, swinging her legs. 'OK, Mummy. Why don't they have money?'

'Not everyone is as lucky as us,' Laura explained gently, closing the lunchbox. 'Some people move to a new country to start over.'

'Why?' Esme frowned thoughtfully.

'To have a better life. But it can be hard starting off, which is why we need to be kind.'

Esme nodded in agreement. 'Nataliya doesn't have many words.'

'Not yet,' Laura said, stroking Esme's cheek. 'But she's learning. And you can help her, can't you? Be a good friend. Even if you don't always understand each other, you can still be kind.'

'I *am* kind.' Esme puffed out her chest. 'I sit next to her. And I showed her my unicorn keyring yesterday. She said "ni-ni-corn!" and laughed!'

Laura grinned. 'That's lovely, darling. And I bet it made her feel happy, knowing she had a friend.' She tucked a strand of Esme's hair behind her ear. 'Now go and get your shoes.'

Esme scurried down the hall. Watching her, Laura felt a familiar ache of love and pride. Whatever else was going on, Esme was her world, her little star. She grabbed her jacket and slipped her heels back on, grateful Shane had given her some space. She didn't want her precious time with her daughter to be tainted by arguments. Shane was keen for her to come home, but they wouldn't be happy in that house while his mother had blood running through her veins. She was quite the philanthropist, Mrs Taylor-Brown, but every gesture of kindness was self-serving. If only people knew how much of a snob she really was.

Laura was grateful that her job afforded her flexible working hours so she could start after nine. She checked the rear-view mirror of her Mercedes before turning towards Aspen Hollow. Not that she could see a lot of the road behind her, given the boxes of designer ornaments, pictures and scented candles obstructing her view. She inhaled the scent of bergamot and lemon zest deep into her lungs. Divine. Dressing the house was an important part of the selling process. The van that was bringing the rest of the items should arrive soon. The house came partly furnished, although some of the previous occupants' belongings had been removed when the bank foreclosed.

She took in the scene as she assessed the area. How different Burton Waters was compared to the small mid-terrace home in which she'd grown up. The marina had everything . . . An eclectic mixture of restaurants and bars, and a small but pretty waterfront. Laura drove down the dip in the road through the permanently open wrought-iron gates of Aspen Hollow, silently promising herself that one day she, Shane and Esme would live somewhere like this. But such communities came at a premium, and she would have to keep working hard.

Tucked away at the edge of the woods, four luxury homes encircled a meticulously landscaped green. Elegant aspen trees dotted the lawn, which was framed by a smooth brick-paved road, providing a loop for cars to navigate. It was picture-postcard perfect, even in the winter. Except . . . She eased her foot off the accelerator of her car as No. 1 came into view.

What the hell? Laura stared, disbelieving, at the sight of a man in overalls scrubbing graffiti from the side of the house. Her spirits fell.

She had worked in undesirable locations – houses where you wiped your feet on the way out. Then there were the homes perched on the edge of busy motorways, complete with blackened windows courtesy of diesel fumes. That's where you'd expect graffiti, not here, in a highly respected suburb. Aspen Hollow was one of the nicest areas she'd worked in.

'Dammit,' she muttered. What sort of history did this house come with? She could check online. A quick internet search was all it would take. But her boss had transferred her especially so she could look at the place with fresh eyes. Whatever had happened was in the past. Still . . . this was not the start she'd envisioned. She took in the van's 'Safe Solutions' logo. Watched the short, stout man switch tools and spray the last of the red paint away. The pressure washer had done its job, and the paint drizzled into a red puddle on the drive. Laura's sense of foreboding grew. The man turned to meet her gaze.

'I'll be out of your way in five,' he called, and Laura delivered a thumbs up, wishing that puddle of red seeping outwards didn't look so much like blood.

She glanced over at the solar panels, dazzling with the reflection of the morning sun. Mentally, she ticked off each selling point. The close was eco-friendly, with rainwater barrels crouching beside vast manicured front lawns. The woodland backdrop completed the look. There were owls, squirrels, even deer. But what she didn't need was a great scrawl of red graffiti on the side wall.

She relayed all of this to Jonathan, who was the first to pick up the phone when she called the agency. Clio, who also worked there, was supposed to be her first point of contact but more often than not she was on a viewing or in the middle of a call.

'Don't worry,' Jonathan assured her as she explained. 'If he can't remove it, my mate Baz has a jet washer that would take the enamel off teeth.'

'It's coming off,' Laura replied. 'But I'm surprised to see it here in the first place. This looks like such a nice area.' She sighed. It wasn't Jonathan's fault that she was going in blind.

'Speak to the security guy . . . Erm, what's his name? He's head of security in the marina, and the residents pay ground rent which pays for this sort of stuff. Anyway . . .' He paused. 'Let me know when you're ready and I'll pop over to record a video tour.'

Suppressing her concerns, Laura said she would and ended the call. Since Covid, online viewings had been all the rage. Some houses, like people, deserved a second chance. She looked around the neighbourhood and decided on her social media strategy. Modern dwellings in harmony with nature. A flutter rose in her chest, the excitement of taking on a new project. But the golden wash of the morning sun did little to warm the day. She glanced around, feeling the prickle of unseen eyes. She was being observed.

As Laura hefted a box from the back of her car, she became aware of someone behind her. She took in the woman's sleek blonde hair as the chilly October air made it dance around her face. Her jeans and white top matched nicely with the mustard cardigan hanging on her slender frame.

'Need a hand with those?' She spoke on a mint-scented breath. 'I'm Scarlett.' She pointed to one of the houses. 'I live right there.'

'Nice to meet you,' Laura said politely. 'Laura. From Ridgeway Residential.'

'Well, Laura from Ridgeway Residential, you look like you could do with some help.' Scarlett wavered slightly as she pointed to the boxes in the back of Laura's car. 'Whoops. These heels are taking some breaking in.'

'Thanks.' Laura flashed her a smile. 'But I can manage.' Judging by Scarlett's wobble, Laura's precious items might not make it inside.

Scarlett lingered, her gaze darting over the boxes crammed with things intended to infuse new life into the home. 'It would be good to see someone living in the place.'

Laura tightened her grip on the heavy box. 'I'll find you some lovely new neighbours.'

Scarlett nodded, but her voice was laced with caution as she peeked at the contents of the box in Laura's arms. 'Nice. But you'll need more than designer smellies to sell the Wilding family home.' Her words were said in a voice that was low and quiet, not meant for Laura's ears. But she picked up on them just the same.

'What was that?' Laura said, her curiosity getting the better of her. Scarlett looked at her blankly. 'About the Wildings,' she continued. 'Were they the previous owners? I'm going in blind, I'm afraid.'

A man stepped out of the neighbouring driveway and offered a curt nod. He was wearing a shirt and tie, with sharply pressed trousers, his short black hair neatly styled.

'Morning,' he said, his attention quickly turning to Scarlett. 'Your breakfast is going cold.'

'This is my husband, David.' Scarlett made the introduction, seemingly unconcerned about her food. 'Darling, this is Laura. She said she's going to find us some nice new neighbours.'

'That's good,' David replied, his words strained with impatience as he gave Laura a smile. 'We love living here, don't we?' He wrapped an arm around his wife's thin waist.

'Mmm?' Scarlett snapped out of her daze. 'Yes. We love living here.' But her words were flat and robotic, lacking any real emotion.

'Right. Well. We'll let you get back to work.' David cleared his throat before guiding Scarlett back inside. Scarlett didn't give Laura a second glance as she was ushered home.

'Um . . . nice to meet you both,' Laura called after them, her biceps aching from holding the box. She watched the couple retreat, a feeling settling in her stomach like a stone. They were nice on the surface. Polite. Affluent. But it seemed Scarlett's husband couldn't get her inside quickly enough. As for the Wilding family . . . did Laura want to know?

At least the Safe Solutions man was packing up to leave. *Here goes.* Taking a deep breath, Laura walked up the freshly cleaned driveway, grateful that the puddle of red was now gone. She watched her step, taking care not to slip on the wet paving stones. Her keys jingled as she balanced the box in her arms and unlocked the front door.

Wow, she thought, her footsteps echoing against the marble flooring of the generous entrance hall. The place was huge, with high ceilings, vast windows and a wide swan-neck staircase adding a touch of opulence. But her initial amazement was replaced as a sudden unwelcome atmosphere sent chills skittering down her spine. The spaciousness engulfed her, making her feel very small. The sense of being watched had followed her inside. She lowered the box to the floor as an inexplicable feeling of vulnerability washed over her.

What happened here? Laura rubbed the back of her neck as she felt a dip in temperature. *Weird,* she thought, clicking the Google Nest thermostat up a couple of notches. It read eighteen degrees. Warmth seemed reluctant to fill the space.

'I'll be off now.' The man from Safe Solutions stopped her on the pavement as she returned to her car for another box. His clothes were splashed damp, his glasses misted from the spray. He took them off to clean them with the corner of his sleeve.

'Can I ask . . .' Laura couldn't stop herself. She needed to know. 'What was it? A tag or . . .'

'A tag?' He raised a bushy eyebrow. 'Only if you consider the word "murder" a calling card.'

CHAPTER 5

Scarlett glared out the window of her self-imposed prison. Another estate agent, another attempt to sell 1 Aspen Hollow. Was this the third or fourth 'For Sale' sign? She wasn't sure. But this lady seemed more determined than the rest. She'd found Laura on the Louth branch page of the Ridgeway Residentials site. Her socials had a decent following. She might pull this off. That did not bode well. To Scarlett, the house was like a dying tooth – decaying, painful and better off gone. Nothing a good bulldozer couldn't fix. But the memories would never leave, no matter what Scarlett did. She picked at the jagged edge of a nail she had broken from falling over that morning. Deirdre, her manicurist, would fix it. But such mishaps were happening more often now. It was why she was safer in the confines of her bedroom, where she couldn't stumble or say the wrong thing.

She sipped the bitter black coffee, standing at the window that gave her a perfect view of the close. The sound of her son's laughter downstairs was a mild irritant as their nanny played 'Baby Shark' on a loop. She couldn't imagine anyone living in No. 1. Why would they want to?

She'd never taken to Ali, who had been too much of a saccharine-sweet girl-next-door type. She couldn't respect people who tried too hard. She'd been nouveau riche, for a start.

Her parents had got lucky investing their money in stocks and shares and left the lot to her. It was obvious that Ali was never going to fit in. But Bruce . . . Scarlett remembered the first time she'd seen him. Those defined shoulders. The tanned forearms. That smile – a mixture of shyness and charm that would make anyone melt. He'd been way too good for Ali, who was obsessed with family life.

Scarlett caught her unkind thoughts and took another sip of her coffee. Alcohol sharpened her edges and made her catty. She'd started early this morning. Just one drink to stop the shakes had turned into two, then three. It wasn't guilt that drove her to booze. Just an unpleasant feeling of regret that she could do without.

Would things have turned out any differently had she been there for Ali? Doubtful. She had always found men easier to befriend. The only female friends she had were ex-colleagues from work, but since she'd had Lou and Harriet, their calls had been infrequent. She couldn't blame them. She was exactly the type of person she used to avoid. But the thought of becoming friends with Ali – swapping recipes and playdates . . . Scarlett grimaced. Not that Ali would be arranging playdates now.

She recalled the morning after. How Bruce had looked so lost as he'd spoken to the police on his drive. The news had spread around the close like wildfire. Her neighbour Graham had never done so much gardening as he did that week. She wasn't sure how she felt about him. At first, she'd thought it would be fun to be friends with a literary agent. He'd struck it lucky in pre-Covid times, with a couple of clients who had dominated the *New York Times* bestseller list. But he was too nosey for her liking. Every now and again he'd stop to chat, his eyes alight with curiosity. He'd be all over the new estate agent. He wouldn't be able to help himself. Scarlett wondered just how much he knew.

At least their close was small, and apart from Graham and his other half, Walter, there was only Billie to worry about. But Billie wasn't the social type. Scarlett struggled to figure her out. She lived in that great big house all by herself, her focus on nothing but her business. At least, that's what she led people to believe. Scarlett stared out the window, her flesh turning cold. Like everyone else on this close, Billie probably had something to hide.

CHAPTER 6

Laura set a vase down on the marble kitchen island that was so big she had to stretch to reach its centre. She only hoped that she could do the place justice, now all the boxes had been carried in. She glanced up at the high ceilings, then her gaze fell to the generous glass windows and the bifold back doors. The air felt still, with an expectant edge. *This house is a dream*, she thought. Her fingers glided over the cool kitchen surfaces as she breathed in the crisp air. How lucky she was, getting to spend time here instead of some stuffy office. *One day*, she told herself, *I'll be living in a place like this.* Her footsteps echoed around the hollow space as she examined each corner of the kitchen. How would you fill all of these cupboards, or the wide built-in fridge? Then there was the wine cooler that would accommodate more bottles than she'd drink in a year. To think that this was *her* listing. A smile spread on her face. She couldn't keep the listing under wraps any longer.

She picked up her phone from the kitchen counter, where she'd left it next to her laptop. A quick Instagram update should whet her followers' appetites for more. She fixed her glasses and finger-combed her hair before grinning for a selfie.

> *Excited to share my latest listing at Aspen Hollow. Who wouldn't want to live here? #WatchThisSpace #LincolnHomes*

Her fingers worked quickly as she added a few more tags for good measure.

She was arranging a colourful cookbook on an angled stand when her first notifications came in.

The fourth comment down caught her attention, and her brow creased in a frown.

Aspen Hollow? In Lincoln? You couldn't pay me to live there!

It might not be the same house, another user replied. Laura scrolled through the rest of the comments.

Not Bruce and Ali Wilding's home, surely. Are they still trying to flog that place?

A slow, nauseating sensation crept over Laura as her stomach began to churn. She'd said she wasn't going to research her listing, but her curiosity made her wonder. What had she let herself in for? More comments were coming in. But were they talking about *this* house? She had to find out. Otherwise she wouldn't know how to respond. Opening a browser, she typed in *Bruce and Ali Wilding* . . . She didn't need to narrow it down any more than that. The articles came up straight away, each headline making her pulse pick up pace. 'Double Murder Shocks Lincoln Community'. *Murder?* Laura's eyes widened as further articles spoke of Bruce Wilding's guilt. 'Wilding Main Suspect in Double Murder Trial – pleads innocent in the murder of his wife and child'. Laura was a born optimist. She staunchly refused to watch the news, or even listen to it on the radio. She protected her thoughts at all times, focusing only on the positives. But now her happy bubble was set to burst.

Her thoughts drifted to the graffiti sprayed on the outside wall. The image of the jarring contrast of red against the beautiful cream brickwork left her feeling uneasy in her skin.

'It can't be this house,' she whispered, then she glanced upwards as she thought she heard a noise. The beauty of this space was quickly turning sinister.

She returned her attention to her phone, skimming through the stories. Bruce Wilding had been convicted of killing his wife, Ali, and child, Cindy, in the bedroom of their home. She clicked on a YouTube link, pressing 'skip' as an ad began to play. There she was – Ali Wilding, in a kitchen that looked identical to the one Laura was standing in now. It was a cookery video recorded by Ali at home for her channel. The video had over a hundred thousand views.

'I'm making spaghetti bolognese tonight. It's Bruce's favourite.'

Ali's voice echoed hauntingly from Laura's phone. Laura hadn't meant to keep watching the video, but she found herself frozen, taking everything in – including the view from the kitchen window behind Ali, which left her in no doubt. Her murder had happened here, in this house. No wonder Laura's boss had told her to view the place with fresh eyes. It hadn't taken long for her resolve to crumble, not when it was so easy to research the place online. Staying out of the know was like holding back the tide. She didn't want to read the sensationalised stories, though. She just wanted a feel for the woman who had lived here. Laura's lips parted in surprise as their similarities hit home. Ali had the same shoulder-length hair, the same stature, and the same intonation to her voice. Laura perhaps weighed a little less, but they could have been mistaken for sisters.

'My secret ingredient . . .' Ali said with a flourish, as she reached for a cupboard door.

Laura touched the same cupboard, and the moment playing on screen came alive. *Talk about watching in 3-D*, Laura thought as the world took a surreal turn.

'Here it is, a dash of Worcestershire sauce,' Ali said, laughing as she gave the bottle a shake. 'It's a bit of a mouthful for our American viewers. Please don't ask me to spell it!'

'Mummy!' Cindy called out. The sight of the little girl's freckled face on her iPhone screen was too much. Laura quickly pressed pause, her throat thickening as her maternal instincts swelled. Because it wasn't just Ali who had died under this roof. She closed the video with her thumb. But she couldn't stop herself glancing at the reams of true crime videos listed beneath.

The titles screamed 'Wilding Family Murders' and 'Bruce Wilding – The Man Who Murdered His Wife and Child' and 'Cindy Wilding – Smothered While She Slept'. Laura stared at the screen in disbelief. Her eyes pricked with tears as she read the video descriptions featuring the grisly details of their deaths. A seemingly perfect family, destroyed in one night. Why?

No wonder this place had been a hard sell. How on earth had her boss, Simon, thought that she wouldn't find out? She scrolled down to a thumbnail of Cindy. Seeing the little girl in the very room that she was currently standing in made it all too real. She wasn't much older than Esme. What sort of monster was Bruce Wilding? How could he physically bring himself to do such a thing? Silently, Laura put her phone face down and brushed away a tear. No wonder her Instagram followers had their concerns.

Her gaze darted around the room as her perception of the space changed. She had been to crime scene houses and seen the aftermath of a police investigation first-hand. But she'd never tried to sell a house where murders had taken place. The agency must have known. She thrust open the PVC windows. The air she'd enjoyed moments before felt tainted now. She imagined the crime scene officers dusting for fingerprints. The army of police who must have traipsed through this home. Then the cleaners arriving in their wake.

No wonder the place felt cold. The residue of violence still lingered. She forced herself to focus on her work. Her OSC candles would fill the home with the smell of jasmine and sandalwood downstairs, while her bergamot diffusers would enhance the luxury bathrooms. The scents were Oprah's favourite for a reason, and nothing was too good for Laura's next big house sale. Because she *would* sell this place, despite its tragic history.

She couldn't bear to think about Ali and Cindy Wilding now. It was time to change the narrative for 1 Aspen Hollow. People didn't just buy a house. They bought how it made them feel. She had her work cut out here, though. Laura touched the glossy white kitchen cupboards – all imports from Italy. Had Ali chosen them, or had her husband taken the lead? They looked like a male purchase, the sleek lines and built-in chrome appliances giving off a sterile gleam.

She took a few snaps with her phone and uploaded a new story. She paused, trying to find the right words. *Dream home, amazing architecture. More coming soon!* A quick addition of a trending tune and her story was complete. But her earlier excitement had faded. She ventured out to the hall and captured three more images before pocketing her phone. Her hand felt heavy as she rested it on the swan-neck banister, one of the most beautiful features in the house. Then she climbed the wide stairwell, towards the upper floor. No creaky stairs underfoot here. The silence enveloped her as she reached the landing. She glanced over her shoulder, willing her heart rate to slow down. How different it all seemed to her now.

She slipped off her shoes and wriggled her toes into the plush carpet, tutting at the sight of the cheap hooks on the walls where pictures had once hung. Another box to tick formed in her mind. She paused outside one of the bedrooms, hesitant as she rested her hand on the door handle, which felt icy to the touch. Then she pushed open the door, taking in the soft pink walls, and the thick cream carpet revealing four craters where a bed had once stood. This had to be Cindy's room. A replacement single bed would arrive today. Laura lingered in the doorway, staring vacantly at the pastel walls and empty shelves. *Mummy!* The sound of Cindy's voice echoed in her mind. The little girl's presence was all around. *Snap out of it*, Laura told herself. It was only natural that she would empathise, given her own daughter was around the same age. Before she could concentrate on the sale, she needed to mentally exorcise the ghosts of No. 1.

Laura only hoped that when Cindy was smothered, her father had made it quick. Her fingers tightened around the door handle as her thoughts turned grim. *Smother, father* . . . The words didn't belong together. *Not all potential buyers will be bothered*, she told herself. *Some might not even care.* But if that were the case, the home would have sold by now. Everybody cared.

The hinges of the master bedroom door complained softly as she pushed it open. The room sprawled before her, barren and uninviting without a bed to anchor it. Her gaze swept across the beige carpet to the wide, curtainless windows. Had Ali stood at that very spot, looking out on to the neighbouring homes? The road was a circular cul-de-sac, and the front bedrooms offered a view of all the other houses.

A flutter of movement caught Laura's eye. A woman sat on the balcony of one of the other houses, drinking from a mug and stroking a fluffy orange lapdog. Her dark braided hair hung past her shoulders. She was dressed in a long puffer coat, wearing flip-flops, sunglasses, a scarf and a bobble hat. Summer and winter . . . The contrast of clothing made her stand out. But it was a nice sunny morning, and there was no crime in catching a few rays, even if they came with a chill.

Laura started as the bedroom door creaked. It was just the wind, wasn't it? But she wasn't the only person to have picked up on the oppressive atmosphere in this bedroom. According to Jonathan, previous viewers of the house hadn't spent long in this space. Now Laura knew why. Jonathan was a useful source of information. The young, handsome man had dated women from several estate agencies. Not so much pillow talk as estate agency chatter. She could do with his company right now. A thick sense of dread trailed after her as she descended the wide stairs.

She straightened her spine, slowed her movements. Her imagination was running away with her, that was all. She checked her watch. The delivery lorry was late. How could she book in viewings if the house wasn't dressed? She exhaled sharply, rubbing her arms against the chill. The place was taking forever to heat up.

She walked out the front door into the weak sunshine and stared down the road. Sounds filtered through her troubled reflections. A backdrop of birdsong. The swish of trees in the breeze. A dog barking in the distance. But no lorry. No traffic at all. Her phone buzzed in her pocket, breaking the stillness. It was bound to be the delivery driver, making some excuse about traffic. But it wasn't a call, it was a text.

Don't go in the house.

The message was short and stark. Laura frowned, her finger hovering over the screen as she considered how to reply. Probably some idiot who'd found her number online. Still, her stomach tightened. She glanced up at the house. The windows seemed so dark now. She should ignore the message. Block the number, even. She jumped as another text message pinged.

Leave while you can.

Her grip tightened around her phone. This wasn't funny. She swallowed hard, her gaze wandering around the close. Three dots appeared, then stopped. Laura texted with trembling fingers.

Who is this?

She stared at the screen, willing a response to come through. Nothing.

'Right,' she said, making a decision.

She dialled the number, ready to give them a piece of her mind, but there was no answer. The slamming of a car door broke the tension, and she looked up to see David deliver a quick wave from behind his steering wheel. *It's a friendly neighbourhood*, she told herself, as David pulled away from his drive. *The murders are in the past.* But the texts weren't . . . and the words had left an imprint in her mind.

Leave while you can.

CHAPTER 7

Ali

Then

I'm standing at my bedroom window for the last time. Shame that it's raining. I hope it clears soon. Today is moving day. I was so excited that I barely slept last night. I trace my fingers over the path of a weary droplet of rain as it trails down the outside of the windowpane. Actually, I don't think it was excitement that kept me awake. Trepidation? Maybe.

I glance around the room, at the cardboard boxes containing too many pairs of shoes. At the zippered laundry bags bulging with clothes. It's unbelievable, how much stuff we've accumulated over the years.

It's six a.m. and Bruce is up, pottering about downstairs. It means so much to him, moving into the home that he created from scratch. I don't think I've ever seen him so excited. We're almost ready to go. Everything has been packed and labelled, apart from the bedclothes and some of Cindy's things. She's still asleep. If she wasn't, she'd be bouncing on my bed by now. I creep around the room, quietly getting dressed. The furniture removals van will be here around eight. It's kind of overwhelming, moving into such a big house, especially when I think of where the money came from.

I can't believe that we're going to be living in Burton Waters – and in such a posh development, too. Who would have thought it when Bruce and I first met? When I think of those days, when Mum and Dad did everything possible to keep us apart. Look at us now.

I check my reflection in the mirror, trepidation growing as I wonder if I'll fit in. God, I miss my mum during times like these. She'd be on the phone now, asking if I've read my meters and arranging a time to come to my new home. My green-fingered father would be waiting to see the garden and ready with advice on the best trees to plant for privacy. A wave of grief washes over me, and I have to catch my breath. Not today. I push it down. Way down, just as I have many times before. Now I'm a parent, I appreciate that everything they did was out of concern. I shouldn't have dropped out of Lincoln University. Had I kept going with my degree, I wouldn't have so many regrets. I swallow down my tears. The old black cloud is back, hovering over my party as I put out the bunting. Losing Mum and Dad in such a short space of time was one of the hardest things I've had to deal with.

I return to the window and take in the view. The rain has turned to drizzle, and the streets are grey and damp. I search my mind for a hopeful thought. At least my inheritance has been used for something solid, something tangible. People assume that Bruce has bought our new home. Given he designed it, it seems only right. It's a big upgrade from our little semi-detached. It's a lot nearer to Lincoln, too. If Bruce gets kudos, then why not? Surely it's better than people thinking the money just landed in our lap? And maybe our lifestyle will encourage him to be more sensible with our finances from now on.

I count another blessing to lift my mood. My online community. They feel like friends. But there are things I can't share with the world.

The front door gently clicks shut downstairs. Bruce has gone for his morning run. I should make a coffee before Cindy gets up. But I can't shake this feeling that something is off. I'm trying to stay positive, but I've had this knot in my stomach all week. Bruce has been working late more often, and when he's home, he's distracted. Sometimes I catch him staring at his phone, and I wonder who he's texting. He's so protective of it. The little things are starting to add up, and I'm scared of what they might mean.

We used to be so close. When we first got together, he worshipped me – but I wonder, was he more in love with the *idea* of being married than spending his life with me? Did he just want a stable family home that was nothing like his own? I had Cindy to try to bring us closer together, but now we sleep back-to-back, and the space between us grows.

I watch him jog down the path, head down against the drizzle. What is he thinking? I wish I knew.

There are moments when Bruce looks at me with that old spark in his eyes, and I think maybe, just maybe, we'll be OK. Here, surrounded by boxes and the remnants of our old life, I'm filled with a strange mix of excitement and dread. The house we're moving to is everything we've ever wanted, but it's also a reminder of everything we stand to lose. If our marriage runs into trouble, our new home will be a battleground.

So, here's to fresh starts, because my family is all I have left.

CHAPTER 8

Bruce stretched in his chair, which was hard beneath his bones. The residue of shampoo made his hair bristle, now it had dried. But there was no way he was returning to the shower block. Not today. He lifted his feet up off the floor and rested them on the bunk bed. The chair was against the wall, but his cell was so narrow that he could easily touch the mattress with his feet. At least, for now, he had the place to himself. The prison was so overcrowded it was unreal, so there was little doubt that he'd have a new cellmate soon. But this was a world away from 1 Aspen Hollow. No, not a world away. A universe. The rusty metal bunk bed came with a thin prison mattress which was no better than a gym crash mat. A small rickety table wobbled when he leaned on it. His two MDF cupboards were screwed to the wall, the kettle was crusted with limescale, and the metal toilet offered no privacy when the prison officers walked in. At least he had an old but workable TV.

He returned his attention to the letter that he'd written to his sister Mags. One more read-through and it was ready to go.

> *Hi sis,*
> *Sorry for filling your mailbox; two letters in two days is excessive. But writing feels like therapy, and even if you don't read my words, at least I've got them off my chest.*

There's a priest here, he's been a literal godsend. I'm not saying that I'm 'born again' – what a cliché that would be. But he has been of comfort during the hardest of days. How are you? Truly, how has life been treating you? Something happened to me today, something horrific, which is why I'm writing so soon. I'm sure it won't make the news. Assaults in prison are an everyday occurrence, but at the time I thought I was witnessing a murder. He was in a bad way. It really hammered it home that life is short.

We didn't see much of each other growing up, did we? With a decade between us, I was just the annoying little brother when you were coming into your own. By the time I hit my gangly teenage years, you were already living in Scotland, embracing the Highlands and university life. I remember feeling awestruck by your independence. I should have told you that. I should have said a lot of things, but as a family we weren't good at sharing our feelings, were we? I don't hold any resentment. I just wish you'd taken me along like I asked. But now, as I sit here, the weight of my confinement pressing down, I have never needed my big sister more than I do right now.

You can probably tell how much today has shaken me. I was taking a shower when it happened. It's where the majority of assaults seem to occur, so I get in and out of that place as quick as I can. My letters are read by the prison so I won't give descriptions or names, just to say that I looked up and saw two shadowy men emerge from the steam. One shoved me so hard that my back slammed against the cold tiles. There wasn't time to register what was going on before they launched at the guy next to me

– I don't know him, but he has a faded tattoo of a sparrow on his neck.

I picked myself up in time to see them laying into him with their shivs. There were these wet, ripping sounds that I can't get out of my head. He didn't even scream, sis, just a gargle of air escaping through blood. I managed to get myself out of there as quick as I could. Sorry, I know. Too much detail. My letters should come with a warning. But it helps to get this stuff out of my head.

I've been lost in depression since getting here, the days bleeding into one another as I go through the motions. But witnessing that violence, the disregard for life – it ignited something inside me. Ali and Cindy deserve more. And it's up to me to find their killer. I'm going to appeal. I need to fight for my freedom, because the truth is out there. Somebody knows. I get a lot of letters from women. Granted, most of them are kinda weird. But maybe someone out there can help me. Maybe even you?

The guy who was stabbed is in the hospital wing. They say he'll recover. It seems it was all over some drug debt – a reminder of how cheap life has become. I've been tempted to dabble, you know? In those darker moments, oblivion calls. But you know what? I won't let this place turn me into a walking zombie. I'm not some low-down loser like the other men here. I'm an architect, for God's sake. I have a master's degree. I think that's half the problem. In prison, you are literally a number. You lose your identity. Everything focuses on what you've been banged up for. I'm not Bruce the architect who likes craft beer and working out in the gym; I'm 78651, wife and kiddie murderer. I'm nothing. I'm lower than the shit you scrape off your shoe. Can you imagine how that feels, being labelled as someone who would kill their own wife and kid?

Bruce stared at the page. He hadn't realised how low he'd got until he saw the words in black and white. He scanned the final few paragraphs, hoping his sister wouldn't be put off responding to his outpouring of emotions.

I've already burdened you with my troubles, but there's something else I need to share. As you know, my house has been put up for sale. I know, it's not mine anymore, especially now that the bank has repossessed it. I should never have mortgaged the place. Ali spent her inheritance buying that house, but mortgaging it seemed like the best way of paying off my debts. She never signed anything – at least, not knowingly. She was never meant to know. I ran with dangerous company back then. Gamblers, card sharks, men who could make paperwork say anything for the right price. But now I'm thinking. If I could find a way of stalling the sale, maybe somehow I could buy it back. I know, it sounds crazy. But nobody's made an offer so far. Another year, that's all I need. One year to prove my innocence. Then . . . I dunno . . . maybe I could get a crowd funder going or something? Go viral, make an appeal? Weirder things have happened on the internet. Or I could sell my story, write a book, or be on Netflix. They eat up stuff like that. Don't get me wrong. I don't want to make this about me. They've stopped looking for the bastard who murdered my family, now I'm banged up for it. I can't let that go.

I know it sounds crazy after everything that's happened, but that house means a lot to me. It's hard to give up the home you've dreamed of your whole life. The nights I spent hunched over my drafting table, drawing lines on blueprints as I planned the development. It was more than architecture to me. Sometimes I close my eyes and take myself back to my office, and I imagine the smell of fresh coffee and graphite and paper as I get ready to dive into the day's tasks. I remember feeling the textured samples of wood, steel and fabric, which helped me bring the house to life. Even now, inside these grey walls, I can close my eyes and walk through each room, feel the warmth of the sun as it spills through the windows, hear the sound of Cindy's footsteps echoing against the floors. They're still there. I can feel it. The memories of life that once filled those spaces is too precious to hand over to a bunch of ghouls.

Could you visit the house? Please? I'm so helpless in here. Could you see if there's any way to delay the sale, just long enough for me to get my bearings, to muster up a fight. I can't shake the feeling that the house might have some overlooked clue. The cops were so busy gunning for me that they didn't consider anything else.

The last thing I want is to pull you into this mire. But you're the only family I have left who cares. You know me, sis. You know I wouldn't be capable of hurting Cindy. I may not have been the best of dads (wonder where I picked that up from, eh?) but I loved her. She was my world. Losing her felt like my heart being ripped out of my chest. And then being accused of her and Ali's destruction . . . It's taken me a year to come back to myself. Anyway, I'll leave it here. Sorry to end on such a bad note. It's all getting on top of me. Please write. Please. Let me know that you're OK.

With hope,
Bruce

He hadn't realised that he was crying until tears blurred his vision. He quickly swiped them away. He'd got it out – all of it. Or at least everything he was able to say. Because he could never admit everything. Not to her. He couldn't bear the shame.

CHAPTER 9

Laura leaned against the counter, her laptop open, her emails checked. Her lunch break was long overdue. Her muscles ached after carrying in the heavy boxes. Yorkshire Tea usually fixed everything in her book. But the heat from her mug couldn't penetrate the chill that had settled deep into the marrow of her bones. She eyed the cool granite surfaces. The house was beautiful. The epitome of luxury. But now that she knew the truth, she couldn't relax. Were her work colleagues laughing at her? Had they taken bets on how long it would be before she discovered the truth? She thought once more of her boss's insistence that she view it objectively. 'If anyone can sell it, you can,' he'd said. But Simon wasn't the type of person to set her up for a fall.

She bit into her sandwich, the crunch of lettuce and ciabatta breaking the silence. The PVC windows framed perfect front lawns, but all she could envision was Bruce, plotting to kill his wife and daughter. Had he stood at this counter, planning their demise? She wanted to hug Esme, to keep her safe from the world, but she had to provide a roof over their heads first. Shane was trying, but his business was new and it would take time to gain enough clients to fund a place of their own. But had she done the right thing by moving out in protest? She loved her husband, but she couldn't live there, not while his parents kept interfering. Her constant bickering with Shane was a testament to that.

A sudden clattering sound jolted her back to the present. It was the heat pump kicking into life . . . Wasn't it? A mechanical heartbeat pulsing through the floors. Though surely new houses shouldn't sound like that? There must be an airlock in the system somewhere.

She turned the thought over like a pebble in her mind. She couldn't wait to lock up the house and sleep at her mum's tonight. She snorted as she snapped back to reality. Looking forward to sleeping at her mum's? Now there was a first. Another sip of tea brought the stark reality home as her eyes danced around the kitchen. She would have to get rid of every reminder of Ali's life. It would be more than a change of decor; the house needed a complete reinvention. But she didn't have the budget for that. She swallowed down her last mouthful of tea as the doorbell chimed.

'Delivery for ya!' The middle-aged man on the doorstep was holding a clipboard, gesturing to the van on the drive. 'Traffic was murder. A lorry spilled its load on the A158.' He ran a hand through his thinning grey hair. 'Bloody beets everywhere!'

Conscious of the time, Laura pushed back her annoyance. A light breeze scattered dead leaves around her feet as she followed him out to the van. He had only come from Horncastle, less than a forty-minute drive away.

'Bit posh around here, innit?' He whistled as he took in the frontage. 'Weird . . .' he continued, rubbing his stubbled chin. 'Have a feeling I've seen this place before.'

Laura didn't enlighten him. 'Yes, well, if you bring it in, I'll show you where everything goes, thanks.'

She watched a sandy-haired lad jump out of the van, wearing a baggy grey hoodie and the skinniest of skinny jeans. The expression on his face hinted that he knew exactly what the address signified.

Laura cleaned her glasses with a tissue as she waited, ready to equip them with overshoes before they came inside.

Fifty minutes later, the middle-aged driver approached her, a faint sheen of sweat coating his brow. 'Sorry, love, we're behind schedule. We've lugged in the furniture. You'll have to bring the boxes inside yourself.' The man nodded towards his younger counterpart, who was taking a selfie with the house in the background.

'I know you're late, I was meant to have this stuff set up ages ago!' Laura said, her annoyance rising. 'So you're damn well bringing the rest of it in!' She stood, hands clenched into fists as she rested them on her hips.

The older man rubbed his stubbled chin. 'I suppose we can help you lug in the heavier bits.'

Laura exhaled, exasperated as the younger of the two asked to use the toilet. 'Go on then, but use the overshoes, and leave the place the same as you find it.' She rolled her sleeves up, determined to get everything unloaded from the van and into the house.

As she put down her fourth box, her thoughts were fully on the property. Lamps would soften the lighting, while strategically placed ornaments would provide viewers with a 'lived-in' feel. She turned around, looking for the younger man. He'd been gone a long time. The sound of a door closing upstairs piqued her curiosity. She massaged the base of her spine before slowly taking the stairs.

'Wow, is that where it happened?'

A young woman's voice filtered from one of the rooms upstairs. *What the hell?* Laura thought. She hadn't let anyone else in. 'Yeah,' a youthful male voice replied. 'He topped her right here. The bed's gone now, though.'

Laura pushed open the door of the main bedroom, just in time to see the driver's assistant on a FaceTime call.

'What's going on here?' Laura shouted, making him jump in response.

'Um . . . Nothing.' He shoved his phone into his jeans pocket before heading for the door.

'It's not nothing. You were FaceTiming. I saw you!'

'It's no big deal.' He glowered as Laura approached. 'Get off my back!'

'Hey! I said, what are you playing at?' Laura followed him out to the landing, but he ignored her protests as they made their way down the stairs.

'There you are!' The other man entered the hall. 'Time's up. We've got to get back.' Laura frowned at the sight of his boots as he trod dirt into the floor.

'Hang on a minute.' Her voice echoed throughout the hall. 'You've not finished!'

'Sorry, love, but we've got other deliveries to make,' the older man replied, his words trailing behind him as he walked outside.

'Oh, for God's sake!' She took in the sight of four boxes left on the ground. Some contained books to fill the library shelves. Others contained kitchen items to add a homely feel. 'I'll be putting in a complaint!' Laura shouted as the van drove off.

Could this day get any worse? As if in answer to her question, a soft speckle of rain kissed the skin on her face. Laura emitted a groan.

Two hours later, Laura was resting her hand on the velvety surface of the new sofa in the spacious living room. She adjusted the plump cushions with care. Each one was a calculated pop of colour against the neutral, muted tones of the house. Her lower back ached from carrying boxes. Laura's gaze swept across the living room. The ghosts of the Wilding family weren't done with the place yet. *Bruce. Ali. Cindy.* Had they spent time here, their laughter resonating in the room?

The sight of the young man FaceTiming in the bedroom had made Laura's skin crawl. Why were some people so fascinated with murder? But, then again, Cally was exactly the same. Not Laura, though. It disgusted her. She could almost hear the heavy stomp of police boots filling the quiet spaces in the aftermath of the crime. Then the hushed presence of detectives as they examined the scene. Each corner of the home would have been filmed, the footage used in court. Revamping 1 Aspen Hollow wouldn't be easy when it was so clearly well known online.

With a practised hand, Laura arranged the stack of agency brochures on the reclaimed-wood coffee table. Their glossy covers promised a luxury lifestyle. Burton Waters had never seen such an ambitious development as Aspen Hollow before. According to an article in *Architecture Now* magazine, locals had protested against planning permission to build the houses in the dip of land. Letters were written about potential flooding, but the developers had a vision and implemented measures to guard against it. Behind the property, the towering aspens played their part, their deep roots providing natural drainage to help make the project a success. So much work had gone into this project, and it had taken just one brutal night to tarnish the image of the house she was standing in.

The rhythmic *tick-tick* of the new oversized clock on the wall underscored the silence. The house was ready for viewings now. She was about to call the Lincoln office when the doorbell delivered a delicate *bing-bong*. Softening her features, she anticipated greeting a stranger. You never knew when a potential buyer would turn up. As Laura opened the door, she was met by not one stranger, but two.

CHAPTER 10

ALI

THEN

I scrape out the last of the Coco Pops into the bin and put Cindy's bowl into the dishwasher. Bruce is sitting at the table. His toast has gone cold as he's engrossed in *Architecture Now* magazine. It came out last week, but he's been rereading it from cover to cover. They've featured Aspen Hollow, and he's on cloud nine. He's come up with a name for the house and it sits proudly over our doorbell: 'Arcadia', which means an idealised, perfect place. Which is exactly what it is to Bruce. I wipe down the counter with my dishcloth, spraying the droplets of spilled milk with the Purdy & Figg counter cleaner that Bruce insists that I use. Today I'm using Grounding Vetiver, which smells like freshly cut grass on a sunny day.

I think of the days when I'd spray my cheap counters using a bottle of Flash that I'd bought for a pound at B&M. Even the air is different here. So clean and fresh, unlike the petrol fumes from cars driving past our last place. Most nights, we hear the owls hoot in the distance. It's taking some getting used to. I've fitted a wildlife camera to capture the hedgehogs coming into our back garden. Esme watches the footage when she gets home from school. Sometimes we catch a glimpse of the deer in the woods, too. Bruce doesn't like the bats, especially the one that swoops into our garden at twilight. I've named him Bertie. It's such a novelty to see them, along with the squirrels that rob our bird feeders at dawn. But it's so dark here at night, especially when the street lights turn off. It's hard to sleep without the comforting glow outside my window.

I can't believe that it's been a whole month since we moved in. I've been so busy. I never imagined what a huge undertaking it would be. We had to throw out most of our old ornaments and pictures. Bruce said that my Dunelm accessories didn't fit in with our new home. But there's the expense of buying things to match . . . I've blown most of my inheritance on the house, but Bruce says it's OK to stick everything else on the credit card. Then there's the extra council tax to pay for all these bedrooms we don't use, and the stamp duty was tens of thousands of pounds. I should be excited, but I'm worried that we're overstretching ourselves financially.

The view from our new home is something else. The close looks picture-perfect – like the Lego houses I used to build as a child. The neighbours are . . . Well, I'm sure I'll fit in eventually. It takes time. I never thought I'd miss anything about our old home. But this place has a different vibe.

I've been scrubbing the same spot for ages, lost in thought. Bruce has finished his toast and is shoving his plate into the dishwasher.

'See you later,' he says, his stubble brushing against my skin as he kisses me on the cheek.

'What time will you be home?' I call after him.

'Not sure, I'll let you know!'

Then the door slams and I'm alone, in this great big house, wondering what I should do. I thought after I was let go from my job that the break from work would do me good. Covid claimed my workplace, as well as the health of the man who ran the Riverside Hotel. It limped on for a year, but it was never the same. Then my parents died, and I haven't had the heart to get another job since. At least I'm earning an income from my YouTube channel. If only they knew that the woman who creates healthy recipes allows her daughter to eat processed cereals for breakfast twice a week.

I stare out the window, watching for signs of life. When a new neighbour moved into our old street, I'd call in to welcome them. Yes, we were all a bit nosey, but we looked out for each other too. Like George, the pensioner who lost his wife five years ago. Or Tanya, the teenage single mum. Or Neil and Aimee, the couple doing odd jobs for cash in hand to keep afloat. I wonder how they're all doing now.

I've had nothing from my new neighbours so far. Not a cheap bottle of prosecco. Not a card. Not even a welcome. Everyone keeps to themselves here. Except for Scarlett and her husband, David, who works as an architect in the same firm. He lost out to Bruce on the contract to design these places. He doesn't hold it against him, though. I'm glad that Bruce has a friend, I just miss the ones I've left behind. My old next-door neighbour Liz came to visit, but I don't think she'll come again. It was hard enough for her when I started vlogging online. But now I've got the house, she thinks I'm showing off. It's not a sin to want to make something of yourself, is it?

A young woman is walking her Pomeranian dog around the close. Their matching pink jackets bring a smile to my face. She's wearing these cute pink braid beads in her hair and white chunky trainers. Should I go out and say hello? Or would that seem desperate? An idea forms as she passes the house. I could invite the new neighbours round for nibbles and drinks. We're overdue a housewarming. It would be nice to get to know everyone. Hopefully they'll like me, too.

There's one new 'friend' that has been following my posts since we made the move. I haven't told Bruce about her yet. If he knew how much she was messaging me, he'd insist I lay off my socials for a while. It's weird, as she doesn't respond to my posts, just messages me directly. It feels rude not to reply, because she always says nice things. She compliments my clothes or shoes, tells me that my recipes are amazing, or says what a great mum I am. It feels nice to hear it. I get nothing out of Bruce anymore, not even flowers. But now my new friend is messaging every day. I keep deleting them in case Bruce twigs that I'm kind of being stalked. At least, that's what it feels like to me. But maybe she's just lonely. She sounds harmless enough. As she says, I have everything she has ever wished for – a loving husband, a beautiful daughter. A home. She talks about how amazing it must feel to wake up feeling loved and secure. Makes you wonder what sort of household she grew up in.

This morning my messenger app displayed ten missed calls. Actual calls. Not messages. Her persistence is slightly disturbing, but it's not as if she's made any threats. She just keeps messaging, saying how great my life is and how much she'd love a little girl like mine. Sometimes she talks about Cindy and Bruce with a false intimacy that leaves me unsettled. I was thinking about blocking her yesterday, then she wrote that my posts are the only thing that get her out of bed. That some days, she feels like ending it all. I couldn't ignore that, because I've had depression and I know how awful it feels. I sent her details of the Samaritans, and told her to look after herself. I tried to make her understand that I can't reply to every comment she makes. I don't want her death on my conscience. The woman needs help.

Another message notification pops up on my phone. It's the price of putting yourself out there on social media, I suppose. She's messaged me again. Her messages always start off in the same familiar way. The weird, off-kilter introduction gives me chills.

Hello sausage!

I mean, what a way to contact someone that you don't even know?

CHAPTER 11

The two men on the doorstep were in stark contrast with each other. The older man peered through thick, black-rimmed glasses that magnified mild, kind eyes. His silver-grey moustache was twirled at the ends with care. His sparse grey hair was neatly combed to one side, his hands clasped loosely together. His companion was a foot taller, with no resemblance to indicate that this was father and son. His skin held the bronze of fake tan, and Laura took in his carefully styled black hair, leather jacket and jeans. This was someone who was hanging on to his youth by his fingernails.

'Evening,' the older man began, delivering a warm smile. 'We're from number three. I'm Walter, and this is my husband, Graham.' His voice was deep and gravelly, with no detectable accent.

'We thought we should introduce ourselves,' Graham chimed in, his blue eyes alight with curiosity. 'Scarlett said there was a new estate agent in town. You must be agent number four, am I right?' He tapped the indent on his chin.

'Nice to meet you both.' Laura matched Walter's amiable tone, despite Graham's unwelcome remark. 'I like your moustache.' She smiled at Walter.

'Thank you.' He delivered a slight bow of the head. 'It has more friends than me!'

Laura smiled. 'Would you like to come in? I was just going to make some tea.' She ushered them both inside, picking up on a subtle unease from Graham as he entered the hall. There was something soothing about the mundane act of greeting neighbours, and she appreciated the company. She watched as they slipped on the overshoes discreetly provided in a basket next to the front door.

'It takes ambition to sell a place like this,' Walter observed, his eyes scanning the home.

'Maybe she likes the danger,' Graham added in a slightly mischievous tone.

'It's a bit of both,' Laura conceded with a smile. These two men represented the community that she needed to get on side. 'I've only been here a few hours, but I have big plans.' In truth, she'd had a horrible start, with one problem after another. The red graffiti, the late delivery, the trouble with the delivery driver upstairs. But she kept her complaints to herself as she showed them in.

The men followed her down the wide hall, their footsteps hollow on the marble-tiled floor. Laura inhaled in appreciation as the scents she had purchased made themselves known. Graham stopped at the open double living-room doors, his lips twitching as he took in each new piece of furniture inside.

'Nice sofa,' he said at last. 'I was thinking of buying one myself.'

'It's from the Amersham range.'

Laura didn't mention that the expensive sofa was rented from a high-end store, as was the rest of the furniture the delivery men had hauled in. She had the aching limbs to prove it, but at least it was done. She'd taken out insurance in case of any accidents, and the furniture was all available for the new owners to buy.

Graham delivered an approving look as he admired the artwork waiting to be hung. 'It would look better on the walls, but it's a good blend of colours and tone.'

'Consider me a transformer of spaces.' Laura gave him a half-smile. 'At least I will be, once I can get a handyman to hang these up.'

'Why pay someone? I'll pop over with my drill. I've got a huge toolbox of goodies.' He delivered a wink. 'We'll have them up in no time.'

'Are you sure? That would be great!' Laura exhaled in relief.

Graham smiled. 'Do you work in the local office? I've not seen you around. We did a lot of house-hunting before we bought our place.'

Laura was happy to answer, grateful for his offer to help. 'I've been brought in from the Louth branch. I specialise in selling houses that need a new lease of life.'

'You're like a fairy godmother for homes.' Walter chuckled.

'Exactly,' Laura replied, leading them through to the expansive kitchen. The evening light slanted through the slim wooden kitchen blinds, laying down alternating bars of gold and shadow.

Minutes later, Laura was handing them cups of tea. There was something about tea that felt so very British to Laura, and the designer tea caddy was well stocked with Yorkshire Tea, Earl Grey and some fruity flavours too. Hospitality was important when it came to selling high-end homes.

'You're not local, though, are you?' Graham peered over the rim of his cup, his pinkie finger sticking elegantly in the air. Everything about him was manicured and polished, and he didn't seem to miss a trick. 'Is that a hint of a Yorkshire accent I detect?'

Laura thought she'd swerved the earlier question about where she was from. 'My father was a Yorkshire man but I grew up on Burton Road in Lincoln. Tell me,' she ventured, keen to change the subject, 'what do you know about the history of this place?'

Walter's cup chinked against his saucer as he rested it on the table. He seemed to give the question some thought as he cleaned his thick glasses and positioned them back on the bridge of his nose. 'It's unthinkable,' he began slowly. 'Bruce seemed so normal. He doted on that little girl.'

'And his wife?'

'We didn't really know her.' He shrugged. 'But they seemed happy enough.'

'I couldn't believe it when I heard.' Graham shook his head. 'The Wildings were just . . . well, an ordinary family. You'd see them out walking around the marina, and they always waved when they drove past in their car.' He tucked his hands into the pockets of his leather jacket and sighed. 'I wish I could have done something, you know? I'm normally good at picking up on these kinds of things.'

Laura didn't doubt it. 'So there was nothing? No small detail that seemed off?' she pressed gently.

A tiny frown creased Walter's brow. 'No. Despite Ali's online presence, they were relatively private people, but not unusually so. And certainly not enough to imagine . . .' His voice trailed off, leaving the sentence to wither.

'We've been asked this question a million times.' Graham picked up where Walter had left off. 'We didn't see anything suspicious.' But as they exchanged a tense glance, Laura sensed that they were holding something back. 'Right!' Graham exclaimed. 'How about we hang these pictures?' Then he was gone, off to get his drill.

'This detects any cables in the wall,' he said upon his return. He was holding a black box, which put Laura's mind at rest. The last thing she wanted was him electrocuting himself.

She and Walter stood watching as he positioned each picture and expertly fitted the attachments needed to hang the artwork on the walls.

'I owe you,' Laura said as she handed him the last print.

'You sure do.' Graham gave her a wink.

'Listen, Laura,' Walter began, as Graham tidied up. 'We just want the neighbourhood to go back to normal. So wave your magic wand and do what you need to do, with our support. It would be nice to have a new family living here. It might get rid of some of the ghouls plaguing the place.' He talked about dark tourists – people who got their kicks out of travelling to crime scenes. 'People have been snooping about in the woods. Then there's the true crime YouTubers, and social media influencers who visit to boost their views.'

Laura gave a knowing nod. 'I've already had that with a delivery driver FaceTiming his girlfriend upstairs. Then there was the graffiti . . .'

'It's not the first time that's happened.' Drill in hand, Graham delivered a weary sigh. 'But Joe, the marina security, does his best to chase them away.'

'But why spray "murder" now? Bruce is in prison. What good does it do?' Laura voiced her thoughts. 'I could understand it if he'd got away with it, but he's been sent down for life.'

'People are still angry,' Walter responded. 'But *we* have to live here. We want to move on.'

Laura liked how the couple answered for each other. She and Shane used to be like that once. They'd been so in tune it was like they could read each other's thoughts.

'Leave it with me.' Laura allowed herself a small smile as she addressed Graham and Walter's concerns. 'Mission Happy Family. I'll turn things around.' She meant every word. This mattered to her.

She switched on a lamp as the room grew dark. Gelling with Graham and Walter was another box ticked.

Walter pushed back his sleeve and checked his oversized watch. 'Thanks for the tea. If there's anything you need, we're two doors down, at number three.'

Laura thanked them both before showing them to the door. But, having removed his overshoes, Graham lingered, as if there was something more he wanted to say.

'C'mon then.' Walter gave him a gentle nudge. 'Claudia will be waiting for her dinner.' He glanced at Laura and smiled. 'Our Persian cat. Quite the drama queen.' Then they were outside, the sweet scent of Graham's aftershave lingering in their wake.

'Bye, now.' Laura's words echoed in the hollow space as she closed the door behind them.

They had been so helpful, but their visit had left her more unsettled than before. Graham seemed observant and keen to be kept abreast of developments. It felt like he knew more than he was letting on. Walter had seemed more genuine, if a little troubled. Perhaps there was a secret behind his smile. She needed to find out more.

But did she? The thought lingered as she walked down the hall. Would questioning the neighbours help sell the home, or was she chasing answers to satisfy her own curiosity?

There was so much work to be done – buyers to convince, and reels to be created for social media. All of that would start tomorrow. A mix of hope and unease churned inside her. Her mind replayed Graham's last glance, before he left to go home.

Shadows crawled along the edges of the house as Laura's gaze circled the living room. In the waning light, she adjusted a painting, tilting it ever so slightly. The image of the marina, with its bobbing boats and still waters, should have brought a sense of peace. Yet Laura's mind was filled with unanswered questions.

A creak from upstairs made her stiffen. *It's just the house settling*, she assured herself. Yet she couldn't calm her growing sense of unease. The graffiti still bothered her. *Murder*. One unnerving word with terrifying connotations.

She climbed the wide stairs, pausing at the door to the master bedroom. Her hand found the light switch and she took in the scene. The new bed looked beautiful. The generous king-size mattress was dressed in crisp linen sheets and a goose-down duvet. She wished that she'd had time to repaper the walls. The cherry-blossom pattern was distinctive, but the dark-pink petals almost looked like splatters of blood. Not that blood had been shed here . . .

Laura looked at the pillows and thought about the amount of pressure needed to smother someone to death. Had he really killed his family like that? Pushed a pillow over their faces while they slept? Laura imagined Ali lying there, her dead eyes misted red.

A door slammed on the landing, and Laura clasped a hand to her chest as she jumped. *What was that?* She tentatively stepped forward, a sense of dread rising. Why did the walls in the room feel like they were closing in? Then sense prevailed as she remembered. The window . . . She'd opened the window in one of the guest rooms to let some fresh air in. Of course. She released a shaky breath. That was it.

But closing the window didn't put Laura at ease. She thought about locking up and doing some work at home. There were plenty of emails to be answered, and she needed to update the office with her marketing plans so far.

She *could* go back to her mum's. Or she could stay and do some filming on her phone. She'd arrange some books next to a throw on the sofa, light some candles, create a cosy scene.

Then a text notification stalled her thoughts. Three words: *I warned you.*

She stared at the screen in disbelief as fear crept over her. It was like she was on the set of a low-budget horror movie. The text was from another number she didn't recognise. She couldn't bring herself to reply. She gathered up her things, turning down the thermostat that insisted it was twenty-two degrees. It felt more like five. Keys in hand, she headed for the door. She wasn't hanging around to see what the message meant.

CHAPTER 12

Scarlett had snorted as she'd seen Graham and Walter pitch up at No. 1. Hadn't taken them long. It wouldn't have been Walter's idea; she was sure of that much. Walter was too nice a man to go around snooping like that. He reminded Scarlett of her grandfather, a kind and humorous soul who saw the best in everyone. She didn't quite get what Walter was doing with Graham, but each to their own. She supposed Graham added a bit of spontaneity to his life. A bit of colour to an otherwise drab day. But being with Graham meant being dragged around to places you didn't want to go.

She had watched them with interest as they both went inside No. 1. As if they hadn't been in that house a hundred times already. With each estate agent, they'd acted like it was their first visit. That was just plain weird. Graham had once told her of his little games – how he liked to play with people and shake things up. He also liked people to be indebted to him. She was sure he was harbouring a dark mind under that charming exterior. He was quite the diva when he'd had a drink or two. He'd even offered her coke once, but she'd politely declined. Things were bad enough as they were. She wasn't ready to jump into the deep end just yet.

She sat on her bed, creasing the duvet that the housekeeper had put on earlier that day. What sort of a life was this – hiding away? She remembered the first time that David had locked her in her room. Well, not everything. She'd been blackout drunk at the time. But she remembered waking up the next day in the recovery position, pins and needles in her right arm, her mouth crusted with vomit, a grey bucket and a pack of wet wipes next to the bed. Faint bruises had dappled her wrists, and she'd still been wearing her clothes from the day before. Her head had felt like somebody was squeezing it in a vice. Bleary-eyed, she'd reached out for the two Panadol that had been left on the dresser, along with the bottle of Evian water. That's when she'd seen the camera sitting on top of the wardrobe, watching her every move. Had David put it there?

She'd groaned as she dragged herself off the bed, with no memory of the night before. At first, she couldn't believe it when the door wouldn't open straight away. It was only after her third or fourth time of rattling it that she'd realised she'd been locked in. Then she'd heard the voice emanating from the camera above the wardrobe. She hadn't even known those things could speak. But it had been David's voice, not the camera, talking. 'I'm on my way home,' he'd said. 'The kids are out for the day.'

Not that she'd asked about them. They were the last thing on her mind when she was like this. She'd burped, and the stink of regurgitated alcohol had sent her reeling. She'd run to the bucket and thrown up whatever was left in her stomach. A mixture of tequila and digestive acid had burned her throat as it appeared.

She hadn't had the energy to be outraged when David arrived home. She'd known by the expression on his face that she'd gone off the rails the night before. 'What did I do?' she'd said, nursing her head as the worst of the pain subsided.

'Later,' David had replied firmly, telling her to go downstairs. 'You need to eat first.'

He'd been unnervingly quiet that day. He'd spoken in soft tones, careful not to upset her as she nursed the mother of all hangovers. 'I didn't want to leave you, but there was a meeting

I couldn't miss. I was checking on you every five minutes.' He'd seemed relieved that she was so subdued. She always was the day after a blowout. She'd promised that she would never drink again.

'It's too late,' David had replied, in a worryingly quiet voice. 'The damage has already been done.'

Fear had lit up her senses. She would never forget the expression on his face. Her normally placid husband had tears in his eyes. That's when Scarlett knew that things would never be the same again.

CHAPTER 13

'I was wondering . . . Can we talk?'

Shane caught Laura just as she was about to take Esme to school. Her daughter had run ahead to the car, ponytail bouncing, singing a Taylor Swift song.

Laura turned to her husband, raising her voice against the rising wind. 'When? My schedule is chocka today.' Lincoln Cathedral's bells rang in the distance, a reminder to get Esme to school on time.

'Anytime. But soon.' His hair still damp from the shower, he stood in his tie, shirt and jeans, ready for his next Zoom call. Shane didn't love being a financial advisor, but he had been railroaded into the job by his parents at a young age. Now he'd started a practice of his own. 'I've tried to give you space but . . .' He shuffled his feet as Laura checked her watch. 'I miss you,' he said eventually. 'Why don't you move back in?'

Laura fought to keep her expression neutral. It had taken a lot to walk out on him. She still loved her husband, but she couldn't go on with the way things were. 'We're not separating, Shane. I'm just taking a stand.'

'All the same. Come home.' His face was fraught with concern.

'I will, as soon as things change. You can't leave it all to me.'

His expression brightened. 'They will. I'm working on it. We'll soon have a place of our own.'

'Well, work harder. I've got to go. Esme will be late for school.'

She pushed down her rising emotions and got into the car. She'd pleaded with Shane for months to aim for a place in both of their names. The townhouse he'd received from his parents had never felt like theirs, especially given the deeds were in his name alone. Laura slammed the car door, face flushed as her grievances came to the forefront of her mind.

'What's wrong, Mummy?' Esme had been watching everything.

'Nothing, sweetie, we were just chatting.'

Laura turned over the car engine. Her resolve was beginning to weaken. Esme deserved a stable home. But she also deserved to be brought up in a space where her parents weren't bickering night and day. She found a cheerful Taylor Swift playlist for them both to sing along to.

The school run complete, Laura negotiated the mini-roundabout that would take her to Aspen Hollow. She was on the phone to Cally, who'd just finished admonishing her.

'How do you think I felt, seeing you in that house? You could have given me a heads-up!' Cally was referring to Laura's social media posts.

'I didn't think you'd recognise it. I was going to tell you when I next saw you.' Laura was used to her sister's protective nature, which was why she hadn't said anything before.

'I'd know that place anywhere! I was obsessed with that case.' Cally's sigh ruffled the phone line. 'Just be careful, yeah? There's a lot of people out there who believe Bruce Wilding was framed.'

'Are you one of them?'

'I was, but now I don't know. There's too much conflicting evidence.' Cally's voice lowered to a whisper. 'Shit. My boss has come in. Bye!'

Laura smiled at the abrupt end to their call. Cally had been advised to cut down on using her phone during work hours. Laura hoped her sister hadn't been caught. She would have loved to get Cally's insights on the case, but equally she didn't want to disclose her own concerns. She couldn't fathom how any father could hurt his family, but why on earth would anyone else have done such a thing?

She slowed as she drove down into Aspen Hollow. The tall wrought-iron gates either side of the road were ornamental, nothing more. The close wasn't as truly secure as the brochures made out.

Her spirits began to deflate like a celebratory balloon with a pin-hole as the house came into view. She should have been elated. Her boss was pleased with her work. They already had a viewing lined up.

Due to the nature of the property, Laura had requested pre-checks on prospective buyers. She had emphasised the need for exclusivity, going so far as to ensure that any viewer had the funds in place to purchase No. 1. The elusive Clio seemed to resent Laura's involvement, probably because she'd failed to sell the place herself. Clio wasn't social-media-savvy; Laura came with more than twenty thousand followers, and that number was growing by the day.

Jonathan was already standing outside the house. She'd arranged to meet him this morning and film a walk-through for the listing. She'd chosen to wear a turquoise dress, despite the October chill. Her auburn hair hung loose in soft waves, and her tan shoes came with a block heel. Trustworthy yet professional was the look she was going for. She enjoyed being centre-stage. This was everything Laura had wanted. So why was she filled with a sense of dread?

Jonathan was slim on the verge of gangly, with piercing blue eyes and thick sandy hair. He was the most helpful person in the Lincoln office of Ridgeway Residential, and his smile rested naturally on his face. As he adjusted the camera angle, he stepped back to frame Laura in the grand living room of 1 Aspen Hollow. They'd been filming for almost an hour, but by the time Jonathan had finished editing the footage, the clip would be just minutes long. Fixing her lapel mic, Laura stood by the marble fireplace, its pristine surface reflecting the light. The sun streamed in through generous-sized windows, yet the house felt colder somehow.

'Follow me . . .' Laura said with enthusiasm, 'to the kitchen, the heart of the home. Where precious memories are made.' Jonathan followed her out. 'It's perfect for entertaining guests, with plenty of open space for a dining area to seat as many as you wish. Isn't it gorgeous?' She went through each feature, every one a selling point. Then they finished where they'd started, in the hall.

'Done?' she said to Jonathan, finally able to relax.

He lowered the camera. 'Yeah, all done here.'

He gathered up his equipment from the island in the kitchen. But his smile faded, his shoulders rising half an inch. It seemed Laura wasn't the only person unable to relax in this home.

She handed him his spare camera battery as he collected up his things. 'What is it? What's wrong?'

'I wasn't going to say anything but . . .' He shoved the battery into his camera bag. 'You'll keep this between us, won't you?'

Laura's forehead creased. 'You have my word.'

'You know how Grimshaw transferred you?'

'Yeah. What about it?'

'Just . . . be careful with this one,' he murmured. 'There's a reason nobody wanted this listing.'

Laura raised an eyebrow. She thought she'd been specially chosen, but in reality No. 1 was a poisoned chalice.

'If you're talking about the murders, I'm well aware.'

'It's not that.' Jonathan sighed. 'I was chatting with Felicity – you know, from Beacon Homes over in Gainsborough. She was one of the previous agents for this place. She said some really weird stuff went on here.'

Laura crossed her arms, yesterday's text messages in her mind. 'Weird how?'

He hesitated, glancing towards the windows as though someone might be listening.

'She said this place gave her the creeps. Then stuff started happening. Things were moved. There were noises upstairs. She started getting these anonymous texts and calls. Then . . . someone started following her. They drove right up her arse one night, nearly took the bumper off her car.'

Laura blinked, her polished composure faltering. 'It's easy to get spooked when there's a murder involved.'

Jonathan pulled on his coat. 'That's what I thought at first. But it got so bad that she reported it to the police. Threatening texts night and day. Being followed. Even her car was vandalised. She was scared, Laura. And she wasn't the only one. Every estate agent who's handled this house has been threatened in some way.'

Laura didn't mention her texts. She desperately needed the commission from the sale of No. 1. 'I had no idea.'

'That's why this place has been through so many hands. Just be careful, yeah?'

'I'll be reet,' she said finally, with a wink as she faked her father's accent. 'Tough as old boots, me. There's Yorkshire blood in these veins.' But their laughter didn't linger and Jonathan wasted no time in leaving the house.

He stood in the doorway, car keys in hand. 'It'll take a couple of hours to edit, but you'll be online today.'

Laura was glad to hear it. But the thought of being stalked was frightening. Who was behind it? And just how far would they go? She had barely closed the door when she heard the sound of laughter. It was coming from inside the house.

What the hell? Had someone come in while she was in the kitchen with Jonathan? Now she could hear voices. Taking tentative steps, she followed the sounds towards the living room. But they sounded artificial, tinny even.

'Happy birthday to you . . .' the voices sang. 'Happy birthday, dear Cindy . . .'

Cindy? Wasn't that the Wildings' little girl? Laura's breathing accelerated. She picked up the bronze ballerina figurine on the hall console table. A heavy enough weapon if needed. The ornament was icy-cold in her palm as she pushed open one of the double living room doors. It sounded like a recording, but how was that possible? The singing descended into clapping.

'Who's there?' Laura's voice was firm, but her pulse had picked up speed.

No response.

She caught sight of her phone, which was sitting on a coffee table in front of the fireplace. It was the source of the sound. Laura looked left and right, checking every corner of the room. No feet peeping out from beneath curtains. No one crouching behind the sofa. She peered at her phone. It was one of Ali's YouTube videos. A birthday party for Cindy. These were the voices and faces of the dead.

Satisfied the room was empty, Laura rested the figurine on the table and snatched up her phone. She'd left it unlocked. Passwords were a nuisance when Esme wanted to play on her apps. The thought of someone being in here, touching her things . . . She shuddered. Then she retraced her last steps. She *had* put her phone down here. It couldn't have played the video on its own . . . could it? But Jonathan's warning rang in her ears. As for the texts she'd received . . . She walked down the corridor, listening for the slightest of sounds. But all she heard was the *boom . . . boom . . . boom* of her heart. As she stood in the hall, she realised that the silence wasn't empty. It was watching and waiting for her next move.

CHAPTER 14

Bruce stared at his last piece of paper. It was cheap and curling at the edges, and if he pressed too hard with his stubby pen, it poked a hole through. 'Canteen' was the term used for the weekly delivery of items that inmates could buy from the prison shop. The canteen sheet displayed his prison number and name, along with the small amount of money that was available for him to spend. He couldn't help but feel depressed whenever it was shoved under his cell door. He'd taken so much for granted in the past. Now, he had to budget like never before. His £10 a week covered the basics, but he could earn up to £20 a week extra if he put himself to work. But that meant mixing with other inmates more than he did now. So, instead, he'd learned to write small, ensuring he didn't waste a scrap of paper, and he only washed his hair once a week. The flimsy sachets of prison shampoo were nothing like the nice-smelling bottles of Molton Brown he'd used at home. He wondered if any of the women who wrote to him would send him some funds. But equally, it disgusted him, the thought of replying to their letters. What did they want from him?

Bruce pushed away the empty page. He could never confess to his sister on paper, as the prison read every word. He didn't hear the footsteps approaching, and stiffened at the sudden rasping of a metal key infiltrating the lock on his door.

'Wilding,' mumbled the guard, a large man with razor burn and an impassive face. Bruce approached him, his thoughts scattering, as the guard delivered a stack of envelopes. There were more. Why? Was it because his house being up for sale had gained traction online? The guard wasted no time in handing the letters over. Bruce sifted through them and one stood out, its edges frayed, as if it had been held tightly by anxious fingers before making it to the post box.

It was from her – the woman who greeted him in the strangest of ways. Her term of endearment was hard to forget. He couldn't shake her off. Then he wondered, why did he keep everything she sent? He debated whether to rip the letters into pieces. But his curiosity regarding her latest communication was stronger than his fear.

The envelope flap separated easily, having already been opened by the prison guards. Such small violations made life in this place that little bit harder. Some bloke was shouting in the distance, making it hard to concentrate on the words on the page. Prison was a place where peace didn't exist.

Bruce sat on the thin mattress, which was slightly more comfortable than the chair.

> *Hello sausage,*
> *I hope you're keeping your spirits up. I had to write another letter, to keep you updated on the house. There's a new estate agent in our beautiful home. Laura is her name. Sounds like a right know-it-all.*

Bruce frowned as he reread the words. *Your* home had now changed to *our* home. Regardless, he was grateful for the update.

Those neighbours of yours have been round. That old fella and his gold-digger husband with the leather jacket. What a fool he looks, with his flashy white teeth and dyed black hair. I call the old fella Walter the wally, with his big glasses and circus moustache, looking like a character from Up! Talk about a mismatch . . . Aspen Hollow is far too good for the likes of those two. I bet you never imagined when you drew up those beautiful plans that you'd have a couple of gays moving in.

Bruce clenched his back molars as he took in the hateful words. His gaze was drawn to his cell window, fury making a home in his chest. What a horrible, ignorant piece of work. But like it or not, Miss 'Sausage' was a link to the outside world. He hadn't heard from his sister in ages. But this woman . . . She was there. On the ground, watching everything. The fact she could report such details about his neighbours left him in no doubt. He drew in a deep breath, inhaling the sterile smell of the prison-grade cleaner that struggled to mask the stench of stale piss. Some inmates enjoyed an odd dirty protest, and left urine puddles by their doors for when the prison guards walked in. A buzzer went off nearby, making his heart lurch. Would he ever get used to this place? He stared at the Rubik's Cube on his tiny desk, one of the few things that kept him occupied. His life was like those coloured squares – a mismatch that wouldn't easily align.

He returned his attention to the letter. The words were printed in the usual Comic Sans font, but he could feel the author's anger seeping through the page.

Scarlett's fooling nobody with her sports bottle. By the way she's staggering around, there's more than water in there. As for that Laura, with her fancy furniture and ornaments, it's as if you never existed, like she's selling a brand-new house. You should see her, dressed up to the nines, driving her big posh car. Her hair is so bouncy, it wouldn't surprise me if she was wearing a wig. But don't you fret. I'll soon see her off. I'm here, ready to roll up my sleeves and put up a fight – and I don't mean metaphorically.

So don't you worry, my love. One way or another, I'll get rid of her.

I've got your back. That's what friends are for.

'No,' Bruce whispered. The woman was becoming wildly territorial. The prison guards must have raised an eyebrow when reading that. Perhaps that was why she'd remained anonymous all along – she didn't want to be questioned about her motives. What did she mean when she said that she'd 'see her off'? Was it all in her mind? An empty threat? A manic fantasy? But she was there, watching. She seemed to know exactly what was going on. He reread the last paragraph. The words of love and friendship. What planet was this woman on?

Bruce shuffled through the stack of other letters. Each one was a reminder of what he was missing in the world outside. Some women talked about their day-to-day lives; others searched for answers about his supposed crimes. Love letters, hate letters, and every damned thing in between. Only one letter worried him enough to use up his last precious page to reply.

The confines of his cell pressed against him as he was consumed by a sense of helplessness. He had to find a way to warn the estate agent without coming across as a psycho.

He paused. He didn't know her surname, or how to address her. There was a good chance the bouncy-haired Laura would be disturbed by contact from a convicted murderer. But he had to try to warn her that someone was watching. Finding religion had taught him that it was never too late to try to do some good. And if she went running for the hills . . . Well, it would give him more time to figure out how to keep the house.

His grip tightened on the clear stubby pen. He missed his beautiful graphite pencils, and how they'd felt so smooth as the tip glided across the page.

Focus, he told himself as his thoughts wandered. It felt like his brain cells were disappearing. He needed to stay on track.

> *Dear Laura,*
> *My name is Bruce Wilding.*
> *You may know who I am. I understand that you've been assigned to sell 1 Aspen Hollow. I mean you no harm and I'm not trying to interfere with your job. But there's a woman who's been writing to me in prison. I've enclosed her letter. I don't know who she is, or why she's doing this. You're welcome to visit me in prison if you'd like to find out more.*
> *I'll understand if you don't. I just thought I should let you know. She obviously doesn't want the house sold. Be careful. It might not be worth the risk. She sounds pretty unhinged.*
>
> *Best regards,*
> *Bruce*

He stared at the blank space on the page. Such a waste when he could have filled it with an outpouring of words. He could tell her that he was innocent. That everything the press were saying about him was a lie. But he knew he'd be wasting his time.

He leaned against the cool concrete wall of his cell, the rough texture grazing his muscled back as he shifted his weight. Was he doing the right thing? Deep down, he didn't want the house to sell.

How strange it was to imagine someone living there while he rotted away in prison. He'd designed every inch of those spaces with care. When he was young and times were tough, he used to imagine his dream home. An odd thing for a young boy to spend time on, but his dream of a better life had offered him an escape from his shitty world. He'd daydreamed about the tall designer windows, the impressive double-door entrance, and the wide polished stairwell. He closed his eyes now as he strained to recall the sound of the marina's waters, lapping against the boats. Then the short walk to the nearby sports bar where he and Ali used to sit in the sun. But now the memory was fading, replaced by Ali's screams of disbelief. People had no idea what had gone on behind the doors of 1 Aspen Hollow.

Bruce's fingers traced the creases of the folded letter, the paper's rough texture a grim reminder of the stakes. Sweat beaded his temples, not from the stale warm air of his cell but from the relentless churning of his thoughts. He slid the letter beneath his pillow. He'd find a way of getting it to Laura. What he had done to Ali was unforgivable. The least he could do was stop another person from getting hurt.

CHAPTER 15

Laura's stomach rumbled in complaint. But she needed to put in the hours so she could move on. Whoever was trying to stop the sale was a bully, and she'd seen off plenty of them in her time. Memories of her childhood brought a smile to her face. She'd always been getting into trouble at school for sticking up for underdogs. When words didn't work, she'd punch them on the nose. Her short, sudden jabs had come out of nowhere – and that was just in primary school. Her father would pretend to be annoyed until he got her home. 'Well done, lass,' he'd say. 'You've got to stand up for yourself in this world.' Perhaps that was why she disliked her mother-in-law so much. But she wasn't dealing with her mother-in-law now. And the question still lingered: why would anyone be so intent on disrupting the sale of the house?

She turned off the car engine and stepped out into the cooling evening air. It had been good to get out of the house and take some photos of the surrounding area. But now darkness was closing in. At least there was no more graffiti on the walls. She peered at the soft lights of the neighbours' houses, their curtains and blinds tightly shut. Her watch read five p.m. She would check that the listing had gone live, share it on her socials, then finish answering her emails.

She let out a tired sigh as she saw a middle-aged woman standing on the doorstep of No. 1. Who was this, at this hour? What did she want? She took in the woman's black Converse shoes and baggy linen shirt and trousers. Her navy jacket was smart, but everything about her appeared mismatched. Both hands tightly clutched a tote bag.

Laura reframed her inner monologue and repeated her usual mantra. *You never know when a viewer will turn up. It only takes one person. Just one. So be nice.*

'Good evening.' The woman's light Scottish accent softened the edges of her words. 'Sorry . . . I know it's late . . . My train was delayed and I didn't want to leave it until tomorrow in case you were busy with viewers.' She smoothed down her frizzy brown hair. 'Sorry . . . I'm Mags. How do you do?' She appeared slightly breathless as she reached out a sturdy hand.

'Nice to meet you, Mags.' Laura smiled through the strongest handshake she'd received in some time. 'I'm Laura.' She looked at Mags expectantly but no response came. 'What can I do for you?'

'Oh! Sorry, what am I like? I presumed you'd know who I am.' Mags apologised for the third time in as many minutes. 'I'm Maggie Wilding, Bruce Wilding's sister. Don't look so scared . . .' An awkward laugh left her lips. 'I mean you no harm.' She tightened her grip on her thick burlap tote bag, which featured a design reading 'Are You Kitten Me?' alongside images of cats. Everything about her seemed homely, but it was getting late.

'Oh . . . Right, I see.' Laura's voice remained steady despite the fluttering in her chest.

'Sorry to turn up out of the blue.' Mags delivered a wide, hopeful smile. 'But I wondered if I could see the place one more time before it's sold.' She took in Laura's face. 'Sorry. I should have let you know.'

Laura should have told her to book an appointment, but she'd come such a long way. And if Laura was honest with herself, she wanted the lowdown on Bruce Wilding. And who better to fill in the gaps than his own sister? But Laura was also trusting. Too trusting at times. Should she let this total stranger inside?

'Of course you can come in,' Laura found herself saying as she looked for the keys in her bag. It wasn't much different than viewers turning up unexpectedly. But the house wasn't fitted with Ring cameras, or any kind of CCTV. Apparently Bruce Wilding had valued his privacy. She recalled something Shane had said when he'd fitted their own home with surveillance. 'The people who worry about being watched are the ones doing something wrong.'

Laura stepped back, granting entry to the unexpected guest. Her mind raced with questions as the woman shuffled inside. Sweet, flowery perfume trailed in her wake. Mags pulled out an old Quality Street tin from her bag. It was the kind that you could buy at Christmas in the eighties, before they'd shrunk in size.

'I baked you a Dundee cake. Some comfort food, given the circumstances.'

'And you brought it all the way from Scotland?' Laura's cold fingers brushed against Mags's warm hand as she took the heavy tin. 'Thanks.' Laura's stomach rumbled in approval. 'I'll put the kettle on.' Comfort food was just what she needed. She rested the tin on the kitchen counter. The smell of candied peel and whisky escaped as she popped open the lid. 'Mmm, smells gorgeous.'

But Mags was barely listening as she stood taking everything in. 'Bruce always loved Dundee cake,' she mused quietly. 'Couldn't get enough of it when he was young.'

As the water in the kettle bubbled and steam rose, Laura turned to make the tea. 'I'm sorry about what happened.' She poured the water into the generous-sized cups. 'It must have been very hard.'

'Aye . . . He's lost everything, sure enough. Ali, Cindy, his home. His letters from prison . . .' Mags blinked, turning her soulful brown eyes back to Laura. 'They're heartbreaking.'

Mags accepted a generous slice of cake with her cup of tea. 'He didn't do it, you know. I swear on everything that's holy, it wasn't him.'

Laura nodded, trying to reconcile the fact that she was eating cake made by Bruce Wilding's sister while trying to sell the home where he'd murdered his family. They sat at the huge kitchen island, drinking from the matching designer cups.

'You must be wondering why I made the journey . . .' Mags spoke in slow, measured tones. 'I mean, why now?'

Laura noticed her habit of breaking up her sentences, as if she was unsure of how to speak. This was a woman who clearly spent considerable time on her own. Laura chewed the Dundee cake, enjoying the rich, moist texture and sweet flavour. Homemade food had been in short supply when she was growing up.

'I wasn't there for Bruce – at least, not when he needed me,' Mags carried on. 'Story of my life. My timing's always been off.'

There's a story there, somewhere, Laura thought, but she allowed Mags the space she needed to carry on.

'I saw your post on social media. I knew it wouldn't be long until you sold the place. I wanted to see it one more time. Put some ghosts to rest.' She paused to clear her throat. 'Is that odd, do you think? I've not been able to visit Bruce in prison, even though he's innocent. It's not him . . .' She paused again. Regrouped. 'I don't do well in crowds.'

Which was most likely why she'd chosen this time of the evening to arrive at the door of 1 Aspen Hollow. The last thing she would have wanted was to bump into any ghouls interested in buying the house.

'Do you need a few minutes? To say goodbye to the place?'

But Mags shook her head. 'Hold on.' She dipped her hand into her tote bag, which had been resting next to her on the marble countertop. 'Read this first.'

Her curiosity piqued, Laura opened the folded page that Mags slid across to her. Then her mouth dropped open. She stared at the prison headed paper. It was a letter from Bruce, written a month ago. 'Hey sis . . .' it began. Bruce then poured his heart out, proclaiming his innocence. He talked about his love for Cindy, and how devastating it had been, being blamed for her and Ali's deaths. He spoke of the times with his little girl he'd taken for granted, and how he wished he could travel back in time. Laura scanned the page, suddenly feeling like a voyeur. This was a man in deep despair. Reluctantly, she folded the letter and gave it back to Mags. Bruce and his family were getting under her skin.

'Now you know I'm the real deal.' Mags gave her a knowing look as she reclaimed the piece of prison paper. 'I'm glad you let me inside, but for your own sake, be careful. Your neighbours . . . They see everything. Someone round here knows what really happened that day.'

The conviction in her voice made Laura feel suddenly cold.

'Bruce didn't have the easiest of childhoods,' Mags continued. 'Our father was a domineering man. We couldn't do a thing right in his eyes. He gave our mother a dog's life.' She paused to sip her tea, her expression filled with regret. 'I left home as soon as my legs would carry me. Then Bruce was left on his own. I'll always feel bad about that.' Laura listened as Mags talked about their childhood, and how obsessed Bruce had been with Ali as a teen. 'I don't leave Scotland often. I felt bad about missing their wedding but they had it abroad. Still . . .' A soft smile rested on her face. 'I visited the house a few times. They brought Cindy to meet me not long after she was born.' Her voice broke at the mention of her niece. 'Poor little mite. A piece of me died the day she left this world.' Mags's eyes glistened with unshed tears as the emotions took hold.

'Is there any chance the truth will come out?' Laura's voice was a whisper, lost in the tragic story that was clearly still raw for

Mags. She didn't know enough about the case to make a judgement either way.

'Hope is all I have left,' Mags admitted. 'I was approached by a lot of reporters . . . but I can't bear being in the public eye. All those people . . . looking at me. Judging. Saying vicious things about my Bruce.' She let out a sorrowful sigh. 'If I were more confident, like you . . . maybe I could help find the person responsible.'

Laura nodded, guessing it had taken a lot of courage for Mags to come here. 'You want my help?'

'Would you?' Mags brightened. 'There was video footage – but it was grainy at best. That could have been anyone driving his car. Bruce said he lost the spare key the week before. I told the police. My brother's been set up. Just because they were wearing his clothes, it doesn't mean that it was him.'

Laura's brow furrowed. From what Mags was saying, evidence *could* have been forced together to fit.

'Cindy and Ali were drugged, then smothered. But Bruce was drugged too. When he woke up . . . Well, you can imagine. It's clear that he was set up.'

'Surely there was more evidence against him?' Laura said. 'Sorry, I'm not familiar with the case.' She thought about Cally, who probably knew it inside out.

'He'd rowed with Ali the day she died. They . . . they weren't happy together, despite her social media posts. He was upfront with the police about their argument from the start. But the scratches on his neck were damning, as well as his skin being under Ali's fingernails.' Mags leaned in closer. 'The police had their wee story. Didn't look any further. Bruce isn't violent. He never raised a hand to Ali, and he wasn't capable of hurting Cindy.' Her eyes widened as she brought her point home. 'Think. Why would he do it? He was an intelligent man. If he didn't want to be married, he could have just got a divorce.'

But Laura wondered how well Mags really knew her brother.

Mags picked at her cake. 'Bruce was in a lot of debt. Money was the root of many an argument, and his online gambling cost them their house. Then there was Ali's life insurance. Bruce was due a payout if she died.'

'I see,' Laura said. 'It's a tough one alright.'

'You'd think they had the perfect marriage, to look at Ali's videos online. But . . .' Her face took on a faraway gaze. 'Truthfully, they weren't right for each other. You wouldn't blame him for seeking comfort elsewhere.'

Laura almost choked on her tea. 'Excuse me.' She covered it up with a cough. She was about to ask if Bruce had been having an affair when Mags spoke again.

'But he's innocent – honest, he is. Whatever went on between him and Ali, he'd never hurt little Cindy. She was an angel.'

In the echoey kitchen, Laura wondered what had really happened that night. She didn't know what to believe. What if Mags was telling the truth? Having money problems didn't make you a murderer. But if not Bruce, who had killed his wife and child?

'Look at the time,' Mags murmured, glancing at her old-fashioned digital watch. 'I should go.'

'Don't rush on my behalf,' Laura replied, not looking forward to being left on her own in the house. 'I've finished work for the day. Would you like to see the rest of the house?'

They paused in the hallway, and Mags rested a hand on the banister. 'Cindy used to race up these stairs. Poor wee thing.' She placed her hand on her chest, as if pushing painful emotions down. 'I have a grief therapist, you know. We speak over the phone. I never knew such things existed until . . . until . . .' She swallowed hard.

'Are you OK?' Laura interjected. 'Can I get you anything?'

Mags shook her head. 'Sometimes it hits me in waves.' She briefly closed her eyes and inhaled a steady breath. 'I'm fine. Let's see what you've done with the living room.'

Having quickly recovered, Mags took the lead, smiling as she approached the bookcase that Laura had stocked. 'Bruce had quite the collection of books. Do you enjoy reading, Laura?'

'Very much so,' Laura replied, glad of the distraction. Her mind had been racing since Mags had turned up, casting doubt on the police evidence that had put Bruce away for life.

'So do I.' Mags delivered a chuckle that filled the room with some much-needed warmth. 'I love romance novels. They're my escape from reality.' She held her tote bag tightly as she delivered a mischievous smile. 'Some of the characters are quite . . . seductive.'

'You know,' Laura began with a twinkle in her eyes, 'I've always found book boyfriends to be far more reliable than real-life ones. They *never* disappoint.'

Mags's eyes brightened with amusement. 'I couldn't agree more. Fictional characters are much better behaved. They don't leave dirty pants lying around, for a start!'

Their soft laughter continued to fill the silent spaces of the house. Laura liked her new-found friend.

'Well, this is just dandy.' Mags nodded to herself. 'But my hotel room is waiting. Thanks for your kindness.'

Laura felt a pang of disappointment at the impending solitude. 'My pleasure. It was nice to meet you.'

As Mags called for a taxi to pick her up, Laura realised that she'd spent more time talking about her brother than touring the house. Perhaps she'd been looking for an ally all along. She waited with Mags for her taxi to arrive.

'Can I ask you something, Mags?' She inhaled the evening air, fresh and cool as it reached her lungs. The close's street lights twinkled, and in the distance she heard the soft repetitive hoot of an owl.

'Of course,' Mags said, both hands clasped over her tote bag.

This wasn't the time or the place, but Laura needed to know. 'Who could have done it? You mentioned Bruce finding comfort elsewhere. Was he having an affair?' Then she told Mags about the threatening texts she'd received, and the problems other agents had encountered with the house.

'The texts only go to prove my point,' Mags said. 'It doesn't surprise me in the least. I told the police . . .' Her eyes narrowed as she glanced around the close. 'Someone here knows what happened. Maybe all of them do.' The beam of car headlights stole her attention as a Handsome Cabs car pulled up in front of the drive. 'Maybe I've said too much,' she said softly, her words tinged with regret.

She had swerved the question about a potential affair. It appeared to be such a painful subject that Laura couldn't ask it again.

Mags waved an acknowledgement at the driver before turning back to Laura. 'Be careful. Don't spend too long here on your own.'

'But who . . . ?' Laura followed Mags as she hurried down the path.

Mags's face was flushed as she opened the taxi door. Laura couldn't read the emotion twisting her features. Was it regret? Fear? 'I'll tell you more, when we have more time. We'll talk it over then.'

'Here's my card.' Laura passed it over. 'Call me.' She wanted to ask her how long she was staying for, what she'd meant and what she knew. But Mags just smiled before slipping the card into her tote bag.

Then she was gone into the night, and Laura was left with a gnawing sensation in her gut. Mags was holding something back. As much as she wanted her brother freed, the woman was scared.

CHAPTER 16

ALI

THEN

I tug at the navy material of my Ralph Lauren dress. It's too tight around my waist. Why did I have to put on weight? It's hard when your occupation revolves around food. 'Never trust a skinny chef,' they say. But now I'm paying the price. I bought the dress in a sale and waited too long to wear it.

The house feels too warm; the dress is sticking to my skin and my armpits are damp with sweat. Summer has arrived and I've had two showers already today. I should have hired a caterer instead of making everything myself. I glance across at Scarlett, with her flawless skin and effortless style, and feel so frumpy in comparison. She's here for nibbles and drinks, along with the rest of our neighbours. A housewarming of sorts. Bruce is in charge of the playlist, and a smooth jazzy tune adds to the ambience in our living room.

I glance around at the expensive decor and designer furnishings. This is a million miles away from when we used to dance to Echo & the Bunnymen in our tiny living room. He was overweight back then, and I was five months pregnant. We had little, but the memory of those nights still brings a smile to my face. He's worked hard to get into shape. But who's he been doing it for?

I cross the kitchen, a smile fixed to my face. Soft lighting illuminates the room, and the kitchen island is laden with food and wine. The beetroot-and-rye tartines haven't been touched, but the smoked salmon blinis have gone down well. There's a few mini arancini carbonaras still sitting there, but Bruce and David have decimated the mini burgers. I stick a carrot baton into my homemade hummus. That's all I'll be having if I want this dress to ever fit me properly again. The music flows over me, and I try to relax. There's a chatter of conversation between our neighbours. People seem to be enjoying themselves.

It feels wrong, not inviting our old friends. But Bruce didn't want to make the wrong impression on our new neighbours. He said it's best to leave our past life behind. I joked that he was becoming a snob, but when free drinks are involved, they *can* go over the top. Our soirée feels dry without them and I force myself to mingle. The gay couple are nice enough, although the younger one . . . What's his name? Graham? That's it. He keeps asking me questions. I think he's trying to find out how we could afford this place.

Billie doesn't say a lot, just watches us all a bit too intensely. I was a taken aback to see her bring her little Pomeranian, but perhaps she's shy.

'Are you OK, Billie? Would Princess like a drink of water?'

She's sitting in a chair in the corner of the room, her dog on her lap, a glass of wine in her hand. It's my third time trying to engage with her, but she just shakes her head.

'Princess only drinks Evian,' she says over a George Benson tune.

I laugh a bit too loudly, then realise she's serious. 'Sorry.' I tap my champagne glass. 'Fizz gives me the giggles.' She smiles and finishes the wine in her glass. 'So, you run an ironing company,' I go on. 'Graham was telling me about your business. You've accomplished so much so young. And your socials – they're on fire! You'll have to give me a few tips.' Billie's socials don't just give ironing tips; she is quickly overtaking the online influencer Mrs Hinch with her cleaning recommendations too. She's done well to be able to afford such a big property so young.

She delivers a polite smile. 'Thanks. And thanks for the invitation. I hope you're settling in.' She scoops up her dog from her lap with one hand and places her on the floor. Would you mind' – she hands me her empty glass – 'taking this, please? Princess needs to stretch her legs.'

As she leaves, I have a feeling that I won't see her again. I rest the wine glass upside down in the dishwasher. Scarlett's laughter grows in intensity. She keeps touching Bruce's arm. I grit my back teeth. Her giggle is just. Too. Much.

CHAPTER 17

The couple booked in for today's viewing looked younger than Laura had expected. The man was no more than thirty – stocky, unshaven, but well dressed in a charcoal suit. The woman wore chunky gold jewellery, and was a couple of inches taller with the help of her Louboutin heels. She played with the ends of her long dark hair as she followed her husband around. Sam and Samantha Golding. Were their names even real?

Their curiosity soon ventured into the macabre. 'So, what's your take on the murders?' Sam asked, his spicy aftershave overpowering Laura as they descended the stairs. 'Guilty or not guilty?'

She fixed her gaze firmly ahead. 'I've no opinion either way,' she replied, her disappointment growing as she led them back into the hall. 'It's amazing, isn't it? The house is so close to Lincoln city, but with the woodlands and the nearby marina, Aspen Hollow offers a real sense of peace and privacy.'

'So he smothered them in their beds, then dragged them downstairs?' Samantha touched her chin with a long red varnished nail. 'Why didn't he just kill them in the kitchen, instead of all that extra work of carrying them down? Makes no sense.'

Laura's patience was being tested today. Samantha had already tried to take photos, but Laura had warned against it. The terms of the viewing had been clearly explained.

'That's what I thought, babe.' Sam's accent became less plummy, and developed an Essex twang. 'He'd already drugged them, so it was premeditated. But he was so sloppy getting rid of them. He must have known he'd get caught. You're right. Makes no sense.'

Laura straightened her posture as she turned to face them both. 'I have a feeling you're more interested in the murders than the house itself.'

'I never said that . . .' Sam's forehead furrowed as he frowned. 'Might be interesting to live in a murder house – a bit of a focal point for conversation . . .' He winked at his wife. 'As long as you don't piss me off.' Samantha slapped her husband's back, sniggering in response.

'Yes, well, I have another viewing soon,' Laura lied. 'So let me know by the end of the day if you'd like to put in an offer. We've had lots of interest.'

'I'm sure you have.' Sam smiled, following her to the front door. His cufflinks glinted in the light as he bent to remove his overshoes. 'But you won't sell this place. No chance.' He cast one last glance around, his wife tottering to keep her balance as she pulled an overshoe from each heel. 'We'll make you an offer,' he continued. 'But for a *lot* less than the asking price.'

'I'm afraid we won't be dropping,' Laura countered. She could have explained the benefits of Sam upping the potential offer he'd mentioned, but after spending the last forty minutes in their company, she couldn't wait to see them go. She closed the door behind them, the annoyance lingering; she hated wasting time on ghouls. Even if they *did* make a realistic offer, they weren't right for this beautiful home. She slipped off her glasses and rubbed the bridge of her nose.

She was becoming territorial. This house was getting to her. It was strange, how she'd begun to both love and hate it at the same time.

Frustration mounting, she returned to her laptop in the kitchen and composed an email to the estate agency. *Hi Clio*, she began.

> *I want to address the importance of vetting viewers more thoroughly for Aspen Hollow. My first viewer, Charles Hart, seemed interested, but his wife wasn't with him as he said she'd 'take some persuading to step foot inside the house'. Given that she wouldn't even come to the viewing, I don't take it as a good sign. He also mentioned that they have yet to sell their own property in Nettleham. I thought we were only entertaining people who were in a position to buy?*

Laura stared at the screen, trying not to sound as pissed off as she felt. Charles had been a nice man, a retired boating enthusiast who would have fit in with the neighbours, but he couldn't decide without his wife being on board. But while Charles had viewed the house as a sound investment, it was clear his wife was repulsed by its history. Laura didn't want to railroad anyone into buying a property they were scared of.

'It can't be that hard for us to drum up more interest now that I've done the groundwork,' Laura grumbled to herself. She had made the house look warm and welcoming, and sold the outdoors lifestyle that came with the prestigious address. It was priced to sell quickly, low enough to attract interest but not so much that it would devalue the neighbouring homes.

It was hard work distracting people from the murders and that awful creepy undertone. A mother and child had died here . . . If there was proof of evil in the world, that was it. And who wanted to live in a home where evil resided? She reread her email, then added a few more lines.

Sam and Samantha Golding (if those are their real names) were only interested in talking about the murders. They seemed quite disappointed when I refused to be drawn in. Samantha wasn't happy when I wouldn't let her take selfies in the master bedroom, and Sam mentioned an offer much lower than the asking price. The whole thing felt like a huge waste of time. As I've already said, it's imperative we ensure future appointments are with serious buyers only. The house is beautifully staged, in a prime location, at a great price. There's no reason why we can't get some genuine viewers in. I suggest that we widen our net, and perhaps focus on people coming down from London who are in a position to work from home. Not everyone is suspicious or focuses on crime.

There, she thought. *I've done it. I've told her how to do her job.*

It was the one thing guaranteed to get her goat, but it also needed to be said. Clio resented her – Laura could tell by the tone of her emails. She was never around when Laura arranged to visit the agency, always conveniently with a client or on a coffee run. She hadn't even been with the Lincoln branch that long.

There were other people in the agency that Laura got on better with. Hetty was a sweet girl who was trying to grow her own social media channel and seemed a little in awe of Laura every time she appeared. Then there was Jonathan, who couldn't do enough to help. So why did Clio dislike her so much?

With the email sent, Laura leaned back in her chair, the stress of the morning's viewings dissipating. She smiled as she checked the views for one of her latest Instagram stories. Her posts weren't all sell, sell, sell. She interspersed some humorous and relatable reels too. Her joke video about her fear of spiders had gained a lot of traction. She'd filmed herself tiptoeing around wearing rubber gloves and holding a small blowtorch, checking each corner of the rooms in No. 1, then appeared as a second, more sensible person, stating newer houses were less likely to have unwanted inhabitants. 'What do YOU do when you find spiders?' she'd asked. 'Burn the house down, or see them on their way?' She'd confided about her own arachnophobia, and pressed 'like' on each comment that came in.

Her thoughts briefly returned to Mags. It couldn't have been easy, losing people she cared about in such horrific circumstances. The press would have hounded her. Why hadn't she spoken to them? Laura recalled her quiet demeanour. Her kindly ways. For whatever reason, she'd taken a shine to Laura.

Perhaps the truth would come out soon. But what was the truth? It was easier to believe that Bruce was guilty than think a killer was stalking her. What did they hope to gain from keeping the house vacant?

Laura switched back to her email. Her inbox held promises of interest, with potential clients eager to view. Despite everything, it seemed her efforts were slowly bearing fruit. She clicked on a new email from Charles Hart, the first viewer from this morning.

I really like the property, he'd written. *Our house won't take long to sell. Let me know if you get an offer, and don't let it go without telling me first.*

A slow smile appeared on Laura's lips. That sounded hopeful. Perhaps he'd persuaded his wife after all. Better still, if she could get a few more interested clients, she might be able to push up the price. She loved a bidding war. As for the truth of what had really gone on in the house . . . was it wise to poke the hornets' nest when she was so close to a sale?

CHAPTER 18

Scarlett sat next to her bedroom window, binoculars in hand. The door wasn't locked. There was no need for it today. She'd even managed a run this morning, although it was annoying to see how unfit she'd become. There was a time when six kilometres had been nothing to her. Then again, there was a time when she hadn't relied on alcohol to get her through the day.

It was exhausting, living in her head. But her thoughts weren't born out of regret or sadness; it was anger, for being put in this situation. Nobody could have predicted the series of events that would lead to Ali and Cindy's murders. Scarlett sighed as she shifted in her chair. She'd always viewed herself in the worst light. Cindy had just been a child. Of course Scarlett felt something. She wouldn't be drinking so much booze if it wasn't to forget. Her children were downstairs, being cared for by the nanny, Orla. She'd barely seen them all day.

Lou was only three – not old enough for school. Such a chatty little boy, with his long brown lashes and deep blue eyes. He was a boy's boy – he was into plastic trucks and made engine noises as he pushed them around the floor. David had bought him a Scalextric for his birthday and spent hours setting it up. Lou had only played with it for ten minutes before reverting to his Tonka truck.

Little Harriet was coming up to eighteen months old. Her blonde curls made her look angelic, although she had a powerful pair of lungs and could scream the house down. She loved to play with her toes and follow her brother around. Lou hadn't been happy when Harriet began walking, babbling as she interrupted his play.

Scarlett raised her binoculars and stared out at No. 1. Some viewers were hanging around outside. She didn't like the look of these two at all. Laura stood at the doorway, her hands clasped, delivering a fake smile. But she wasn't fooling anyone. She could stick up as many reels as she liked, but that house would always belong to Bruce. Laura hadn't a clue what he was really like. But Scarlett did.

The ring of her phone pulled her from the moment. Her husband's name flashed up on the screen.

'Yes?' Scarlett snapped, unable to hide her irritation.

'Everything OK?'

'I'm not swinging from a rope, if that's what you mean.'

Silence. She could sense his disapproval from here.

'I'm fine,' she continued, wishing he'd just go away.

'I thought we could go out for dinner tonight – there's a new Indian restaurant in town . . .'

'I'm on a diet.'

'Why? There's nothing left of you as it is.'

Scarlett wished she could shave off her hard edges. She never used to be this way. *He* had done this to her. Turned her into something dark. Made her act on impulse. Forced her to feel emotions that made her want to lash out.

'Fine,' she relented. 'But book Thai No. 1 instead. Indian food gives me horrible indigestion.' She hung up, because she knew there was a lecture coming otherwise. 'How much have you drunk today?' would be the first question. Then, 'Have you spoken to anyone?' She also knew what tonight was about. Coming up with a battle plan for the future, because neither of them could afford for anyone to discover the truth.

CHAPTER 19

'You're popular.' The stocky female prison guard handed Bruce his latest wad of letters. 'Got a proper fan club going on here, ain't ya?'

'Thanks.' Bruce gave her a weak smile. Her name was Ms Barnes and she wouldn't allow anyone to use her first name – not even her colleagues. Sometimes her gaze lingered on him as they spoke, but Bruce had never seen her smile. But then again, smiles were too much effort in this place.

She was right about the letters. The number he received each time was growing. The renewed interest in the house had brought more women out of the woodwork. He rifled through the envelopes, stopping at the one with the Comic Sans printed address. Everything about this writer was anonymous.

> *Hello sausage,*
> *How are you keeping? I have news, dearest one. I know that you live for my letters. Lots of women write to you, I'm sure. But it's my letters that you can't open quickly enough.*
> *I wanted to send you a treat. I had this idea in my head, that I'd sneak into your house – sorry, our house – take some little trinket and send it to you. Something to remember the place by. I know how much it means to*

you, even now. But then I remembered that anything I send will be examined by those dreadful prison guards and most likely taken away. It's disgusting, that's what it is, their sticky fingers all over my personal letters before you even get to look at them. They take away your freedom and then rob you of your privacy to boot.

Some prison guard was trending on X this week. She was having it off with one of the inmates in prison. Disgusting, it was. You could see the lot! And there was the other fella, his cellmate, smoking weed and filming the whole thing. The video went viral. Dirty woman. Dirty, filthy, dirty, dirty woman.

Do you have female prison guards? Because you must be lonely. A good-looking man like you. You must have needs. Stay faithful, won't you? Sorry. I shouldn't ask. Because I know you wouldn't do that to me. You slide my letters under your pillow, don't you? Then you reread them again and again, imagining your life on the outside. I suppose I'm a bit of a tease, aren't I? I'm laughing. I'm a nice person, really. I don't have many friends, but when I do . . . well, I never let go.

How quickly their imaginary relationship had blossomed in her head. If there was ever a case of magical thinking, this was it. Or was she a journalist, trying to be clever and garner his trust? Bruce rubbed his chin. It was doubtful that even a journalist would go this far. Wasn't it against some code of ethics? Or maybe that was the police. He frowned, continuing to read.

Anyway, where was I? Oh yes, the house. I went there to get your trinket. I should have realised that there was nothing left to take. The estate agent has got rid of nearly everything already and replaced it with garish designer muck. But don't worry, we'll soon fill it with things of our own.

This woman's out of her tree, Bruce thought. *Why am I even reading this drivel?* But he knew why. He had to know what was going on.

The letter-writer seemed to pre-empt his thoughts.

Yes, I've been to the house. Not just from the outside, I've properly been there. I've visited our bedroom. I lay on the new bed, imagining us waking up in that space. Imagining other things too. I stared out our window at the moonlight, although it's nicer when the street lights go off. That Laura woman, she doesn't even know when I'm there. You should see what she's done with the place. Are you allowed on social media? Have you looked at her posts? So blooming disrespectful. Well, don't you worry, my love. I'll soon have our house back to exactly the way it was. I just need to get rid of that estate agent first. I'll make it quick. And don't worry, I won't get caught.
Mags has been hanging around Aspen Hollow. I don't know what she thinks she's doing in Lincoln. Maybe she wants to see the place before it's sold. Maybe that's why she's not been writing back to you. Cindy and Ali's deaths have affected us all, in so many ways.

'She's crazy,' Bruce whispered beneath his breath. Was she talking about finishing Laura off? He stared at the letter in disbelief. He'd have to report these threats. And as for Mags . . . Was she really in Lincoln, or was this woman making it all up? She knew about the street lights going off, although most councils had such energy-saving initiatives these days. But how did she know that Mags hadn't written to him in a while? Guesswork? Doubtful. She sounded so certain. He scratched the side of his neck. This woman was making his skin crawl. How could she possibly know this kind of stuff? Surely it was only him, the prison guards who read his letters, and John, the prison chaplain who visited once a week. Reluctantly, he returned his gaze to the page.

> *I'm taking some time off work, so I can be here for you. Can't stand that place anyway. Bossy cows, the lot of them, telling me what to do. Do you feel it, Bruce? Destiny is calling. I made you a promise. I'm going to make it happen. I love you. All of you. Right through to the marrow of your bones. It's why I'm doing everything to stop the sale. Nothing, and I mean nothing, will take our happy home away.*
> *The place is more than walls and windows; what came from your mind is now an extension of us both, and I'll be damned if I allow anyone else to live there.*
> *Wait for me, Bruce. Because I'm here, ready to welcome you home.*
> *Until then, my dearest, hold on. Our time is coming.*

Bruce clenched his teeth as the shrill drill of an alarm sounded without warning. Someone was kicking off – again. He took a breath, reread the letter, lingering over each word. The sound faded into the distance, because Bruce wasn't really in his cell. He was back in Lincoln, standing in his bedroom in Aspen Hollow. Back on that awful day, when he'd said goodbye to his child, filled with dread and regret. Did he deserve this prison sentence? Being stuck in this hellhole that was eroding his mental health piece by piece?

Another shrill bell. Heavy footsteps passing his door. Would this prison ever be done with him?

CHAPTER 20

Laura checked each of the five bedrooms, ensuring that everything was right before her next viewing arrived. She had just finished going through her inbox. Clio from the estate agency had delivered a sharp three-line reply to her earlier email, saying that all prospective viewers were thoroughly vetted and that 'challenging homes' such as 1 Aspen Hollow would naturally prove harder to sell. Laura wished that she hadn't composed the email to begin with. She hated bad feelings amongst her work colleagues. She'd bring in some doughnuts the next time she popped in. There was no shortage of bakeries in Lincoln, and plenty of places to buy sweet treats.

She switched on the landing light to chase away the shadows as the late-afternoon sky cast a gloom through the windowpanes. It was barely four p.m. In a few short weeks it would be Halloween. Then the Christmas ads would be playing on the television. It was a terrible time of year to try to shift a property. Few people wanted to move during the holiday season, so time was not on her side.

There had been problems at the initial planning application stage of these homes too. According to an article Laura had read online, not everyone had approved of the section of woodlands being bulldozed to make space. Demonstrations had taken place and the proposed number of houses had been halved from eight to four. She thought about the graffiti and wondered if bad blood still lingered.

Laura heaved a sigh, reframing her thoughts. Aspen Hollow houses had generous grassy back gardens, the rear bedrooms offering a view of the woods in regular use by dog walkers. The garden fences had been kept deliberately low so as not to obstruct the view. The low fence, the sterile kitchen, the glassy bifold doors. Bruce's work had featured in architectural magazines and his stamp was everywhere. But to Laura, it didn't feel secure. Perhaps the man had been more trusting than her. She'd build a six-foot fence with lights, cameras, the lot. Maybe have a dog too, although Esme would prefer a cat. She'd been nagging Laura to get a kitten for weeks.

Laura snapped out of her daydream as she stared out of the window, her fingers lightly touching the pane of glass. She gasped as she saw a figure darting away from the back fence of the house. Had they been in the garden? Or just snooping around? Laura stared into the darkening woods as the person ran and hid behind a tree. They weren't one of the usual dog walkers. They were dressed completely in black. Motionless, Laura watched them peep towards the house, before they ran deeper into the woods and out of sight. What were they up to? Then another thought occurred to her. Had she locked the back doors? She took the small spiral staircase down from one of the guest rooms. It led to a boot room with bench seats, coat hooks and even more storage space. She tried the handle of the boot room back door, satisfied by its firmness. Locked. As it should be.

But a lingering feeling of unease brought her back to the kitchen, to the bifold back door. Should she check the garden, just to be safe? When it came to the design of the house, the rear garden was the most underwhelming part. A tiled patio led out to a generous lawn, with a separate decking area and hot tub on the side. A garden shed was tucked away, and a seating area for six was neatly situated beneath a folded-up parasol.

Laura unlocked the back door and stared out at the swaying aspen trees. Their leaves shimmered in a kaleidoscope of yellow, gold and orange in the light of the setting sun. But there was nobody outside. There was nothing but the soft coos of pigeons roosting on branches. Laura almost stepped on the bright-orange Nike shoebox on the doorstep.

'What the . . . ?' She glared at the offending object. Her mind quickly did the maths and came up with something alarming. The figure in the woods . . . Had they just deposited it there? It wouldn't be difficult for someone to climb the low back fence.

She jerked as her phone rang in the pocket of her suit jacket.

'Cally,' Laura gasped. 'You almost—'

'Frightened you to death?' Her sister laughed. 'Gave you a heart attack? Jeez, I'm going to text before I call. You're so jumpy these days.'

But Laura wasn't in the mood for jokes. 'Um . . . It's nothing. I'm alright. Something weird just happened.' Her gaze was fixed on the shoebox at her feet. There could be anything in there.

'Spill the beans,' her sister insisted. 'What is it? Do I need to come down there?'

Laura was surprised Cally hadn't asked to see the place sooner, given she was such a true crime enthusiast. It would take her less than an hour to drive from where she lived and worked in Louth.

'There's a box, on the doorstep . . . A shoebox,' Laura added. 'There was someone sneaking around in the woods at the back of the house. I think they left it here.'

'Ooh. Well, you're going to have to open it, aren't you?' her sister said, a bit too gleefully. 'You can't just leave it there.'

Laura stared at the box, contemplating her actions. 'I'm not touching that thing with my bare hands. There could be a bomb . . .'

She was met with a giggle. 'Or a stick of TNT? Maybe the Road Runner left it there.' There was another soft laugh. 'Get a broom, you numpty. Give it a poke.'

Laura couldn't help but laugh in response. As a child, she'd been fed on a diet of Warner Bros cartoons to keep her quiet during the day. Road Runner, Tom and Jerry, Bugs Bunny . . . She'd loved them all.

She frowned. 'But . . . there could be anything in there.'

'Then get the guy from security to check it out.'

That wasn't a bad idea, but Laura didn't want to look like a fool. Besides, he worked for the marina, not Aspen Hollow, and she hadn't seen him about. 'I can't afford for this to get out.'

Cally's motherly sigh sounded on the line. 'Do you need me to come over there?'

'No, it's just a shoebox, and I have a viewer coming any minute.'

'OK then.' She could hear that Cally's words were carried on a smile. 'Then pull up your big-girl pants and get a bin bag. You've got some, haven't you?'

'Yes.' Laura always came prepared.

'OK then, put me on FaceTime. Get a bin bag and a broom. If there's anything in the box then throw the lot in the bag and tie it at the top.'

Laura loved her sister's no-nonsense attitude, and Cally had watched enough crime shows to be mindful of forensics.

Two minutes later and Laura was standing with a bin bag in one hand and a slim broom in the other. She rested the open bag on the grass, her pulse picking up speed as she grabbed her phone to give her sister a better view.

'OK. Let's do this.' She took a deep breath, stepping back as she nudged open the lid of the box with the broom.

'What is it? What's in there?' Cally's face filled the iPhone screen.

Laura peered cautiously into the box. 'I can't see any—'

Her words came to a sudden stop as she emitted a scream.

Dropping her phone, she whacked the box as if she were holding a golf club instead of a broom. She watched it fly into the air, its contents deposited squarely on the patio as the box landed on the recycling bin. With a quick yelp, Laura ran back to the door.

'What is it? What's wrong?! I can't see!' Cally shouted from the phone, which was face down on the outdoor tiles. 'Pick me up!' she shouted.

Hands flapping, Laura ran outside, snatched the phone from the ground, and darted back inside.

'Oh my God!' Laura's legs were weak as she locked the back bifold doors. 'It was a spider, a great big one.' She sat the phone up on a nearby shelf. She rubbed her skin as she was overcome with a sensation of spiders crawling everywhere.

'Oh, for pity's sake, is that all?'

'It was huge, as big as a mouse!' Laura protested, scratching an imaginary itch.

'I can't believe you locked the door.' Cally was still laughing. 'Did you think he was going to climb up, then reach with his little spider hands and open it?'

'Look at it!' Laura turned the camera around as the spider scuttled off the patio and into the grass. 'I'm lucky I didn't break my phone.'

'Oh, it *is* quite big. A cardinal spider, by the looks of it. Its bite is pretty painless.' But Cally didn't stop laughing. She was obviously quite entertained by it all.

'Well, I'm never going outside again. You know how scared I am of spiders. Cally, why would anyone do that?' Laura paused for thought. 'They must follow my socials. I said I was scared of them in my last video.'

Laura rubbed the back of her neck. She couldn't stop her skin from crawling. Cally used to be fascinated by insects. She'd chased Laura around the house with spiders and crane flies when they were young. It was hardly any wonder she'd spent her teenage years as a goth.

'I've got the heebie-jeebies now.' Laura peered at the phone screen as her sister wiped a tear from her eye.

'I haven't laughed so much in ages!'

'I'm never going out there again.' Laura forced some steady breaths into her lungs.

'The box probably blew over your fence from a neighbour's house, and the spider climbed inside. They like dry, dark spaces. He won't bother you again.'

But Laura wasn't convinced. Cally could laugh all she wanted. This felt personal.

'Are you OK now?' said Cally. 'I've got to shoot off.'

Only now did Laura absorb the fact that her sister wasn't in her flat, but sitting in her car.

'Where are you off to?'

'Hot date.' Cally's dimples were on display as she grinned. 'And I'm going to be late, so . . .'

Laura let her go. Cally was always coy about her dates and Laura knew she wouldn't say any more than that. She stood in silence, thinking over her options. This was more serious than Cally realised. Her story of a shoebox randomly blowing into the garden didn't ring true. Laura's hands were still shaking, but she wouldn't be forced out. She just needed to be more mindful about sharing her fears online. But it begged the question – how much was Laura being watched?

CHAPTER 21

ALI

THEN

I flick through my Instagram page. Two hundred new followers today alone. But this isn't how my evening was meant to end. Bruce's dinner is stone cold. Beef Wellington, made from scratch. I filmed myself making it for my socials and I've had a crazy number of views. But even that can't lift my spirits. It's eight p.m. now. Bruce was meant to be home by five. I got sick of waiting for him and ate on my own. I'm wearing the red dress that he likes. I even styled my hair in a French plait. A complete waste of time. Cindy's on a playdate with Sasha, her friend from school. I feel like going around there and picking her up early. I know. I'm a helicopter parent. But I can't help myself. When she's gone it feels like a piece of me has been wrenched away.

Cindy was an early baby. A whole two months, in fact. There were times when she came close to not making it. I pissed off the nurses at the time as I wouldn't leave her side. Once, I heard them whispering about me when they thought that I was asleep in the chair next to her incubator. Their words were spoken out of concern, but to them, babies came and went as part of their working day. Cindy has always been my world. I can still remember the strength of her grip as she wrapped her hand around my little finger for the first time. She's such a little fighter, my sweet girl.

The clock ticks away every second. The place seems so empty without her. She'll be back in an hour, full of pizza and ice cream, and ready for bed. I count the minutes as they pass. Wasted time Bruce and I would have had to ourselves. But as usual, I'm eating alone. Sighing, I stare at my phone. At least the table setting looks good. All I'm missing is my husband in the photos for our 'romantic night in'. I film my videos for YouTube and repurpose them for Instagram – and, if I've time, TikTok too. I used to predominantly only share videos and reels of me making food. My first family video almost came by accident, as Cindy joined in one day. Now I include her and Bruce whenever I can. But what's portrayed on social media is a world away from our real lives. If people knew about our rows they might not gush quite so much. We largely avoid each other now, because when we clash . . . it's explosive.

Bruce often loses track of time now that he's taken up golf. He and David go to the driving range in Lincoln twice a week. I'm glad that they're such good friends and there's no animosity between them. Bruce did pretty much steal the contract for these houses from under David's nose, after all. And if their friendship gets Bruce away from those silly poker game apps, then it's all good with me. But I don't like how David's wife Scarlett is with Bruce. She's clingy and desperate for attention. She actually has a nanny – Orla, she's called. Some twenty-something hipster who cycles past my house every morning on her way to take care of her kids for the day. Meanwhile, Scarlett jogs around the marina with her high ponytail and Lycra sports gear, acting as if she's better than everyone else.

At least Cindy is happy. She loves her new princess bedroom. I decorated it in pastel colours, with paintings of unicorns and pretty fairy lights hung above her bed. She was so excited when she saw it, almost hugging me to death. It's comforting to feel so loved.

My stalker loves her too. I blink, taking a second to correct myself. She's not really a stalker. @Miss53 is just a very lonely soul. I know how that feels. I probably shouldn't encourage her, but sometimes in the middle of the night when I can't sleep, we message each other online. I'm careful about what I share, but it's nice hearing from someone who looks up to me. Bruce used to be like that once, until he got to know me better.

Speak of the devil – he's here. A car has pulled up on the drive. My husband is home at last. I feel like giving him a proper telling-off, but I'll listen to his apology. Because I need a steady life, and Cindy needs a father. I don't have the strength to do it all alone.

CHAPTER 22

Shadows slowly crawled around Bruce's cell. He was so used to watching them that he could tell the time by their movement – unless it was raining, which was pretty common these days. He was glad the summer had been a washout. Missing out on sun-soaked weather would only have intensified his pain. He sat on the bottom bunk, working his wedding band around his finger. It had grown so loose that it tended to fall off. He didn't even know why he wore it – in the last few years, his marriage had been nothing but a sham. But if he didn't show allegiance to Ali, people would think he was guilty for sure.

The shadows found his small desk, where he wrote his letters to his sister. Perhaps Mags sensed that he wasn't being honest in his words. She'd always said that she'd believed in his innocence, but now . . . Her lack of response told him all he needed to know. The journalists and armchair detectives who hounded him were relentless. What had it been like for her, his dear introverted Mags?

Soon he would have another cellmate. The last two weeks alone had been a luxury. He touched the scar on his neck. If he hadn't woken up in time . . . and if the prison guard hadn't been close . . . His last cellmate had barely nicked him, but it had been enough for Bruce to get the place to himself for a while. There were too many incidents that could cost you your life in this place. The guards did their best – they were never far away, although he doubted they really cared. Convicted child killers had a price on their heads. It was only a matter of time until Bruce's luck ran out.

In the background, the usual clamour of inmates' shouts and jeers echoed down the corridors. If they weren't demanding phone calls, they were screaming at their fellow inmates to shut up. Some sang to pass the time. Some cried. Others shouted at the voices in their heads. The outside world was ceasing to exist. It was just Bruce, in the bowels of this hellish place, where he was nothing more than a number to the guards who kept watch. Each day, his universe became smaller as the stars in his sky petered out. If he was struggling now, how would he feel in ten years? Would he even make it that long?

The steady cadence of footsteps approaching his cell freed Bruce from his downwardly spiralling thoughts. Someone was outside the locked door. He straightened his spine, and pushed back his muscular shoulders, preparing himself for whatever cellmate was about to be introduced. Should he stand? No. That might look like he was worried. He would sit, narrow his eyes, resting pissed-off face. Look strong. Not stiff. Present, but not rattled.

Fuck it, he thought, *I'll stand. Don't want him looking down at me.* First impressions were everything.

The jingle of keys was followed by the click of the lock disengaging. Bruce braced himself as the cell door groaned open, steeling himself for the worst. Then the tension drained from him as Father John Shanahan came into view. Clad in black from head to toe, the only contrast was the sliver of white of his dog collar. His jeans and trainers weren't traditional, but this was a man who didn't fit the usual mould. He was younger than Bruce by a few years, and leaner, with hair that was longer and less kempt than you'd expect of a Catholic priest. His clothes carried a familiar scent – a mix of cigarettes and mints, a faint and bittersweet reminder of the world beyond the prison bars.

'You requested a visit,' John said, taking a seat in the only chair in the cell. The guard looked Bruce up and down before retreating back into the corridor.

Bruce settled back on the bed, momentary relief relaxing his muscles once more. 'Thanks for coming. I didn't expect to see you so soon.'

'You don't ask unless it's important.' His soft Irish accent was a pleasure to listen to. The prison was rich with diversity, but prisoners' words were usually coated with frustration, their intonation harsh. John – as he preferred to be called – was one of very few people whose voice didn't grate.

'Thanks for your time.' Bruce gave him a feeble smile. His relief at getting to spend another night alone washed over him. 'I've been getting weird letters. They're enough to keep me awake at night.'

'I know of a fella who's written some good stuff. It'll make you feel better than whatever's in those pages.' John's face warmed with a smile. Nobody could question the chaplain's dedication to his faith. Bruce couldn't understand how someone John's age could commit to a lifetime of chastity, but then again, now that he was in prison, he'd done the same.

'I've read the book, watched the movie. Not totally convinced just yet,' said Bruce.

'Well, you know I love a challenge. Now, what's in these letters that's made you so concerned?'

Bruce nodded in acknowledgement. For a brief moment he felt normal, like he was chatting with a mate down the pub. But John's time was precious – he was on the clock. Bruce wasn't the only inmate he had to visit tonight. Suicide was commonplace, although rarely reported in the news. And even if it was, nobody seemed to care.

Bruce slipped the letters out from under his pillow and handed them over. He watched John's brow crease as his eyes darted left to right, taking in the words.

'Hmm . . .' He rested the pages on the small worn table next to the chair. 'She's quite the troubled soul.' He paused, giving it some thought. 'Infatuation often stems from deeper mental health issues. This isn't just about you.'

'You're right there. But I'm worried this estate agent might get hurt.' Bruce thought it best to get straight to the point. 'I wrote a letter to warn her, but I haven't sent it . . . I don't know how she'd take it, coming from me.'

'Aye, sure enough.' John crossed one long leg over the other, softly bouncing it as he thought. 'Maybe you could speak to the police?'

Bruce gave an involuntary snort. 'I hardly have the best of relationships with the cops.' He shook his head. 'If something did happen to her, they'd probably say I orchestrated it.'

A few seconds of silence passed as John absorbed his words. 'Sure enough. I'll keep her in my prayers.'

Bruce raised an eyebrow. 'That wasn't quite what I had in mind.'

The smile on John's face relayed that he already knew. 'You want me to speak to this Laura.'

'If you could. Please.' Bruce said. 'I know it's a big ask, but I don't know what else to do.' He would have preferred to talk to his sister. A visit from her could solve everything. She had a gentle manner about her. She'd get the message across. He'd written her countless letters since he'd got here and had treasured each response. But he couldn't get through to her on the phone and she wasn't responding anymore. For now, a priest was a better candidate to approach Laura. 'Give her the letter, so she can see the threats for herself.'

'Right we are. I'll see what I can do.' John pocketed the letter before pulling back his shirtsleeve and checking his Apple Watch. 'Sure we've got time for a prayer before I go.' It wasn't a request. It was a religious quid pro quo.

'Go on then.' Bruce smiled. 'It can't do any harm.'

'Good man.' John grinned.

CHAPTER 23

Laura plugged in her laptop to charge on the worktop of the gleaming kitchen. She had given the counter another dusting, in between checking work emails and taking calls. She rubbed the base of her spine. Her childhood mattress was too soft to sleep well on but it was unlikely her mother would be upgrading it anytime soon. She groaned as her back made its own protest. The temptation to pack her bags and return to her marital home was strong. This morning her mother had seemed better on her feet, and had even been making Laura's favourite breakfast – French toast. But as Laura had thanked her, her mum had put her in her place. 'It's not for you,' she'd said, before asking when she was going home.

Laura sighed as she took the stairs, her thoughts still with her mum. She'd hoped to connect. To give her another chance. She'd ironed her clothes, cleaned her house and made her numerous cups of tea. But this morning had proved that things were never going to change. Today was hump day in more ways than one.

This afternoon had been strange. The first viewer had cancelled, and now the next one was twenty minutes late. She frowned as she stared at the rumpled bedspread on the master bed. She hadn't noticed that earlier. She was sure she'd done a better job of making it. She smoothed the ivory bedding, plumping the pillows until they were just right. A sudden shower of rain tapped at the windowpane. The weather had been forecasted to turn.

She checked her watch as the doorbell chimed. Her second prospective buyer of the afternoon was here.

The woman was called Kimberly, but preferred the title of 'Ms Langthorn' according to details the agency had passed on. Clio had taken a few days off work, and Laura hoped it wasn't because she had pissed her off. Surely she was made of sterner stuff than that? But still . . . Laura felt guilty for having had a moan. Life was hard enough for women in business, without them taking chunks out of each other. Downstairs, she checked her reflection in the mirror before opening the front door.

'Ms Langthorn, I presume?' The woman was tall, nearly six foot, with a statuesque build. Her short dark hair brushed against her shoulders in a blunt bob. Her skin was Botox-smooth, so it was hard to judge her age, but Laura guessed her to be in her late forties. A light application of make-up gave a soft glow to her skin. She shook out her umbrella, already wet after making the short transition from her car to the front door.

'Yes.' She smiled, offering a slim hand. 'Nice to meet you.' Her handshake was strong, her skin ice-cold. A chilly gust of wind swept through the hall as Laura let her inside.

Apparently, Ms Langthorn was a businesswoman, high up in some multi-level marketing company – according to the bio Jonathan had emailed earlier in the day. She was interested in the property as a base, but travelled overseas much of the year. A serious buyer, in Laura's eyes, and she wasted no time in starting the tour.

'Would the property be just for you?' she asked, engaging in small talk as she showed her around.

'For now,' Ms Langthorn replied, not giving too much away.

Fair enough, Laura thought. She'd entertained many different types in house viewings over the years. Some loved to talk about themselves, or all about their family and what they did for work. Ms Langthorn was one of those people who maintained a professional veneer. She didn't seem the superstitious type, but as they stood at the master bedroom door, Laura began to wonder if she'd judged her too soon. She'd seemed happy to allow Laura to go through her spiel as they entered each room, but now she sensed the need for silence as Ms Langthorn stood in the bedroom, her expression tight, her arms folded. Laura was about to show her the view from the generous window when she spoke.

'You shouldn't sell this place.'

'Sorry, what was that?' Laura tilted her head to one side.

'They're still here. Their energy. I can feel it.'

Laura inwardly groaned. She wanted to tell her that she was wrong. But the words wouldn't come.

'They're not ready to move on.' Ms Langthorn's hand went to the small gold cross that she wore around her neck. She was looking around the room as if something was about to jump out at her. 'This place . . .' Her words were haunting. 'It's not time. Take it off the market.' She turned, her steely grey eyes landing on Laura. 'Did you hear what I said? You can't sell this house. Something dark lives here.' Then she reversed out of the bedroom, as if afraid to turn her back on it. Her breathing accelerated as Laura followed her out. The woman seemed genuinely scared.

'Who are you?' Laura demanded as she followed her down the stairs. 'Some kind of psychic?'

It wasn't until they got to the bottom that Ms Langthorn spoke again. 'I'm a genuine buyer. I've viewed lots of houses. I thought that if their spirits had moved on . . . that maybe this place would be alright.' She paused, her gaze creeping upwards. 'It's a good price, and exactly where I want to be, near the water and trees.' She returned her attention to Laura. 'But you need to have a blessing, at the very least. There's something here . . . but it's low-level, I can't quite reach it.'

Laura couldn't disagree. The house was filled with a sense of depression, as if it were a living thing. But she was flooded with disappointment at yet another wasted viewing. She exhaled a long sigh, her words flat with disappointment. 'If you change your mind, let me know. I'm sure it won't be long until it's sold.'

As they got to the front door, Ms Langthorn squeezed Laura's arm. 'I'm serious. Be careful. I know you think I'm crazy, but I'm not. I run a seven-figure business. I'm no timewaster.'

Dumbstruck, Laura showed her out. 'Yes, I do think you're crazy,' she finally mumbled as the door clicked shut. But was she, though?

Laura stiffened as the doorbell chimed. What now?

CHAPTER 24

ALI

THEN

Sometimes I think that if we could just live in our own little bubble, everything would be OK. I scroll through the photos of Disney World, each one a precious memory that never fails to make me smile. It was frivolous, spending money on a holiday so soon after moving in, but I knew that if we didn't go now, some big household expense would come to swallow it up. Cindy loved every second in Florida. She dressed like a princess every day and her little autograph book was full in no time. It was adorable when the characters came up to us and asked for *her* autograph! My heart melted as she wrote her little Cindy squiggle, beaming with pride as they called her an honorary Disney Princess. That night, she asked if we could stay at Disney World forever. Our own little bubble for sure . . . I didn't enjoy the long queues for rides, and the price of food was extortionate, but we felt like a proper family unit again. Bruce barely let go of our hands the whole time we were there. I can still hear the 'It's a Small World' tune in my head. It was lovely to have some time in the sun, and we even got to spend a few days on the beach in Fort Lauderdale. Bliss.

Bruce strides into the kitchen, and then is pulling open the cupboard drawers. 'Keys. Have you seen my car keys?'

'No, I—'

'You were in it last,' he interrupts, his irritation growing as he goes to check the utility room. He's dressed in a new designer suit, his hair still damp from the shower. He works on Saturdays now. 'Got them,' he says triumphantly, and I hear them jingle as he takes them from the hook on the wall.

I sniff as he gives me a perfunctory kiss on the cheek on the way out. 'New aftershave?' I don't recognise the smell as I inhale a fresh spicy kick.

'Oh . . . Dior Sauvage. I fancied a change.' He gives me a heart-stopping grin and I want him to draw me close, just like he did at Disney World.

'Bruce . . .' I say. I'm always chasing after the man I married. So energetic in the morning, tired at night. 'Fancy a date night tonight? I could get a babysitter . . .' But his eyes crinkle and there is the beginning of a frown. He stands there, looking pained as he rubs his freshly shaven face. 'I can't. Card night tonight, remember? Soon, though. Yeah?'

Card night. Of course. He goes into Lincoln once a fortnight to play at some new club he's joined. He pulls up the sleeve of his crisp white shirt to check the time. Billie's ironing company did a good job. He said it's worth the investment to have them done properly, especially when he spends so much on his clothes. The 'Ironing Angels' do a collection and drop-off service to the close once a week.

Bruce goes into the living room to give a cheery goodbye to Cindy before popping on his shoes in the hall. She's still in her pyjamas, watching her favourite Barbie movie on TV.

I'm drawn to the window in the kitchen, and watch his car leave the drive. With his gym-toned body and holiday-tanned skin, he's not your typical architect. When he's happy, his boyish grin still makes me giddy inside. And it's not just me. A good percentage of my online audience appreciate him when he makes an appearance. The reels of him walking poolside gained so many heart emojis. Not to mention all the gushing messages from my biggest fan, @Miss53. I think she's a little in love with him. He's so charming on the surface that it's hard not to be. But there's another side to Bruce shown to only a few. It's dark and troubled, like he's deep underwater, where no one, not even Cindy, can reach him.

'Why is Daddy sad?' she asks at times like that. I just tell her that we're all sad sometimes and it will pass. Then I add that *I'll* always be happy for her.

I clear away our breakfast things: the remnants of the blueberry pancakes, a half-empty pot of natural yoghurt, empty coffee cups. The Alexa speaker plays Absolute Eighties radio, and the music lifts my mood. Alison Moyet. Now there's a blast from the past. I'm thinking about going for a walk in the woods when Cindy's voice rises behind me. 'Can I play this game, Mummy?' She's holding her father's iPad.

'Where did you get that?' I take the iPad from her hands. 'That's Daddy's. For work.' He must have left it behind in his rush to get out the door. 'Why don't you get dressed? We'll go looking for deer in the woods.' I've already laid out her clothes on her bed.

'Can we feed the ducks too?' Her face is bright with anticipation and I agree.

'Yay!' She forgets about the iPad as she runs out to the hall and bounds upstairs.

I glance back out the window but there's no sign of Bruce's car. I don't get any enjoyment out of snooping, but given his behaviour it's entirely justified. His iPad is linked to his phone. I stare at the 'game' that Cindy wanted to play. It's a gambling app.

He's always loved card games. That's what I thought he was playing – games. Like the bingo games my friends used to play online. A bit of harmless fun. A way of letting off steam. It would be worse if he was addicted to porn – or so I thought. But my legs grow weak as I stare at the notification: *Deposit confirmed: £500.*

I sink on to a kitchen chair, the iPad resting heavily on my lap. 'This can't be right,' I whisper, swiping past the garish colours and flashing jackpot graphics into Bruce's account history. My mouth drops open as the transaction history reveals just how much he's spent. £100 here, £200 there – dozens of deposits over the past month, all adding up to thousands of pounds. I feel sick as I scroll through page after page of losses, the occasional win only a fraction of what he has spent. I grip the iPad tighter as I read the text at the bottom: *Lifetime deposits: £12,800.* He's only had the app for a year. My breath catches as I return to the home screen, where there are dozens of apps like these. A creeping sense of betrayal rises, along with the question: where has he got all this money from? I would have noticed the withdrawals from my bank account. Has he got a secret credit card? How does he afford to pay it back?

I quickly fix my face as Cindy skips into the kitchen, dressed in her favourite dungarees.

'Do me a favour, sweetheart, put this back where you found it. We don't want Daddy to be cross.'

She gives me a solemn nod of the head and takes the iPad from my grip. It's hard to let it go. There's so much I need to check. But I know my husband, and he'll soon realise his mistake. He's probably already on his way back.

I can't confront him. Not yet. I don't know how he'll react.

Bruce's childhood was fragmented. He didn't come from a loving family. His parents couldn't stand each other and his sister left the first chance she got. When Bruce gets angry, he's not always in control. He frightens me when he lashes out.

I don't get angry. I sulk. I usually fume, bottling everything up.

In the quiet times, when Bruce is remorseful, he tells me that he doesn't really know who he is anymore. Perhaps his gambling is a midlife crisis. But he needs to get it under control, because we don't have any savings to speak of. The equity in our home will see us through our retirement, but how do we manage this gambling habit in the meantime? It's scary and I can't let it go. But how on earth do I approach him about this?

There's nobody I can talk to. I miss Mum at times like this. Actually, that's a lie. I miss her every day. As an only child, I've never known what it's like to have a sister. But I didn't need one, because Mum was everything to me. She voiced her concerns about Bruce, but after I got married she came into her own. She adored Cindy. She couldn't do enough for us both. How I wish that I could still turn to her for advice.

Cindy returns to the kitchen, just as car tyres scrunch on our drive.

'Let's not mention the iPad,' I say to her. 'It'll be our little secret, yeah?' She nods in agreement. I don't want her to witness any confrontation. I'll deal with this in my own way. I touch her shoulder. She's growing up too fast. 'Why don't you go get your coat?'

I try to act surprised as Bruce pops his head round the door. 'Only me. Forgot something.' His face is flushed as he checks my expression. 'You OK?' There's a guilty edge to his voice.

I smile, clearing the thickness in my throat. 'I'm fine. We're just going for a walk in the woods.'

I clasp my shaking hands together as Bruce says goodbye for the second time. This is about more than a gambling problem. The look on his face tells me that I've only scratched the surface.

CHAPTER 25

After her odd encounter with Ms Langthorn, Laura was taken aback to find a priest at her door. Was this some kind of sick joke? It took her several seconds to find her voice after he introduced himself as Father Shanahan, but asked her to call him John. His brown eyes were deep and inviting, and his wavy hair brushed against firm shoulders. With his black jacket, matching shirt and jeans, he was the epitome of a trendy priest, blending piety with a touch of rebellious charm that no doubt made teenage girls crush hard during Mass. But it was the sound of his Irish accent that gained Laura's trust. She'd always had a soft spot for the Irish.

'Sorry,' the priest apologised for the second time. 'I didn't mean to alarm you.' She'd brought him into the kitchen, mainly because Graham, the neighbour, had been hoovering his car interior and watching their every move. The wind had not abated, but the rain had stopped for now.

John refused Laura's offer of refreshments, saying he'd just had a coffee in the marina after his drive from Wakefield. The penny didn't drop straight away.

Laura stood at the kitchen island, feeling very much on the back foot as she accepted his apologies.

'I'm Bruce Wilding's chaplain . . .' He waited for a response but Laura offered none. 'At Wakefield Prison? Where he's serving time.'

'Oh. I see.' Laura's heart fluttered at the mention of Bruce's name.

'There's nothing to worry about . . . Well, if there were nothing to worry about, I wouldn't be here . . .' His eyes crinkled at the corners as soft laughter left his lips. 'Right. Get to the point, John. Bruce asked me to get a message to you.'

Laura looked at him blankly. What did Bruce Wilding want with her?

'Yes,' he said, 'I can see this has come as a surprise. Would you like to see my ID?'

'No.' Laura waved it away. 'No need. What's the message?' She was too disturbed by his visit for formalities. How could this friendly, amenable priest be speaking on behalf of a man found guilty of such vile things? Laura wanted nothing to do with Bruce Wilding, but she would hear the priest out.

John delivered a patient smile. 'First, Bruce bears you no ill will. He knows you're selling the house and he's fully accepting that this place is a part of his past.' He paused, his eyes lingering on her face. 'He still maintains his innocence, and to be honest I believe him. I've spoken with him at length and I've come to know him well.'

'Then what does he want with me?' Laura's words were imbued with confusion and fear. John was the second person to protest Bruce's innocence, but she wasn't buying it.

'May I?' He gestured towards one of the leather-and-chrome bar stools at the kitchen island.

'Of course,' Laura replied, taking a bottle of water from the fridge. She sat down on another stool, taking the weight off her feet. The seats were high but comfortable, and she sipped her water as she waited for John to explain.

'Bruce has been getting letters – quite a lot of them, in fact,' John began. 'Some of them are . . . well, as you would imagine. There are a lot of angry people out there. Then there are the letters from women, a strange fan club of sorts. He finds those more disturbing than the hate mail. He doesn't understand why anyone would be bothered with him.' He slipped a hand into the pocket of his black jacket. 'Perhaps it's better if you read this for yourself.' He handed her two folded pieces of paper.

Laura reluctantly took the letters and slowly read each word. The first was from Bruce, and it took all of her self-control not to drop it on to the counter. *Dear Laura*, it began. *My name is Bruce Wilding* . . . The room fell quiet as she read, the distant rumble of a car passing outside. She finished reading Bruce's message and picked up the second letter. Her lips parted as her blood turned cold. The letter was unsigned, with a weird introductory 'Hello sausage'. The more Laura read, the more worried she became. Was this connected to the strange text messages she'd received? Was someone trying to stop the sale so she could have the house for herself? Was that who had left the spider on the doorstep? Because that was weirdly personal. But still, there was a warning voice. She didn't know this priest, or the convicted murderer he claimed to represent.

'Did Bruce *really* get this letter, or did he write both of them himself?' Laura finally met John's gaze. 'Because I've heard he's very attached to this house.'

John took the letters back, a slight smile playing on his face. 'I understand your scepticism.' He folded over the pages. 'But prison guards have confirmed that the letters were sent to Bruce in prison. They're keeping an eye on it. She's been writing for some time. As for this house . . .' He glanced around the kitchen. 'It really is something. But he lost it to the bank some time ago.'

That was true. 'Then this woman . . . She clearly has mental health issues.' Laura sighed. Was this the same person who was putting potential buyers off with the graffiti? What about the previous estate agents – had she interfered with them doing their jobs too? This was all Laura needed.

She turned and closed the kitchen window as the sound of Graham's hoover interrupted her thoughts. His bloody car mats would be bald at this rate.

'Indeed,' John agreed. 'She seems like a disturbed soul. One to watch out for, for sure. But Bruce doesn't have a hidden agenda. He's concerned for your safety, that's all.'

The thought of being on Bruce Wilding's radar felt somewhat surreal. 'Why get you to come? Couldn't he have asked his sister to pass on the message? She's been here.'

'He's tried. She's not answering her phone.'

Laura suppressed an involuntary shudder. It felt like someone had walked on her grave. 'This stalker . . . She could have been here at the same time as me.' The danger of the situation was not lost on Laura. She'd heard enough of Cally's true crime stories to be aware. 'But how? I lock up every time I leave.' She rested her feet on the rung of her stool as more questions arose in her mind.

John glanced at the ceiling. 'Is there an alarm? Bruce mentioned that there wasn't. It really is quite something, this house.'

'There's no alarm,' Laura snapped as John gazed around the rest of the house. 'But for God's sake keep that to yourself. I doubt the estate agency would fork out for one now. They just want to get rid.' Colour rose to her cheeks. 'Sorry, I didn't mean to snap. But she's infatuated with him, and I'm enemy number one!'

'Best to exercise caution.' John clasped his hands together, resting them on the cool marble countertop. He looked thoughtful for a moment. 'This woman . . . She said . . .' He took the letter from Laura's hands and read the words aloud. 'She said Mags has been hanging around Aspen Hollow. You haven't shared her being here on your social media or anything, have you?'

'She came for a chat. Why would I mention that online? All of this business with Bruce . . . I get the impression that it's not been easy on her.' Laura met John's eyes. 'Losing your niece and sister-in-law, then finding out your brother is responsible.'

'So the courts say.' John's voice was low and calm. 'I'll let Bruce know that you spoke to his sister. He hasn't heard from her in a while. Perhaps it's wise if you take some extra precautions in the meantime. Report anything suspicious to the police. Because if Bruce didn't kill his wife and child, then somebody else did.'

'I'll be careful.' Laura set her jaw firmly. 'The quicker I sell this house, the quicker I'll be out of here. I'm no quitter. But if I run into problems, then I'll call the police.' The hoovering outside finally came to a halt. Laura chewed on her bottom lip, spreading her hand over the cool marble worktop. Why was everything so hard? 'My last viewer . . . She was either psychic or out of her tree. She said that this place needed a blessing. I don't suppose you could . . . ?'

'Delighted to oblige.'

'Thanks.' Laura checked her watch. 'I've got half an hour before my next appointment – that's if they don't cancel on me.'

'I only need a few minutes in each room.' He slid off the stool, appearing genuinely pleased to have been asked. He took a small bottle of holy water from his pocket, along with a small gold cross. 'Where would you like me to start?'

They stood solemnly on the upper floor. The priest's voice was steady as he began the prayer. It felt like they were disturbing something best left alone, and Laura was feeling increasingly uncomfortable. This was a house which had been left silent for too long. To think, the last child who'd lived within these walls had ended up dying here . . .

She watched as John made the sign of the cross, his small gold crucifix catching the light.

'Almighty God, we ask you to purify this home.' His words resonated in the stillness. 'May your light drive out darkness and your peace rest upon those who dwell here.' He moved slowly along the landing, sprinkling droplets of holy water. '*Omnipotens Deus, benedic domum hanc et expelle ab ea omnes spiritus malignos . . .'* The air seemed to hum around him. Laura followed, rubbing the hairs rising on her arms. John's voice was smooth and velvety. She allowed his words to flow over her, a reminder of her childhood when her father used to take her to Mass.

They left the master bedroom until last. Laura wondered what her social media followers would make of this. John placed his hand gently on the doorframe and whispered, 'Let no harm enter here again.' He stood in silence for a few seconds before turning to Laura. 'I hope this brings peace.'

Laura showed him to the front door, lost in thought. 'Why do you think Bruce contacted me? I've nothing to do with him. Why would he care?'

'Things have a habit of keeping you awake at night on the inside. God knows the poor man could do with some peace of mind.'

'You really believe he's innocent, don't you?' Laura took in John's expression, searched his face for clues. But all she saw was warmth reflected back at her.

'I probably shouldn't say. But after speaking to Bruce at length . . . yes, I believe that he was framed. Somebody murdered his wife and child and now he is paying the price.'

'Could I speak to him?' Butterflies rose in Laura's stomach at the thought. It was frightening, the thought of coming face to face with Bruce. But the priest had sowed an element of doubt about the man's guilt. She needed to make her own mind up.

John tilted his head to one side. 'I'll pass on your details.' The outside breeze wafted in as Laura opened the door to let him out. The close was unnervingly quiet as he cupped his hand against the wind to light a cigarette. It seemed that even priests had their vices. Head down, he walked to his vintage Ford Cortina.

Laura clicked the door shut. Her gaze darted to the ceiling as the same oppressive atmosphere returned. It would take more than the power of prayer to bring peace to this place.

CHAPTER 26

Spice, heroin, crack, cannabis. It was all readily available on the inside if you knew where to look. And lately it had felt like the prison was turning lawless. Understaffed, underfunded and overcrowded – the place was falling apart. The building was literally crumbling. The shower blocks were a rusted wreck and the toilets barely flushed. Not a day went past that Bruce didn't smell skunk drifting from someone's cell, and then there was the homemade hooch that would give weedkiller a run for its money. Given Bruce's addictive personality, he steered clear of drugs, but that wasn't to say he was never tempted.

Tonight was one of those times. There had been another suicide on his wing, and thanks to information from an unusually talkative female guard, Bruce had discovered that he'd known the dead man. For a second, he'd envied his escape from the hell they'd found themselves in. He'd been known as Reefer, a fifty-year-old pothead who treated the prison gates like a revolving door. Bruce didn't know what he'd been sent down for; it wasn't something you asked about. If you did, you'd discover that everyone in prison had been 'set up' for one crime or another.

According to the prison guard, Reefer's long-term girlfriend had broken it off with him two weeks before. Bruce had only spoken to Reefer a couple of times, but he'd seemed OK. Without that link to the outside world . . . Evidently it had got too much for him. Drugs could offer respite, but they could also open the door to suicide.

Bruce drove his hand through his hair, unable to shake off his bleak reflections. He had nobody left now his sister wasn't responding. He'd had a family once. Ali and Cindy had loved him, despite the ups and downs, and he'd thrown it all away. He thought of the last time he'd spoken to Ali. Of the row they'd had that night. He thought about their trip to Disney World, and how Cindy had insisted on holding his hand. He'd been so proud of his little princess. She'd always been polite when she met the Disney characters, allowing other children to rush forward as she waited patiently to be seen. The pain of her loss would torture him every day.

The police had seemed suspicious of him from the off. Would it have happened if they'd stayed put in their old house? But then, their arguments had been gaining momentum before the move. He'd dreamed of his new home in Aspen Hollow for so long, and all it had brought him was pain. Yet still he could not bear the thought of anyone else under his roof. How messed up did that make him?

CHAPTER 27

'No. Please, no.' Laura groaned in disbelief as she checked each car tyre in turn. She was standing on the drive, keys in hand. All she wanted was to go home.

'It's definitely been gouged.' Scarlett Chaplin stood over her, a sports bottle in her hand. Judging by her bleary expression, Scarlett wasn't quite with it today. But Laura had bigger problems to worry about now.

'You think someone used a knife to do this?' Laura asked. Thankfully the attack had been focused on just one tyre, probably because cutting four would be too conspicuous.

'Well, they didn't use a spoon, hun,' Scarlett said dryly.

Laura crouched as she shone her iPhone torch on the tyre. She was grateful for the company, even if it came with smart remarks. Scarlett had come out of the house just as Laura discovered the vandalism to her car.

'Are you sure you didn't see anything?' Laura touched the hole in the tyre in disbelief. Scarlett was always at that window, watching.

Scarlett shrugged. 'It's too dark to see anything until the street lights come on.' She looked around her as they were suddenly illuminated in an orange glow as one by one each light automatically switched on. Scarlett delivered a shrill laugh. 'Well, look at that! Just like magic.' Except she said 'jush', wobbling slightly in her black high heels. Laura frowned. Was she . . . drunk? It was only just gone six p.m.

Laura turned at the sound of footsteps approaching. Billie was dressed casually, in jeans and a long coat belted at the waist. But it was the dog that she was walking that got Laura's attention. Such a sweet little ball of orange fluff.

'Nice pooch,' Scarlett said. 'Shit-something, isn't it?' She crowed a laugh.

'Shih Tzu? No. Pomeranian.' Billie's voice was flat. She looked Scarlett up and down, failing to hide her disapproval. Then she turned to Laura. 'Are you alright?'

'Someone slashed my tyre. I don't suppose you saw anything?' Laura knelt to pet the dog, who wagged her tail furiously.

'Sorry.' Billie shrugged. 'I was inside making a reel. My socials keep me busy when I'm not working. I didn't see anything.'

'She's gorgeous.' Laura smiled, despite her troubles.

'She is,' Billie agreed, her face clouding over as she took in the sight of the deflated tyre. 'Those are thick tyres. That would have taken a bit of strength. You'd better report this to the police, to be on the safe side.' She turned to Scarlett, giving her a withering look. 'Your husband's looking for you – *again.*'

Laura glanced over to see David on his doorstep, gesturing at Scarlett to come inside. Every curtain, window and blind in their home was firmly shut.

'Fuck's sake,' Scarlett muttered, before turning on her heel and going back to her house.

'He doesn't seem to let her go far on her own,' Laura observed, lowering her voice. 'Has she been drinking?'

'You don't know the half of it,' Billie sighed, her braids shadowing her face as she bent to pet her dog. 'C'mon, Princess, time for pee-pee. Maybe you can water Scarlett's lawn.'

'Wait,' Laura called, a sudden wind whipping her hair on to her face. 'Is there anything I should know?' It seemed like an odd question, given she was barely acquainted with the woman, but she couldn't help but feel that more was at stake here. 'It's just that . . .' she continued, 'weird things have been happening. I've not felt very welcome in the close.'

Princess pulled on the lead, suddenly keen to leave. 'I've no problem with you being here,' Billie said. 'But I can't speak for anyone else. Who knows what goes on behind closed doors?'

Laura trotted after Billie. 'What do you mean?'

Billie glanced up at the neighbouring houses before meeting Laura's gaze. 'Nothing. I was being silly. This is a great community. Just sell the house. Take what you can get for it and leave, yeah?'

'That's what I plan on doing, but . . .' Laura continued to follow.

'Good.' Billie walked steadfastly on, her face fixed in a rigid smile. 'Now can you please go?' Another glance at a neighbouring house. Laura followed Billie's gaze to see Graham staring out of an upstairs window. Then the light flickered off, as if he'd realised he'd been seen.

Laura watched Billie half walk, half trot away from her up the road. Had the sight of Graham watching them scared her away? The monochrome sky offered little comfort as fear muscled its way in. Then a memory returned, of Graham bragging about his 'toolbox full of goodies'. Was that a knife that had punctured her car tyre, or a drill? She shivered as her worries brought a tightness to her chest. She was in way over her head.

CHAPTER 28

Laura suppressed a yawn. It was turning out to be a long day. She'd lain in bed last night, staring at the ceiling. The incident with her car had left her ultra-vigilant, listening for every little sound. She'd forced herself to return to Aspen Hollow for another day's work. Now she looked out the kitchen window, checking her car on the drive for the umpteenth time. With no solid offers for the house coming in, she was losing hope. She'd booked in five separate viewings, but only two couples had turned up. The evenings were getting darker. The weather was turning cold. Soon it would be Halloween. She needed to sell the place before winter closed in.

'Mummy, did you know why the pony couldn't sing a lullaby?' Esme's gap-toothed grin beamed from Laura's phone screen.

'No, sweetie, I don't.' The corners of Laura's eyes crinkled with amusement. She hadn't been able to see her daughter this evening, so a FaceTime call would have to suffice.

'Because she was a little horse!'

Laura joined in with Esme's infectious laughter. Esme could have her moments – she was like her mum in that respect – but today she was the jolliest little soul. Esme wanted to be a dancer. Like many girls her age, she was at her happiest in the limelight, lip-syncing to the latest pop song.

'Brilliant. Just brilliant,' Laura said as Esme's giggling subsided. 'Now, don't forget to brush your teeth.'

They said their goodbyes, and Laura was about to hang up when Shane's face appeared on the screen. The new unshaven look suited him, and his smile . . . Laura's heart still gave a little jolt at the sight of him.

'Hey, love, everything alright?' Shane's tone was light.

'Oh, it's going great, thanks!' Laura's answer was prepared. She couldn't disclose that her car tyre had been punctured last night – he'd tell her to get out of there. One of the first things her dad had taught her when she bought her first car was how to change a tyre. It was a skill she hadn't needed until yesterday. What had happened with the spider was bad enough, but the thought of someone roaming the close with a weapon scared her more. Billie's behaviour troubled her, too. Was she covering something up? Then there was Scarlett. Laura thought back to the first time they'd met, when she was unsteady on her feet, and how she'd seemed that way the last time too. It seemed she was a bit of a lush. Was that why her husband wouldn't let her out of his sight? And what about Walter and Graham? Were either of them capable of causing harm? Her tyres were thick, made to withstand all kinds of pressure. It would have taken considerable force to cause the puncture. She'd reported the incident to the police, and a local PCSO had conducted house-to-house calls on the close. Apparently, Graham hadn't been in when the PCSO called round, and nobody else on the close had seen a thing. But someone had been on the driveway. How could that go unnoticed?

Shane's voice broke into her train of thought. 'Hot date tonight, is it?' He let out an awkward laugh. In the background, Laura could see Esme's latest sparkly drawings stuck to the fridge. Shane was a good dad. It was a shame he'd allowed his parents to come between them both. Loyalty was everything to Laura, and

Shane should have stood up to them. But his mother had never got over Shane dumping the wealthy Charlotte Beaumont-Wells for Laura. A reunion would be on the cards if his snobby mother had anything to do with it.

'I'm hosting an open house this evening, for people who can't view during the day,' she relented, giving him some details of her plans. 'Nibbles, drinks. I've invited the neighbours for afterwards, so I can address any concerns.'

'The neighbours? It's a bit above and beyond for an estate agent, isn't it? What concerns would they have?'

Laura sighed. She didn't want to go into all that now. The less Shane knew about what her sister deemed 'the murder house', the better. 'Oh, nothing. The place has been empty for a while. We've got a lot of viewers lined up and I need to keep them on side.'

'Well, as long as you're not funding it out of pocket. I hope the estate agency is paying for it.'

'They're covering the nibbles. A few bottles of prosecco won't break the bank.'

Shane had always been sensible. *Too* sensible at times. Still, it was nice that he cared. 'Why don't you come home afterwards? This is silly . . .'

But Laura wouldn't back down. 'I told you. I won't sleep in that house another night.'

'But Mum's asking questions.'

Laura rolled her eyes. 'I bet she wet her pants with excitement when she saw that I was gone.'

'It wasn't like that,' Shane sighed. 'I soon put her straight. She knows we're saving for a place of our own.'

'I'll be over in the morning,' she replied. 'Give Esme a kiss from me.' She ended the call as she heard a soft thump. She held her breath, listening. Had the sound come from upstairs?

An unsettling silence enveloped her as she stepped into Cindy's old bedroom. The atmosphere felt thick with something she couldn't decipher. But she'd searched each room in turn, and there was nobody there.

'I'm so sorry you both died.' Laura didn't want to think about ghosts, but if felt like someone was listening. She had hoped that the priest's blessing would have the desired effect. But it was still there, lingering in the upper floor of this home – the inexplicable feeling of being watched. She shivered, the room's pastel walls vibrating with a little girl's cries. Only Cindy hadn't cried, as far as Laura knew. She'd been drugged, then smothered in her sleep. Laura shuddered at the thought. The sooner she sold this place, the better.

CHAPTER 29

Laura stood back from the kitchen island, pleased with how the evening had gone so far. Several viewers had said that they'd be in touch, and one was returning tomorrow with their partner. Laura had scheduled the viewings from five until six forty-five, and had invited the neighbours round from seven to eight. Her feet were tired from standing all day, but at least she'd got her steps in. She washed and dried the last piece of glassware, ready for the arrival of the neighbours. It gleamed under the soft glow of the overhead lights. She placed each piece in alignment with the porcelain plates she'd refilled with posh crisps and snacks. Soft music played in the background. She lit candles to add a glow, their flames casting shadows on the walls. The kitchen was a picture of elegance. She pushed thoughts of Ali away.

Pausing to capture the moment, she got out her phone, framing the perfect shot. With a few taps and swipes, the images found their way on to her social media pages. Then the chime of the doorbell got her attention, and she patted her hair before striding down the hall. This evening, guests didn't need to worry about overshoes. This was a relaxed, informal setting designed to put the neighbours at ease. Someone was hiding something. She just needed to find out what.

'Welcome,' she said as the neighbours began to file in. Glasses of prosecco were poured and she told them to help themselves.

She found David and Scarlett in the living room. 'I like what you've done with the place.' His gaze lingered over the decor. It was the most he'd said to her so far.

'Thanks. It's all about finding the right touches.' She smiled, studying his face for clues. A flicker of emotion. A look of regret. But he was too preoccupied with the decor.

David was dressed smartly, in a shirt, tie and pressed trousers, but Scarlett's flowing polka-dot dress was a stranger to an iron. Something told Laura that this was out of character.

Scarlett was draining her glass of prosecco and already unsteady on her heels. 'So . . .' she said. 'Have you had any luck?'

'This place won't be empty for much longer.' Laura smiled. 'I'm confident we'll sell soon.' She took a deep breath. 'Do you think they'll settle in OK? Your new neighbours. I got quite the fright when my car tyre was slashed.'

Scarlett snorted, mumbling something about running for the hills. David steered her towards the door. 'Sorry to hear about your car. We're going to get some water.'

Laura followed them out to the kitchen, where the rest of the neighbours had congregated. The conversation held little interest for Laura as they talked about home security, how businesses were doing on the marina, and the new influx of people who were buying houses as holiday homes.

'The problem is, they only turn up for a few weeks of the year,' Graham said. 'How can local businesses stay open without customers?'

'Occasional tourists, I suppose,' Walter chimed in. 'We don't want this place being overrun with families. I like the quiet pace.'

'Too right.' Billie was the last to arrive. How long had she been listening in? She was wearing jeans paired with a satin blouse, without her dog for once. 'Quiet is good. It's why I came here.' She eyed up Scarlett and David, who were standing angled away from each other.

'Billie.' Graham handed her a glass of prosecco. 'Nice to see you. No Princess tonight? I thought you were glued at the hip.'

'She's not well.' Billie took the glass from his outstretched hand and sniffed its contents before taking a tiny sip.

Laura watched as David leaned over to Scarlett, his voice a hushed reprimand. 'Slow down with the wine,' he murmured, his jaw tight. His efforts to switch her drink to water obviously hadn't worked.

Scarlett's sharp, sudden laughter filled the room. 'Why? Afraid I'll let the cat out of the bag?'

Oh my God, Laura thought. *Is she talking about an affair with Bruce?* Because Laura had already put her in the frame. Mags had said Bruce had sought comfort elsewhere. But had she been talking about Scarlett?

Walter cleared his throat. 'So how did the viewings go? I saw a few people coming in and out.'

'I've had lots of interest,' Laura said, watching Scarlett down another glass of prosecco, much to her husband's disapproval. She picked up a glass for herself. She would soon be driving home, but a sip wouldn't hurt. She returned her attention to Walter. 'I'll have it sold in no time.'

Billie stared into the distance, her attention seemingly anchored elsewhere.

'Did you hear about my car tyre?' Laura turned to face Graham. 'Someone slashed it, right on the drive.'

'Yeah, I heard. Sooner you move on, the better, eh?'

'But what about the new owners? Do you think they'll have trouble too?' There was a part of Laura that was concerned for their welfare. She'd feel a lot happier if she discovered who was behind the threats and strange happenings.

'I suppose we'll have to wait and see.' Graham gave her a wry smile.

'Of course they'll be alright.' Walter glared at his husband. 'Graham's just pulling your chain.'

'I hope so.' As she placed her glass on the table, Laura realised that Billie was missing.

'Excuse me,' she murmured, leaving the room. She surely wouldn't have left already?

After trying each downstairs room, Laura took the stairs. Slowly, she crept up each step, listening for signs of life. But silence rebounded around her as she searched for her missing guest. Eventually, she found Billie standing at the vast window of the master bedroom, her form framed by the light of the moon. Laura flicked on the light. Startled, Billie spun around, her breath catching as their eyes met.

'Oh! I . . . I just wanted to see the view from here,' Billie stammered, resting a hand on her chest.

'Billie,' Laura began gently, bypassing her excuse, 'what's your connection with the Wildings?'

'Nothing. No connection, apart from being neighbours.' Billie swallowed hard. 'I . . . I'm just sad for them. It's difficult being here, in this house.'

Then why come to their bedroom? Laura thought. *Because this is where it happened. This is where Ali was murdered.*

With a tight smile, Billie turned to leave. 'Thanks for tonight,' she whispered, more to herself than to Laura. 'I need to get back to Princess.'

'Wait. Don't go,' Laura urged.

But when Billie turned to face her, her eyes were filled with tears. 'I'm sorry, but this place is toxic. I . . . I can't.'

'What do you mean?' Laura followed her out. 'You know something, don't you?' But her words were ignored as Billie trotted down the stairs.

Laura shook her head. Why was everyone living on this close so damned odd?

When she returned to the kitchen, her guests were ready to leave. Laura's smile was fixed as she followed them to the door.

'It's been . . . interesting.' Graham's eyes twinkled as he tied his scarf.

'You're very *interesting* neighbours,' Laura replied.

'Well, thanks for a lovely evening.' Walter rested his hand lightly on Graham's back.

Scarlett swayed slightly, her words slurred but sharp. 'Oh yes, lovely. Just like one big happy family here in Aspen Hollow.'

David took Scarlett's arm, his features grim as he steered her away with a firm grip. 'Apologies, Laura. She's had a bit too much to drink.'

The cool night swallowed them up as they stumbled into its embrace.

Graham snorted as Laura stood outside. 'She's always on the sauce these days.' He looked like he was about to say more when Walter guided him away.

'Not the time or the place, dear heart,' Laura heard him say.

Whatever they knew, they weren't going to tell her. What a waste of time.

She embraced the quietness of the house as she walked upstairs to watch the neighbours from the window of the master bedroom, where she'd found Billie minutes earlier. What had Scarlett meant about not letting the cat out of the bag? And what were Graham and Walter being so secretive about?

The neighbours dispersed like billiard balls towards their respective homes. The evening had raised more questions than answers, Laura thought. Scarlett had clearly been upset – but about what? And as for Billie – why had she come into the master bedroom, and was it really her dog that had made her leave so suddenly?

Tension turned to nervous anticipation. Laura was closing in on the truth. She could feel it in her bones.

CHAPTER 30

ALI

THEN

It's taken me two weeks to get access to Bruce's phone. Two weeks of pretending that everything is alright. The soft glow of his mobile lights up the nightstand, the screen dimming a few seconds later. Bruce stirs in the bed next to me, his breath sour with the scent of whisky. At last – he's out of it. I pretended to be asleep when he got in twenty minutes ago, tugging off his clothes and stumbling into bed. There was some big celebration at the golf club, apparently. At least, that's what he told me before he went. Funny how I'm never asked to these things.

I creep out of bed in my pyjamas and slide his phone from the nightstand. A small voice in my head asks if I really want to do this as Bruce's snores rebound around the room. He doesn't normally get this drunk. This might be my only chance. Holding my breath, I pick up his phone and tilt it towards his face. For a split second, his eyelids flutter, and I prepare to make up some excuse about checking his breathing. But then the phone vibrates gently in my hand, unlocking with a quiet click. Relief floods through me, followed by a wave of guilt and fear. Bruce snores again, turning on to his left side. I angle the screen towards me. This isn't curiosity anymore – this is me finding out what the hell has been going on.

My footsteps are quiet on the landing as I take his phone downstairs into the kitchen. My fingers peck at the screen. I can't let it lock again.

Sitting in the darkness, I feel physically sick. There is nothing in his texts, just some messages from work and the occasional one from David asking if he's up for a round of golf. I flick to his WhatsApp. I wasn't aware that he even knew how to use it. I check his work group chat first, which comes with the usual stupid gifs and memes. I try the next conversation down. It's from 'Anon'. What the hell? Bruce has actually saved their name as Anon. Time stops as I scroll through the messages. I can barely catch my breath.

> *Anon: Coming out tonight? I need to see you.*
> *Bruce: Not sure if I can get out. Might be pushing it a bit.*
> *Anon: C'mon, you can find a way. Unless you don't want to?*
> *Bruce: You know that's not true.*
> *Anon: Doesn't hurt to say.*
> *Bruce: You already know. But situation isn't good at home.*
> *Anon: It's no walk in the park for me either. But I'm worth it, aren't I?*
> *Bruce: Always. I can't wait to touch you again.*
> *Anon: Then tonight. Use David as an excuse :-)*
> *Bruce: Good old David. Alright then. Usual place and time.*

The usual place and time? The betrayal is like a knife in my gut. The 'use David as an excuse' message was sent just days ago. I shouldn't be surprised. I've had my suspicions. As bad as the gambling apps were, I had a sick feeling that the betrayal didn't stop there. I force myself to stand. I can't go back to bed. I'm not just furious for me; he's betrayed Cindy too. My body seems to move on its own as I pull on my coat and boots. The front door softly clicks behind me and I pocket the keys. I check the time on his phone. It's just gone two a.m. The night air swirls around my pyjama legs and the close is deathly quiet. The phone has locked, which is fine with me. I can't bring myself to read any more anyway. I walk, numb with disbelief.

The lights of the marina are twinkling as I take Scarlett's usual jogging route. The bitch. It's her. It has to be. Who else would joke about David? Know to use him as an excuse? The more I think about her smug face, the more murderous my anger gets. Before I know it, I'm pulling my arm back and launching the phone into the water. *Plop.* I stand there in shock as it sinks.

With hindsight, that was a stupid thing to do. Because now that I've had time to think, I want to know more. Were there pictures? Voice notes? Maybe it's best that I didn't see. That sneering tone. The mocking wink. Bruce doesn't deserve Cindy. Our family is too good for him. What I'm feeling is beyond anger. How dare he do this to us? I've been suspicious about Scarlett for a while, but how would a fling with Scarlett work? David's hardly going to cover for Bruce carrying on with his wife . . . unless they get David so blotto that Bruce brings him home, gets him to bed and then has it off with Scarlett. But they have two little children. Would Bruce have it in him to do such a thing – betray not just one family, but two?

Dejected, I plod home. Maybe he spends an hour with David then meets Scarlett afterwards. Unless he's seeing someone else? But there's only Billie on the close. I can't see it being her. She's too young, too standoffish for him. Someone at work, maybe? Now I'm almost tearing out my hair. Why the hell did I throw away his phone? The clouds blot the moon above and my thoughts grow morose as I reach the Aspen Hollow footpath. Bruce won't even notice that I'm gone. I'll tell him off for 'losing' his phone when he gets up in the morning.

My thoughts darken as I form a plan. It doesn't matter who he's seeing. He's the one I need to focus on. I'm in the driving seat now. And if he wants to leave me, I'm not going to make it easy. Whoever he's seeing can rot in hell. I won't let him go.

CHAPTER 31

Laura groaned as she placed the last of the dishes into the dishwasher. She couldn't leave until the place was spotless. Work was catching up with her. The viewings, the reels, the editing and planning, replying to every comment online, then the endless stream of emails. Sometimes she forgot to eat. She was pushing herself too hard.

Her body ached as she cleaned off the counter. This house was sapping her energy and her spirit. She thought of the bullies she'd faced in her youth, and how she'd never backed down. An uncomfortable thought rose above the rest. What about the family who bought this place? Would the threats carry on? She couldn't allow that to happen. She'd tried emailing Mags for more information but was yet to receive a response. She was OK, though, wasn't she? Laura wondered to herself.

Bang! The sudden noise made her jump.

'What? Who's there?' She stood bolt upright, dishcloth in hand. Her heartbeat hammered in her ears.

Bang!

Was there movement in the house? She was sure everyone had left. *Calm down*, she told herself, but she moved on shaky legs.

Bang!

The sound came again, like the sudden slamming of a door. Sweat prickled Laura's armpits. Should she call the police? But to say what? That she'd heard a door slam? Was it even coming from inside the house? And where was her phone? She rooted around in her bag but it wasn't there anymore.

What do I do? She wished she'd just gone back to her mum's. But then she told herself to face the threat head on.

Shadows danced on the landing as she crept upstairs.

'I've called the police!' she lied. 'They're on their way!' Her head swivelled left and right. Nothing.

She strained to listen but all she could hear was the sound of the blood pumping in her ears. She needed to catch the person behind this, to put an end to their treacherous campaign. Her mouth was dry, her limbs trembling as a shot of adrenaline took hold.

Bang!

She walked along the landing, reluctantly checking each room in turn. She couldn't remember where she'd left her phone. She shouldn't have had that small glass of prosecco. Tiredness and alcohol had lulled her into a false sense of security. Made her relax more than she should. She'd always been a lightweight when it came to booze.

'Hello?' she called out as she heard a soft creak. 'Anyone there?' Her heart felt like it was going to beat its way out of her chest. She was passing Cindy's old bedroom when she heard it: the *bang, bang* of wooden blinds flapping hard against a windowpane. Had she left the window open? The wind had picked up pace and was blowing a gale outside. Was that all that this was? She forced herself to breathe as she approached the room. She wasn't ready for the scene before her.

The beautiful space she'd dressed with care had been totally ransacked. The toys she'd positioned were strewn across the floor, children's books yanked from the shelves, their pages crumpled and torn. A teddy bear lay decapitated, its cotton innards spilling out on the floor. Laura stood in disbelief as fear took hold. Who had done this? And when?

Amongst the chaos, a doll caught her eye. It was sitting on the single bed, staring blankly back at her. Hadn't Cindy had the same one? She'd seen it in Ali's Instagram reels. Who had done this? Then another, darker question rose in her mind. *Are they still here?*

Bang!

She shrieked as the blinds flapped hard against the open bedroom window. Forcing her feet to move, Laura pushed the blinds aside and slammed the window shut. Had she really left it open to begin with? She knew she should call the police, but it always came back to the same thing: if news of a stalker got out, she could kiss goodbye to her house sale. She was so close. She'd put in so much work. An offer would come in any day now, she could feel it. Whoever was stalking her would have to accept the sale once it went through.

She tried to remember the last time she had been in Cindy's room. It was *after* the last set of viewers, which was hours ago.

Riiiing, riiing. The sound of her phone rose from downstairs. It was loud and abrasive, tearing through the silence. She knew she should leave, but she was compelled to find her phone. Where the hell was it? *Riiiing, riiing*, it continued, taunting her. She went into the kitchen, but her bag wasn't where she'd left it anymore.

'What the . . . ?' She opened the microwave door to find her phone. Snatching it from the plate, she put it to her ear.

Help. She needed help. But the person on the other end wasn't saying a word. All she could hear was a long heavy breath. Biting her bottom lip, Laura ended the call.

She felt violated. Someone was touching her things. They were also still in the house. *Why are you wasting time?* The voice of her sister echoed in her mind, as it always did when she was in trouble. *Get the hell out of there!*

'Where's the bloody car keys?' Laura muttered, pocketing her phone. She found her bag on the floor, far from where she had left it. But she couldn't think about that now. She couldn't stand another second in this place. She had to get out.

It was a relief to close the front door behind her, her chest heaving as she forced a breath. But then she was plunged into gloom as the street lights switched off, one by one. Laura fumbled with her car keys, her nerves on edge as a scream sounded in the distance. It was a fox, that was all – wasn't it?

'Fuck!' The keys dropped from her clumsy fingers.

'Are you alright?'

The deep voice made her jump. She took in Graham's form in the darkness.

'Sorry,' he said. 'I didn't mean to frighten you. Just putting out the bins for the morning. You look like you've seen a ghost.'

Laura had, of sorts. The ghost of Cindy's doll. She grazed her fingers against the gravel as she snatched her car keys from the ground. 'I need . . .' Her words stumbled over a jagged breath. 'I need to go.'

'Hey, what's wrong? Are you OK?' Graham took one look at the house and began to lead her away. 'Come over to ours. We're making hot chocolate.' She followed, more shaken than she wanted to let on.

It wasn't until Laura got to Graham and Walter's house that she was calm enough to relay what had happened. Their home was similar to Bruce's but had fewer bedrooms, and instead of a rear stairwell and boot room there was an orangery and a smaller downstairs toilet. The furniture was decadent, most likely chosen by Graham. Their kitchen was an open-plan kitchen and diner, and they sat around the sturdy marble table as Graham handed out mugs of hot chocolate.

'Have you called the police?' Walter asked, sitting there in his plaid dressing gown. Without his usual twist of wax, his moustache drooped at the ends, softening his facial features.

153

Laura shook her head in response to his question. 'I can't. If this gets out, I can kiss goodbye to selling the house.'

'Do you think someone broke in?'

She shrugged, blowing on her beverage before taking a small sip. 'It could have happened during the open house, but I have all their details – I don't get why they'd trash Cindy's old room.'

Graham tapped the table with his fingernails. 'Where did Billie go? She left abruptly, didn't she?'

Laura frowned. Of course. In all the confusion she'd forgotten about Billie. 'I found her in the master bedroom, staring out the window. She was upset.'

'Over what?' Graham's finger-tapping suddenly stopped.

Laura shrugged. 'Over what happened there, I suppose. I don't know why she went upstairs, though.' She took another sip of hot chocolate, which was doing a good job of reviving her. She mentioned her slashed car tyre again, as well as her phone and the threatening texts.

'You should call the police,' Walter interjected. 'Whoever is behind this could still be in the house.'

Graham agreed. 'This sounds dangerous. Maybe it's best if you step away from the sale.'

'Like hell I will.' Laura cradled her mug in both hands. 'What really happened in that house? You must know something, Graham. You know everything that goes on around here.'

Graham gave a gasp of mock disgust. 'Are you calling me a nosey neighbour?'

Laura's lips twitched in a smile. '*Observant* is a better word.'

'We'd rather not get involved.' Walter exchanged a furtive glance with his husband.

'It's just me,' Laura pleaded. 'I won't say anything. But I need to know what I'm dealing with here.'

Silence fell between them.

'Bruce was having an affair,' Graham blurted out, before his husband could stop him. 'His marriage was a sham.'

'I guessed as much,' Laura said quietly.

'How? Because the police didn't even know that. He covered his tracks well.'

'His sister, Mags, came to see me. She said he'd found comfort elsewhere.'

'Then you know what we know.' Walter rose from the table.

'But who with?' Laura answered. 'Was it Scarlett? Is she trying to stop the sale of the house?'

Graham opened his mouth to speak but Walter raised a hand. 'We're not getting involved.'

Laura was crestfallen. 'But—'

'Sorry,' Graham interrupted. 'Final answer. Walter's right. You're welcome to stay over. We'll go to the house in the morning and check that the coast is clear.'

Laura considered it for a moment, but then recalled that Graham was the first person she'd bumped into when she rushed out of the house. Had he really just happened to be there? His sudden appearance felt off.

'Thanks for the offer.' Laura rose, taking her cup to the sink. 'But I'll pop home to Mum's for tonight.'

Walter and Graham were still hiding something. This was about more than an affair. A woman and her daughter had been murdered. Laura didn't trust the neighbours enough to sleep under their roof.

CHAPTER 32

Ali

Then

Why is my life such a car crash? I was brought up in a sensible household. My parents were accountants, for God's sake. They didn't believe in corporal punishment, and the worst thing they did was ground me whenever I went off the rails. We prayed before every mealtime and I was brought to church every week, but it was only because they wanted to steer me on to the right path. They didn't approve of boys with long hair, and heaven help me if I brought one home with a tattoo.

I've tried to analyse where I keep going wrong. My father was sixty-eight when Mum had me. She was fifty-three. I was a surprise baby, arriving long after they'd come to terms with Dad's supposed infertility. Mum thought she was going through the menopause. According to her stories, she didn't know she was pregnant until I gave her a firm kick. Even then, she panicked, thinking something serious was wrong with her gut. I may not have been planned, but I was incredibly loved. They wrapped me up in cotton wool from day one. But I still cringe when memories of being picked up from the school playground raise their ugly head. The other kids used to tease that my grandparents had arrived. My clothes, my hair . . . Nothing about me fitted in until I was old enough to change it myself. I suppose that's why I flew off the rails. I started drinking at thirteen, smoked cannabis a year after that. Anything to gain the respect of my peers. I straightened myself out eventually, and I even returned to the church. But my grades suffered as a result. After I had Cindy, I apologised to my parents for what I'd put them through. I'm glad I got to make peace with them before they died. Their deaths were horrendously sudden. I'll never, ever get over it. If they could see me now, they'd be mortified. Almost as ashamed as they were the day I dropped out of university.

But no matter what I do, it only seems to make things worse. I don't want Cindy to end up like me. I've worked out what she needs most in the world. She doesn't need a broken home. She doesn't need a one-parent family. She doesn't need to see me calling out her father as a liar and a cheat. It's hard to think these thoughts, but I need him to see what he'd be missing if we split. I can't let him go. Not yet. I've thought about who his bit on the side could be. I might be wrong about Scarlett, I might not. I reckon it's been going on for some time. I imagine her out there, stalking us online. My videos are her window into our world. I dwelled on it all day after finding the messages, and I've come up with a plan.

Today I rang the golf club to speak to my husband. I was told that he hadn't been there all day. He'd taken his clubs this morning. He was in a good mood. He's been gone for hours. But I've texted his new phone. Now he's on his way home. Enough is enough. I'm taking back control. I won't be a helpless bystander in my marriage anymore.

I stand before my live video feed after warning my viewers that I have something to share. Bruce won't see it, he's driving and hates social media, but I bet that *she* will. The slut who's been screwing my husband. The bitch who's trying to break up our home. The thing is, Bruce won't ever leave me. He loves this house too much. His plans for Aspen Hollow came from drawings he made as a teenager. He is way more invested than an ordinary architect would ever be. He earmarked this house from day one, but could only buy it with my inheritance. When we posed for our photo at the front door, it felt like I was living in a dream world. But dreams don't last forever and our bubble of happiness has finally popped.

I'm putting the finishing touches on the cake I've just baked. My live feed is a success, hundreds of people are watching, and I smile at the emojis as I announce, 'Bruce is here!' I smooth down my hair. 'Are you ready to hear my news?' I giggle with excitement. I'm laying it on thick. Bruce doesn't see the camera at first. Cindy is in her room, headphones on, playing a new game on her Nintendo Switch. Bruce takes the car keys from his navy golf trousers and rests them on the side.

'Welcome home, honey!' I grin. 'Say hello to my viewers.'

He freezes as he sees the camera. Suddenly he's shy. Awkward.

'Hi!' he says, stepping towards me. 'What's going on?' he mumbles, soft and low.

I produce a cake with pink-and-blue icing. I show it to the camera before allowing him to read the top. It reads WELCOME HOME DADDY. I watch as he reads the words, then looks at me, puzzled.

'From your second child,' I reply, this mad grin fixed on my face. He looks at the cake. Then he stares open-mouthed at me. Then he looks at the camera and back at the cake.

'What's this?' All the blood has left his face and his expression is strained.

'I'm pregnant,' I blurt out. 'We're having baby number two.'

His eyes widen, and I know what he's thinking – that this is nothing short of a miracle. We barely sleep together these days.

'Wow,' he says, catching his breath. 'Wow.' But the second *wow* comes out flat and he pulls me towards him. Then he whispers into my ear, 'Turn off the camera. Now.'

I turn to the screen, real tears in my eyes. 'We're a bit emotional, folks. I'm going to leave it here. Thanks for sharing this moment with me! Will it be a boy or a girl? Leave your comments below.' I am pushing the algorithm, as always. 'We're going to have some cake.'

I swipe away my tears. I've done it out of anger and it has backfired massively on me. I wonder what my viewers really think. Bruce goes to the sink for a glass of water. Already, the comments are flooding in.

> *He's not very happy about that.*
> *Give him a break, anyone could see the poor bloke is shocked!*
> *It's big news, it's still sinking in.*
> *Did you see the look on his face? Shoot me now!*
> *She should have told him in private. What an attention seeker.*

I rest my phone face down. My plan is to say I've had a miscarriage, later on. But I'm already regretting everything.

Bruce is shaking his head, his features stony. 'What in the actual fuck, Ali? You could've told me in private. Are you really pregnant?'

'Of course I'm pregnant, I wouldn't just make it up.' I throw him a hurt expression, even though that's exactly what I've just done. He doesn't blink as I tell him the due date. My stomach is churning. 'Cindy's upstairs on her Switch. I haven't told her yet.'

I'm not sure how I should act, so I give him a watery smile. 'Would you like some cake?' I follow up.

Bruce curls his fist and makes me jump as he hits the countertop. 'No, I don't want any bloody cake! How did this . . . how did this happen?'

'You mean, how could you possibly be accused of sleeping with your wife?' I spit, one hand over my stomach for effect.

He has the decency to look shame-faced.

'I'm three months gone. It only takes once.'

'I thought you were on the pill.'

'Why would I be? Santa comes in this house more than you do!' I scream, pausing to double-check that I *have* turned my camera off. 'Most husbands would be thrilled. What a great way for this baby to start its little life.'

Bruce heaves a sigh. 'Look, when it comes to personal news you can't turn on the camera and film it. How would you like it if I shoved a phone in your face every time I had something big to discuss?'

But Bruce never discusses anything. He just goes ahead and does his own thing. His face is flushed, his body tense, as he stands over me.

'Isn't it what you signed up for when you married me?' I stare up at him. 'For better for worse, in hashtags and in health?' My words are tinged with bitterness.

'Are you punishing me? Is that why you put me on the spot?' Bruce is right. But he has no idea how far I am willing to go. As if I'd let him leave a marriage I've invested my whole life in.

'It's the only way I can get your attention!' I'm crying now, big ugly sobs. 'You've just made me feel like shit.'

'Well, ditto,' he fumes, poking me in the chest. 'Because you should have discussed this with me. Now we don't have . . . options.'

I stare as the words fall from his lips. Because I am mortally offended for the baby that doesn't even exist.

'You want me to get rid of it? Is that what you're saying?'

He calms. Takes a step back. 'I'm saying we can't afford another mouth to feed.'

'And whose fault is that?' I counter, barely able to speak through my sobs. 'Because it was your idea to put all our money into this place.'

We shout at each other for a while, then he storms out, probably into the arms of his mistress. I'm left to pick up the pieces and answer my congratulatory posts on social media. I hate him so much in this moment. Some women are treated like princesses while I'm treated like dirt. I could have mentioned the gambling apps. The destruction of the phone he thinks he lost on his drunken night out. But I keep it to myself, because I need to know more.

Now I'm heading out through the back garden with Cindy, ready to feed the ducks who live in the pond in the woods. I open the gate that leads to the woodland trail and allow her through. At least she didn't hear our argument. That's one good thing about living in such a big house.

I hand her a small bag of food.

'Heeeere, duck duck duck!' she calls, just as I've taught her. Their quacks sound like laughter as they swim towards us. I stand beneath the shade of a tree, watching my daughter feed them at the edge of the pond.

'Careful!' I call as she gets a little close to the water. She's not in any danger, I just like to keep her close. If only Bruce was as protective of us both. I fight back my tears as I come to face the truth. My husband doesn't love me anymore.

CHAPTER 33

As night closed in around her and the car crawled past 1 Aspen Hollow, Laura didn't dare to look up at the windows for fear of what she might see. She remained focused, the headlights carving a path out of the dip of the close. She would slip into her mother's house tonight and leave first thing in the morning. The rear-view mirror reflected a tarry darkness, all the street lights extinguished now. Trees flanked the road, their skeletal branches swaying in the night breeze. She gripped the wheel a little tighter, the chill from the leather seeping into her skin. Who had been in the house tonight? The ferocity of their destruction was evidence of their temper. This was about more than scaring her off.

It was a relief when the familiar outline of her mother's house came into view. She lived on a narrow street, each red-brick terrace house a copy of the one next to it. Few people took pride in their front gardens, and most were paved over – the only greenery the errant weeds that forced their way through the cracks. An eerie army of black waste disposal bins stood sentry on the pavement, the overspilling plastic bags ripe for the crows who came at dawn. Laura parked her car, her keys in her hand as she approached the front door. A lone dog barked from a neighbouring home as she fumbled with the house key. Why wouldn't it work? Laura jiggled the key in the door frantically, denial giving way to realisation as the truth dawned – her mother had changed the locks.

Surely there was an explanation. Had her mum lost her key and forgotten to give Laura one when she had it replaced? Or had the house intruder switched them somehow? She stared at the coloured fob. Found the scratch on the inside. It was the same key. Laura stood back, glaring up at her mum's bedroom window. It was gone eleven p.m. A curtain quivered. She was up there. Laura could sense her presence.

'Mum?' Her voice was a whisper, but loud enough to reach the bedroom window, which was open slightly to let the cigarette smoke out. No answer came. It wasn't the first time Laura had been locked out of the house, but it would be the last. She had tried so hard to bridge the gap between them since her father died. But her mum simply wasn't interested. She never had been.

'Fine,' she muttered, turning on her heel. 'I know when I'm not wanted.'

She scanned the once-familiar neighbourhood in the hollow quiet of the night. Esme would never be made to feel like this. Laura would make sure of it. No wonder her marriage was having problems. Latchkey kids, that's what the neighbours had called her and Cally. Their father had sold property abroad and was away for days or even weeks at a time. Their mother was never home, and when she was she was either drunk or sleeping it off. After school, she and Cally would let themselves into the house and Cally would make them both jam sandwiches from stale bread.

Laura dismissed the memories. Her past did not define her. She would do better with her own family. Gathering her resolve, she started the car engine. It was time to swallow her pride. She knew where she needed to go.

Outside the house in the Cathedral Quarter, she got out of the car, stiff and tired but looking forward to her bed. Only now was she seeing the problems she and Shane had been having were more about her than him. She was the one who couldn't accept his parents' interference when they'd offered to pay for everything. Laura had grown up independent. She couldn't adjust to a family where parents were so involved. Not a day passed that Shane's mother didn't ring, or make some comment about Laura's parenting skills. Shane struggled to stand up to his mum, but Laura could have at least met him halfway. A mother who cared too much was better than one who didn't care at all.

Laura was in the kitchen when Shane came down, in his boxers and T-shirt. He would walk around the house with no top on rather than turn down the heating. Such was the privilege of being born into wealth. His mother never had to dry her Primark knickers on the radiator.

'Sorry. Did you think there was a burglar?' Laura watched him rub his eyes with the heels of his palms. It was something Esme also did. Those two were so alike.

'It's OK. What's wrong?' Shane asked, masking a yawn with his hand.

'I was working late. Mum's changed the locks and I can't get in.'

'Jeez, your mum . . .' Shane tutted, shaking his head in disgust. 'But at least it's brought you home.' He raised an eyebrow. 'You're staying, aren't you? Until we get a place of our own?'

Laura nodded. 'I've been a silly bugger, haven't I?' She allowed her father's Yorkshire accent to slip through, knowing it would make him smile.

'Aye, lass. Now go and brew us a cuppa tea!' Shane came back with one of his own.

'That was awful,' Laura laughed. 'Just stop. Dad will be turning in his grave.'

Shane's eyes were deep with affection as he delivered a heart-melting smile. They stood across from each other, in the sad hours of the night, neither of them ready for sleep.

Shane opened his arms for a hug. 'Welcome home.'

Laura closed her eyes as she accepted his embrace, breathing in the faintest remnants of his musky aftershave. When it was just their little family unit, all was well in the world. If only it was just the three of them.

An involuntary shudder drove its way down her back.

'Sorry,' she said. 'Someone just walked over my grave.'

Shane seemed unperturbed. 'Hey, I've been watching this K-drama on Netflix. *Queen of Tears*. Fancy checking it out?'

They had met over their love of K-drama in a random Facebook group, and been shocked to discover that they lived just a few miles apart. The Stokes tea room had become their weekly meeting place, and in the summer they walked around the greenery of The Lawn's car park, discussing plot lines and characters. It was a romance all of its own – Shane, an only child from a wealthy Lincoln family, and Laura, the ambitious, independent woman making her own way in the world.

Now, they snuggled on the sofa that had been chosen and paid for by his parents, much like the rest of the furniture in the house. Shane pulled a soft throw over them both. Laura relaxed, enjoying the comforting reassurance of being with her husband. It wasn't perfect. Not yet. But it would be . . . as soon as she sold 1 Aspen Hollow. Tension seeped from her bones as she dozed in Shane's arms.

CHAPTER 34

'Let me out!' Scarlett hammered on the door. This wasn't happening again. It couldn't be. 'I know you can hear me, David!' She marched over to the camera in the corner of the room. 'If you don't open that door, I'm going through the window. I mean it!'

David wasn't at work. The nanny had Fridays off. The children were either downstairs or with their grandparents. Either way, David was home. She sat on the bed, listening for movement outside the room. She waited for the click of a lock being opened. But today, the door stayed shut. Stillness returned.

This was another one of those times she wished she had never set foot in Aspen Hollow. Scarlett had picked up on a weird feeling the moment she came to live here. She'd always had a bit of a sixth sense. In her early childhood, she used to talk to her nan. She'd be in the space between wakefulness and sleeping when she'd see her on the end of her bed. It would have been fine, had her nan not died the day after she was born. Scarlett didn't remember much of it, but her mother used to ask her questions about the woman she'd never met.

'What did Nana say last night?' she'd ask, as Scarlett's father rolled his eyes.

'That she doesn't need all those flowers on her grave,' Scarlett once replied. 'You should save up the money instead.'

Her mother had both laughed and cried, saying it sounded exactly like her. But as Scarlett aged, her grandmother's visits had come to a halt. Perhaps she'd stopped seeing her, or maybe the 'visits' had been Scarlett's way of pleasing her mum. She couldn't say for sure. All she knew was that the close never felt like a restful place. They'd had a reasonably happy life before coming to live in Aspen Hollow. But bit by bit, she and David had changed. He certainly wasn't the man that she thought he was. And as for No. 1 . . .

She pulled herself out of her thoughts, got up and pressed her hand to the door. Someone was sobbing on the other side.

'David?'

'I'm here.'

His response came quickly but he made no effort to let her out. This was bad. Very bad. She'd never heard him cry before.

'Open the door.' The heat was leaving her voice. Her mouth was bone dry, her hands trembling with the need for booze.

No reply. Just a long, shuddering sigh. She thought of her hiding places. David had found them all.

'Is it about last night?' In truth, she remembered little of the party at No. 1.

'You came so close,' David said. 'So close to telling them everything. Do you know what kind of social media following that estate agent has? Thousands. Do you understand?'

'Where are the children?' It was all she could think of to say. Because 'sorry' wouldn't cut it today.

'Do you care? You barely look at them these days.'

'Of course I care . . .' Sadness overcame her through the severity of her hangover. 'I . . . I'm struggling. I need help.'

'I've tried. You won't let me in.' He sniffed. 'I think we're at the end of the road.'

No! Scarlett's thoughts suddenly sharpened. She was in pain. She was an addict. But she didn't want to be alone. Mistakes had been made. Cataclysmic ones. But they had to salvage what they could.

'I'll go to rehab,' she said, because she couldn't bear to hear her husband suffer anymore.

'Are you sure?' He paused to clear his throat. 'You're not just telling me what I need to hear?'

'I'm saying what I need to do.'

Scarlett waited for a response. There was the soft click of a bolt turning in the door. The sight of her husband's face was enough to strengthen her resolve. She accepted his arms as he opened them and she fell into them. Regardless of what had happened, they had to learn how to move on.

CHAPTER 35

Laura hadn't stopped all day. Breakfast had been nice, but had ended abruptly when Shane's parents walked in on them both. It was hard to tell whose smile was more fake, hers or Mrs Taylor-Brown's. She'd then returned to the house at Aspen Hollow, grateful for Graham's presence as he helped her clean the place up. She threw out the messed-up books and toys, as well as the decapitated teddy bear. As for the doll – well, it wasn't as if Mattel had made just one. Laura needed to stay firm in her conviction that she could sell this house – which was why she hadn't informed the police of the threats to date.

She'd completed another viewing before driving to Lincoln. The city had been filled with shoppers today, as well as the usual buskers and novelty acts. Lincoln was small but packed with life, and she'd enjoyed her visit to the estate agency office to discuss the viewings so far. Had Clio not made herself scarce, she could have availed herself of the tray of goodies that Laura had bought from Doughnotts.

Now she was driving back to the close, her spirits lifting at the sight of Mags sitting on the doorstep of No. 1, kitten tote bag in hand, clearly waiting for her to return. But what if she'd been gone for the day? Why hadn't Mags just texted? She certainly was an odd little soul. But odd or not, Laura was glad to see her. She liked Mags; the woman had a comforting nature about her, maternal almost. Laura wondered if she had children of her own. She hadn't seen a wedding ring on her finger when she'd looked.

'I hope you haven't been waiting long,' Laura said as she approached.

'I've nothing else to do,' Mags said in her soft Scottish lilt. 'And I don't want to get in the way of your work. The neighbours have been giving me funny looks.' She rose from the step, patting down her baggy black dress.

'Come in,' Laura said, gesturing to the door, wishing the neighbours had shown as much interest when her tyre was slashed. 'I was hoping you'd get back in touch.'

'Yes, sorry, I saw your emails,' Mags said. 'But I prefer to speak to people in person. I'm a bit old-fashioned like that . . .'

'You're not alone,' Laura's voice echoed in the hall. 'I've noticed it more and more. People use their phones for everything except speaking on. I suppose we've become a bit more insular since social media came on the scene.'

'I've always been insular,' Mags admitted, with a shrug. In that moment she looked so sad that Laura wanted to know more.

'I'm parched,' Laura said as they reached the kitchen. 'Fancy a cuppa?'

Mags didn't refuse. Laura busied herself making tea while Mags talked about the weather. It was only when they were sitting facing each other that Laura divulged what had been going on.

'It's scary, and it's dangerous. Whoever's doing this, they're emotionally involved.'

'Then it's the same person who killed Ali and Cindy.' Mags was hunched over her mug of tea, her knuckles whitening as she gripped it a little tighter. 'They have an agenda.' Her breath was laden with grief. 'I'll never get over it. And now my brother is paying the price. I feel awful, really I do. It gives me the most terrible stomach ache.'

Laura sipped her tea, desperate for Mags to get to the point.

'I've been to the doctor for my nerves. I can't sleep. Can't think straight. All I want is for Bruce to be able to escape from this nightmare.'

'Do you think the neighbours might be involved?' Laura asked.

'It's not a stranger, that's for sure.' Mags glanced towards the window. 'Just think . . . if you could find out the truth. What a difference that would make.'

'I wish I could,' Laura replied. 'But I've not been feeling all that safe here myself . . .'

'Then do yourself a favour and leave, before they get to you too. I'm going straight to the train station after this,' Mags continued. 'I've had enough of this place.' She seemed out of sync today, a ball of grief and anxiety.

'Mags . . .' Laura leaned closer. 'The last time we met, you said something about Bruce having an affair. Were you talking about Scarlett?'

'Did I say that? Goodness . . .' A creak of the door made Mags start. Suddenly Billie was standing there, watching them both.

'Am I interrupting? The front door was open. I presumed it was still an open house.'

Mags clutched her tote bag, nostrils flaring as she met Laura's eyes. 'Thanks for the tea. I . . . I have to go or I'll miss my train.' She barely acknowledged Billie as she marched past, her head down.

'Do you want me to call you a taxi?' Laura called after her, but Mags was already walking out of the house, one hand raised in a quick goodbye.

'No need!'

'Was it something I said?' A small smile played on Billie's face.

But Laura was too annoyed by the interruption to be amused. Mags had rushed off as if her backside was on fire. Laura left Billie standing as she followed Mags out. 'Mags, wait. You were about to tell me about Bruce's affair.'

'Sorry,' Mags said, eyes shining with emotion. 'I can't. All of this. It's too much. I need to go back to Scotland.'

'Please,' Laura begged. 'I need answers.'

But Mags ignored her pleas as she trotted down the road. She'd come here to help. What had changed her mind? Laura turned back towards the house to find Billie standing in her path.

'Everything alright?' Billie said.

'I've had better days,' Laura sighed. 'Did you want something?'

'I want you to put my house on the market, after you've sold this place.'

'Really?' Laura was still annoyed by her intrusion. 'Can I ask why?'

Billie's chunky mustard jumper slid off a bare shoulder as she pushed her hands into the front pockets of her jeans. 'I came here for peace. It's been anything but.'

'I'm sure things will die down once the house is sold. I've more viewers lined up, offers are coming in.' It was true about the offers, but they'd been way too low to sell. The psychic woman who had viewed the house a few days ago had put in an offer to buy. But Laura wasn't letting it go for such a pitiful amount.

Billie's expression hardened. 'When I say I want peace . . . I'm not annoyed by the viewings, I'm talking about our beloved neighbours. I've had enough of their dramas, their arguing all hours of the day and night.' Billie glanced around the close. 'I see people walking around outside at all hours. It's unsettling.'

'Oh. Will you be buying another property elsewhere? I can keep a lookout for you . . .'

But Billie shook her head. 'I'm going to travel. Take some time off.'

Laura nodded, thoughtful. 'Sorry the neighbours have been giving you grief. Have you tried having a word?'

Billie's laughter was short and sharp. 'It's not up to me to sort their marriage out. Then there's Scarlett and David, slamming car doors in the middle of the night.'

'Wait . . . what? When you said the neighbours were arguing, I thought you meant them. Do Walter and Graham fight too?'

'Oh yes, it's never-ending with my delightful neighbours.' Her phone buzzed in the back pocket of her jeans. She glanced at the screen. 'I have to go. What I said . . . Keep that to yourself, yeah? I don't want to be dragged into their drama.'

'Of course. Discretion is my middle name. When do you want to put it up for sale? I'll have to do a valuation.'

'It's pretty identical to this one . . . without the Wilding family history.' Billie scrolled through her phone. 'Get as much as you can for this place, because that will affect the price of mine.'

'Don't worry, we'll work out a strategy,' Laura reassured her. 'Are you absolutely sure you want to sell?'

Billie nodded, resolute. 'Aspen Hollow isn't what it was cracked up to be.'

Laura couldn't disagree. At this rate, there wouldn't be any neighbours left.

Once Billie had gone, she checked her watch. She'd cleared the next couple of hours from her schedule. She had somewhere important to be. Mags had suggested that she make a choice: leave, or unravel the truth. And Laura wasn't a quitter. A prison visiting order had come through. Butterflies danced in her stomach at the thought of meeting Bruce Wilding in the flesh.

CHAPTER 36

Bruce felt like he was on a first date instead of sitting in the prison visiting room with all the other men. His knee bobbed up and down beneath the metal table, the heel of his Nike trainer tapping against the cold cement floor. Everything in prison was cold, metallic, hard and rough. But the woman approaching him was anything but. His lips parted in surprise. He hadn't expected her to look so much like his wife. She was soft and bright and curvy, and smelled sweet and fragrant as she got close. Bruce inhaled the gentle scent of her perfume. Vanilla. It was something with vanilla in it. Just like the scent Ali used to wear. Living in acrid air made you appreciate the finer things even more. If he ever got out of this place, he'd surround himself with nice smells. Every day would be about living life to the full, and he'd never take things for granted again. He used to buy Ali all her perfume. When he travelled he'd bring her back a bottle of something nice from the duty-free shops. Cindy had loved the giant bars of Toblerone, and Ali would allow her one segment a night. Bruce blinked, grounding himself. He went to stand in acknowledgement of his visitor, but Laura quickly took her seat.

'I didn't know if we're allowed to shake hands or not.' She blinked behind her glasses, her blue eyes darting towards the guards before settling back on him. She looked nervous. Unsettled. As anyone would, in a place like this. But there was something more behind her eyes as she glanced at him. Fear. She was scared of him. 'I've, um . . . never been inside a prison before.' Her words stumbled over each other as she sat before him.

'At least you recognised me.' Bruce smiled in an effort to put her at ease. Her nervousness was palpable. She rested her forearms on the table, tightly clasping her hands. She was wearing a navy-blue scoop-necked dress and a jacket to match. More businesslike than casual, like something you'd wear if you worked in a bank. 'I'm guessing I'm still quite well known in the outside world,' Bruce said, filling the gap of silence.

'You are to me,' Laura said. 'I've learned a lot since taking on your old home.' She paused, a flush rising to her cheeks. 'Sorry, is it a sore subject? I'm nervous. I don't know what to say.'

'It's OK.' Bruce smiled. 'Take a breath. They'll let you leave, I promise. Thanks for coming, it's nice to get visitors – especially normal ones.'

'I never said I was normal. Let's not set the bar too high.' Laura relaxed her posture, her shoulders dropping half an inch.

Bruce liked her already. 'I would have sent the letters directly but I didn't want to freak you out.'

'John mentioned that. And if I'm honest it did. But he's a nice man. He's got a lot of faith in you.'

Bruce dropped his hand as he realised he was touching the small silver cross around his neck. 'I'm glad someone does. I'm worried he'll be transferred to another prison. It sometimes happens. Allegations are made, then nothing comes of it . . . but it doesn't look good so they move on somewhere else.'

Bruce glanced at the couple nearby. He had come to know many of the inmates and the people who visited them. Gerald was a sixty-year-old investment banker who'd been imprisoned for fraud. The woman across from him was quietly crying. On the other side of the room, a man named Jericho was arguing with his brother. Jericho had been imprisoned for slitting a rival gang member's throat. He was only twenty-two. It took all sorts.

'Anyway—' Bruce quickly looked back to Laura as Jericho caught his gaze. 'You didn't come to hear me complain. Everything OK? Nobody's hurt you, have they?'

'No, nobody's been hurt, just . . . just a stick in the spokes of life, as my father would say.' She delivered a small, tight smile. She told him about the threatening texts she'd received, then damage to her car and, finally, how Cindy's bedroom had been trashed. Her frown deepened. 'I get the feeling that I'm not alone in the house.'

'Sounds like my stalker. Who else would go to the trouble of finding a replica doll? Fucking sick, that's what it is.' Bruce shifted in the hard, uncomfortable bucket seat. 'Excuse my French. But this . . .' He ran his hand through his hair, unable to find the words. 'Stay safe, yeah? Don't go in there on your own.'

'We're checking any potential buyers.' Laura's throat clicked as she swallowed. This was a woman who was playing things down. She paused with the look of someone who had an important question to ask. Not any question. *The* question. Bruce didn't want to hear it. Not again. He always felt like he was on trial when people brought up the deaths of his wife and child.

'John said she's been writing for some time. Any idea who she is?'

Bruce was glad he'd read Laura wrong. Perhaps she wouldn't ask after all. He thought for a moment. It was hard to think when the chatter in the room was so loud.

'I honestly don't know. She started sending letters not long after I got here. She never signs them and she doesn't give her address. At first, I could kind of understand, because everyone wanted something from me back then. And I suppose . . .' He rubbed his chin. 'It was good to hear from someone who didn't want to sell me out to the press. Her letters were pretty ordinary

176

to begin with. Listening to her talk about work and politics and traffic and global warming . . . All those ordinary mundane things we worry about on the outside. It made me feel connected, without the pressure of having to write back, you know?'

Laura nodded in response, her gaze briefly flicking to Gerald's wife, who was drying her eyes with a tissue.

'I used to look forward to her letters,' Bruce continued. 'It's weird but I think she knew. She seemed to know a lot about how I was doing. And for a long time I wondered what she was getting out of it. Maybe she was being strategic, gaining my trust . . . I don't know. It's been going on for a long time. But then she started getting intense.' His foot began tapping as he thought of how things had escalated in the past few weeks. 'She's furious about the house being up for sale. She's always said I'm innocent and she knows that beyond a doubt.'

'How do you think she knows, though?' Laura said, leaning in, as if he was going to impart some big secret to her. Bruce watched her closely, reading her face for clues. What did she really want from him? Prison had made him mistrustful of everyone.

'But then she said that I have to hurry up and get out of prison before the house is sold. As if it's that easy.' Bruce emitted a dry laugh. 'But she did make me realise that I couldn't keep going the way that I was, sitting on my grief. Wallowing in self-pity. I had to make a change.' He stared deep into Laura's eyes. Past her glasses into the flecks of blue and grey. Saw that likeness to Ali again. Or maybe his brain was fucked up from the time he'd spent inside. 'I didn't kill my wife and daughter. I was set up.' He studied her reaction. Waited for the sceptical nod.

'I want to believe you,' she simply said. 'I wouldn't be here if I didn't.' And he supposed that it was true. She was wearing a wedding ring. Carried a certain maternal sense about her. 'This woman . . . Could it be anyone you know?'

Bruce shrugged. 'I don't see what they'd get out of being anonymous. Although she knows my letters are read by the prison guards. She's fairly pissed off about that. It feels like she's unravelling. It doesn't help that there's so many videos of me online. I hate those things. I wish I could take them down.'

Laura shook her head. 'I do a lot of stuff online, and believe me, the internet never forgets.'

'Did Mags pay you a visit? I've been worried about her.'

'Oh, yes,' Laura said. 'She's lovely, a really nice woman. She made me a Dundee cake.'

Bruce raised an eyebrow. 'Mags baked a cake? And you're still in one piece?' He chuckled. 'She can't bake to save her life.'

'Well, she must have been practising . . . It was very nice.'

'Now Mum was a great cook. She could turn her hand to anything. But Mags . . .' Bruce grimaced. 'Mum used to say that she'd burn tea if she could.' A soft smile rose to his face. 'I miss her, you know? Tell me about her. I want to hear everything. You'll do that for me, won't you?'

And so Laura did. She spoke about Mags's sudden appearance, describing what she was wearing so Bruce could paint a picture in his mind. She relayed everything she'd said, and discussed Mags's concerns.

'She's worried about you.' Laura's features became strained. 'Is there . . . is there any way she might know who framed you for murder? I think she's trying to find new evidence, to help in whatever way she can.'

Bruce shook his head. 'I don't want her getting involved. She might get hurt. My sister . . . She's a private person. I just want to know that she's OK.'

'I got that impression,' Laura said. 'But I'm happy to act as an intermediary if it helps. Anything you want me to pass on?'

'Just my best wishes. Tell her I miss her letters. And tell her . . . tell her not to get involved. I'll sort this out on my own.'

But Laura's nod of acknowledgement was slow in coming. His eyes crept to the clock on the wall as it ticked the minutes away. Soon their visit would be over, and he would be back in his cell, ruminating on their conversation.

'Is there anything I can get you?' Laura said. 'I feel bad, coming here empty-handed.'

'It's not a dinner party. The fact you came is enough in itself.'

'Still. I'd like to bring something. I feel so bad about everything.'

'Stationery. I like to write, but the paper here is crap. Any kind of loose paper. Nothing with wires, like ring binders . . . If you don't mind.' He hated asking, but it wasn't a big request.

'Bruce, can I be really frank with you?' Laura asked.

'What is it? Are you after a scoop? Because if you are . . .'

She straightened, looking so horrified that Bruce immediately regretted his words. 'Oh God, no, not at all!' Her gaze crept back to him. 'I know it's none of my business, but . . .' She nibbled her bottom lip, waiting for permission.

'What is it?'

'Were you having an affair? It's just that . . .' Her cheeks reddened to a brighter shade of pink. 'Well, I wonder if it has a bearing on what's happening with the house. Mags mentioned that there might be someone else involved. Someone from the close?'

Bruce groaned. Was this why his sister hadn't been in touch? Did she know that he'd tell her off for getting so involved? He tuned back in to Laura, who was staring at him intently.

'Anyone I need to watch out for in the close?'

Her question hung in the air as she smoothed the ends of her hair with manicured fingers. The chatter in the room grew, and Bruce wished they could have met somewhere, anywhere, without the incessant noise. Oh for the days when he used to sit at the marina, coffee in hand, watching the world go by.

'Bruce?' Laura said.

He was doing this more often lately, zoning out when he should be paying attention. He didn't like the question. Didn't want to face up to it yet.

'You're right, it's none of your business.' He watched her face crumple a little, like an errant child who'd been told off. 'You've nothing to worry about from any of my neighbours. They're not capable of hurting anyone.'

'Sorry. Yes . . . You're probably right. The house will be sold soon and—'

'And I don't know what Mags is up to, but she should keep her nose out,' Bruce interrupted. The possibility of his house being returned to him was fading away.

'Look. The way I see it . . . Mags means well,' Laura continued, oblivious to his growing irritation. 'She really cares about you, Bruce. But she's scared, too. I just want to get to the bottom of it. The last thing I want is the new owners of the house being stalked.'

Bruce didn't want to think about anyone else living in his home. He hadn't meant to snap, but he was sick of being treated like a criminal. He didn't trust Laura enough to tell her anything now.

'Thanks for coming, anyway. And if you could tell Mags to get in touch, I'd really appreciate it.' But as he rose, Laura stayed put.

'Wait, Bruce . . . I'm really sorry. I didn't mean to offend you. I can't imagine how hard this has been.'

'I'm glad you can't imagine it,' Bruce said, wearily. 'Because I wouldn't wish that on anyone. Take care of yourself, Laura. Look after your family. Because that's all that really matters in the end.' He nodded at the nearby guard. 'I want to go back to my cell.'

CHAPTER 37

'Oh my God, sis, I can't believe you met Bruce Wilding. What was he like?' Cally's voice rose from Laura's car speakers as she made the journey home. Cally was talking about Bruce as if he were some kind of A-list celebrity. 'Was he as gorgeous in real life as he is in those YouTube videos?'

Her sister had always been dark. Laura still had the photographs of her gothic teenage years. Now, her love for true crime had no boundaries and she couldn't see when she was being insensitive.

'Dunno, I didn't notice,' Laura said dully, regretting bringing her visit up. But Cally had asked where she'd been and Laura couldn't bring herself to lie. 'We were too busy talking about his stalker.' She filled her in, to a certain extent.

'I doubt she means any harm. Lots of women write to men in prison. She's probably just some harmless woman with a crush,' Cally replied. Usually, she saw the worst in everyone. Her perception of the world was slightly skewed.

'Yeah, probably.' Laura had glossed over the woman's obsession. The conversation moved on to brighter things, as Cally talked about some man that she'd met. But Laura was only half listening. Thoughts of Bruce lingered as they ended the call, and she barely took in the journey as she negotiated the motorway.

She wished she hadn't opened her big mouth and questioned Bruce about his affair and what Mags had said. Of course he'd feel upset by his sister's involvement. But Mags was trying to help in the only way she could. But how did she know so much? How many times had she visited before the murders took place? It was like trying to complete a puzzle that had too many missing parts. Yet Laura got a feeling that the answers were staring her in the face.

She continued to mull it over, driving on autopilot. Surely Bruce knew his own sister wouldn't sell him out . . . Unless he was scared of what she was about to reveal. He'd been on edge the whole visit. She'd felt like she was walking on eggshells from the moment she got there. Her heart had been hammering when she first walked in, but gradually she had relaxed in his company. Could he really be an innocent man?

Laura gripped the wheel a little tighter. To think, he'd been dependent on the rambling letters of some strange woman to hear news of the outside world. She supposed she could write to him, keep him up to date with all the latest goings-on. She could . . . She reeled in her wandering thoughts as she drove around a roundabout. What was she doing? Shane wouldn't approve of that. And what about Esme? Because there was still a strong chance that Bruce was a murderer. And if he was proved innocent and got released from prison, did she really want to get involved?

The rest of the drive to Aspen Hollow passed quickly as Laura thought about Bruce's family dynamics. His upbringing had been difficult, according to Mags. But then again, so had Laura's, and she had turned out OK. As for Mags . . . She had scurried away quickly after Billie made an appearance at the house, and Laura hadn't heard from her since. She'd already emailed her a couple of times this afternoon, asking if she was OK. But what if she wasn't? What if she'd been hurt by somebody with too much to lose?

CHAPTER 38

The metallic clank of a cell door being shut in the distance jolted Bruce from his shallow slumber. His visit with Laura had set him back. Seeing the questions in her eyes had made him want to retreat to the so-called safety of his cell. Had he become cage-bound already? No longer capable of facing up to the outside world? He'd heard of it happening to other inmates, who on their release would commit crimes just so they could return to a place ruled by routine. Inside, they had three square meals a day, a roof over their heads and a bed for the night. But Bruce didn't have the excuse of the prospect of homelessness. If he cleared his name, he had a job to fall back on. Skills he could utilise. Friends who would return once they discovered he'd been wrongly convicted. He wasn't so sure about family, though. Mags . . .

A long-drawn-out sigh escaped his lips. He'd thought he could depend on her.

He sat up on the thin mattress as footsteps approached. The sickly smell of antiseptic hit the back of his throat. It was a mixture of lemon and bleach. There had been a clean-up in the corridor, which meant something had gone down. He didn't want to know any more. All he could see was the expression on Laura's face. He'd seen her judgement. Been reminded of how much of his old life was being dismantled and sold to the highest bidder. Would the people who bought his home honestly appreciate it? Or would they use it as a talking point with their friends?

He swivelled his head towards the cell door as the footsteps came to a halt outside. His nerves were frayed from constantly worrying about what was about to happen. *Please not a new cellmate*, he thought. *Not tonight.* His muscles grew taut as he gripped the metal frame of a bed that allowed little sleep. His senses were heightened. Whatever came through that door would alter the course of his day. Nothing good ever came from surprise visits.

The door opened and Bruce's heart beat a little faster. The sight of the man he'd come to know as a friend brought instant relief. But beneath the bleak prison lights, he took in the solemn expression on Father John Shanahan's face. Bruce waited, unsure that he wanted to hear the bad news the priest was obviously going to impart. The world offered no sympathy when you'd lost everything; it just found more ways to grind you down.

'What's wrong?' Bruce asked, his voice tight with worry. 'What is it? What's happened?'

For a moment, neither man spoke. John took the chair across from him and nodded to the guard, who left them both alone. This wasn't good.

'Is it Laura?' Bruce uttered. 'Has something happened to her?'

He shouldn't have treated her so harshly. She was only trying to help. Bruce's ruminations careened down the darkest of paths as he waited for it to be confirmed. Had there been another death in his house?

John delivered a slow pivot of his head from left to right.

'It's not Laura,' he murmured. 'Bruce . . .' His voice was thick with sympathy against the backdrop of the constant noise. Doors clanged, buzzers rang out, voices shouted, men cried. But all Bruce could hear was the voice in his head that told him it was happening again. It rang with deadly certainty. Somebody in his family was dead.

'It's your sister,' John carried on, putting words to Bruce's worst fears.

'No.' Bruce's chest tightened as grief made a return visit. He didn't want to hear it. Not Mags. Please. Not her. He couldn't breathe. He couldn't . . .

His world became fuzzy at the edges. His heart was pounding too hard.

'Slow your breathing,' John uttered, suddenly by his side.

'Can't . . . breathe . . .' Bruce uttered, his hand clasped to his chest.

John rubbed his back in circular motions. It was so long since Bruce had been physically touched by another human being that the small act of comfort helped him return to himself.

'You're having a panic attack,' John went on. 'Bruce. Focus on my voice. Breathe with me. In . . . one . . . two . . . three . . . Hold it for four. Now out . . . two . . . three . . .' he continued, until Bruce slowly sucked in air. They waited, nothing between them but the sound of Bruce's breath. Another wave of grief washed over him. It couldn't be true. Not Mags.

'How . . . ?' Bruce asked, as hot tears welled in his eyes and blurred a world he wanted no part of anymore.

'She was found in her flat with a head injury. I'm sorry, Bruce. Police will speak to you about it soon. I just thought the news would be better coming from me.'

'It's not her. It can't be.' Bruce couldn't stop his tears.

'She's been identified by a neighbour. She was worried about your sister. She had a key and let herself in.'

'No,' Bruce repeated. 'Mags is all I have left.' He scrunched his hand into a fist and bit down on it to stop the sobs. John stood and opened his arms. Bruce rose and accepted the hug.

'You're not alone,' John whispered, softly patting his back as Bruce cried into his shoulder.

CHAPTER 39

Scarlett admired the greenery in the room, and ran her fingers over the glossy leaves of a *Monstera obliqua*. A humidifier added moisture to the air. Even the carpets were a soft green shade. The furniture was in keeping with the setting, with comfortable beige cushions and soft footstools.

'Do you like it?' Josie watched her admire the assorted exotic plants. 'That one's new.'

Josie, her therapist, did not come cheap. But Scarlett's problems were complex and would not be solved easily.

She realised that Josie was waiting for a response.

'They're all so soothing,' she replied, her eyes dancing over the areca palm trees in their huge ceramic pots, and at the yucca plants with their sword-shaped leaves. Scarlett had always liked indoor plants, but there were varieties here that she didn't know the names of. It took her focus off her own problems for a short while.

Josie was wearing a long tan skirt with flat leather shoes and a silky cream blouse. Her wispy brown hair was threaded with grey and was pulled off her face into a clip at the back. Her blue eyes homed in on Scarlett as she took a seat. 'Have you had a drink today?'

Straight to the point, Scarlett thought, withering beneath the strength of her gaze. It was as if Josie could see into her soul. The woman was old enough to be her mother, and had a firm-but-fair vibe.

Scarlett couldn't lie. She nodded meekly, no longer able to meet Josie's gaze.

'David – my husband – found all of my hiding places. Except for one.'

Her hands found each other on her lap and she began to pick at her jagged nails. She was sitting in jeans and a sweatshirt. Her heels were the only remnant of her usual style. She'd been wearing high heels since she was thirteen years old, and her calves always ached when she put on trainers to go for a run. There'd once been a time when her appearance was everything, and she wouldn't let David see her without make-up, never mind dressed like this. How far she'd fallen in the last year.

'I want help. Otherwise I wouldn't be here. But the shakes . . . They get so bad. Everything hurts when I stop.' She swallowed the growing lump in her throat, unable to say more.

Josie considered her for a moment. 'OK. Scarlett, firstly, I appreciate your honesty. Secondly, it's not as easy as just quitting. Rehab will help treat the physical problems of AWS, but I'm here to help with your emotional issues.'

Scarlett nodded as Josie spoke about alcohol withdrawal syndrome. She'd already had a thorough intake exam with the detox team at the rehab unit. Her bloods had been taken, and they'd spoken about her health and what support was available to her. Drugs would be prescribed, both to treat her ongoing depression and to help with the discomfort that going cold turkey would bring. But it was the therapy that had worried Scarlett the most. David had been so scared of what she might say, yet here he was, placing her in a position where she'd be encouraged to open up.

'You can have as many therapy sessions as you need,' Josie continued, crossing her slim legs.

'Are they . . . confidential?'

'Of course. If there's one thing I need you to take from today's session, it's that we stand by our code of ethics. Whatever you tell me won't go outside these four walls. You have my word.'

'When you say "whatever" . . .' Scarlett sighed. She had kept her secrets for so long, they were eating her up inside.

'I'm here to help. I suggest we begin by discussing what led you here.'

There was an undertone to her words. A seriousness that Scarlett instinctively trusted. No judgement. The woman wanted to help.

Today she would tell Josie everything. About Bruce, Ali and the whole tragic story. Because she had pieced together the memories of the night that they'd died.

CHAPTER 40

Laura placed her hand on the banister. She'd been so engrossed in her work that she'd thought she was imagining the small keening sound. She'd almost completed her social media strategy, updating reels, listings and posts to drive interest. She'd been hammering home the fact that she was close to a sale. Yet each time she made an update, her stomach twisted just a little bit.

Outside sounds filtered in through the windows. Billie's dog excitedly yapping as she took it for a walk. The low, droning sound of the Red Arrow jets as they flew to the Waddington airbase. The soft creak and groan of the trees when the wind whipped up. The miaow of Graham and Walter's cat as she took a stroll around the neighbourhood on her own. None of these sounds were similar to what Laura had just heard echoing from upstairs – the soft, whining cry of a child.

But had she heard it, or was it in her imagination? Last night, she'd watched YouTube videos of the Wilding family in this home, and now the sounds of their voices were replaying in her mind. *This is getting ridiculous*, she told herself. Her imagination was playing tricks on her . . . wasn't it? She was about to return to the kitchen when the heard the sound upstairs again. This time it was louder. This time she knew it was real.

She rested her hand over her mouth to stem the cry welling up in her throat. Someone was really up there. As she quietly picked up her handbag, she didn't hang around to find out what was going on. It was clocking-off time. She wasn't about to confront whoever was upstairs. She tried to focus on her breathing as she stood at the front door. There it was again. The sound of a little girl's cries. But it didn't last long. She waited for it to play out. There. It was on a loop, maybe . . . a recording . . . wasn't it? A soundbite snatched from an Instagram reel, perhaps. If she thought for a second that a child was really in trouble she would be galloping up those stairs.

Most of Ali's posts had been happy ones, but there were a couple in which Cindy had fallen off her bicycle or come home crying because of something minor. Laura had binge-watched so many. She recognised the pattern. But it wasn't the sound itself that worried her; it was the person playing them. This house didn't have ghosts. It had an intruder.

She slipped out the front door and locked it firmly behind her, taking a moment to breathe as she reached her car.

She wasn't going to her mum's. Gloria had already called to say that Laura's old bedroom was no longer available. She had taken in a lodger, apparently. Someone who would keep her in booze and cigarettes. Laura would never understand her self-absorbed mother.

It felt natural to return to Shane. Maybe they could change the locks on their Lincoln house. But it wouldn't be worth the hissy fit her mother-in-law would throw if she couldn't let herself in. Laura could be honest with her husband, though. This time she would tell him what was happening. The prison visit, the letters, the sounds and the texts. She shouldn't have to face it on her own.

She quietly slipped into the house, using her key. Shane didn't hear her as she entered the hall. The sound of her mother-in-law made Laura swear beneath her breath. Of course she was here. The living room door was open. There was no way Laura wanted to see the woman, but as her voice rose in defiance, Laura couldn't resist listening in.

'Just because a rat is born in a stable it doesn't make it a racehorse,' Mrs Taylor-Brown quipped, defensive as always. 'She'll *never* fit in.'

'No, Mum.' Shane spoke with a firmness Laura hadn't heard before. 'You don't get to talk about Laura like that anymore.'

Laura's eyes widened in disbelief. Is that what his mother really thought of her? That she was akin to a rat? It was a relief that Esme was a heavy sleeper. She would have hated for her to hear that. She clenched her fists as quiet fury rose. What if Esme had been here, listening at the door?

'I'm only saying—'

'Well, from now on you can keep your nasty opinions to yourself!' Shane shouted.

'What? How dare you . . . ?' she gasped. 'How dare you raise your voice to me, your own mother—'

'But it's perfectly fine for you to compare my wife to a rat? I'm sick of your snide comments. You almost broke up my marriage and you're still not happy . . .'

'I'm just saying, it's time you got a divorce. You should never have split up with Charlotte. Laura isn't cut out for this family.'

'No, she's not . . . You're right there,' Shane agreed.

Laura's heart sank.

'She's a million times too good for the likes of us,' he continued. 'She's worked hard to get where she is. Nothing's been handed to her on a plate. She treats everyone with kindness and all she does is expect the same in return.'

Laura sat on a rollercoaster of emotions. This was what she'd been waiting to hear.

'So no, there won't be any divorce,' Shane went on. 'And if you don't like it then *you* don't belong here anymore.'

'Give up your family and you give up everything,' his mother retorted. It wasn't the first time such a threat had been made. Laura held her breath.

But Shane wasn't backing down. 'I'm not a kid anymore, Mum. Laura and Esme are my family now. It's about time I stood on my own two feet.'

'She won't have you without our money . . .'

Laura couldn't stand to hear any more. She pushed through the door, cheeks burning.

'That's where you're wrong.' She took Shane's side with a flourish. 'This "stable rat" is here to stay.' Her arm slid so easily around her husband's waist in that moment. She watched the colour visibly drain from her mother-in-law's face. This had been a long time coming.

Physically, Mrs Taylor-Brown had never been intimidating. She was a couple of inches smaller than Laura and built like a reed. But her authoritarian manner made grown men duck out of sight whenever she made an appearance. Laura was no stranger to her vitriol, but she had never taken things this far. Then again, her mother-in-law hadn't known that Laura was listening in.

Shane appeared shocked but pleased as he placed an arm around Laura's shoulders and gave her a squeeze. 'Mum, you owe Laura an apology.'

'No need,' Laura said, trying to sound unfazed. 'Since the knives are out, we may as well call a spade a spade.' She looked the woman up and down, finally having the freedom to say how she was feeling for once. Shane had always tiptoed around his mother before now. 'Things are going to change, if you want to be a part of Esme's life. I won't have you disrespecting me in front of her.'

'I would never do that.' Her mother-in-law's face tightened. 'I only want the best for my son.'

'That could have been Esme, not me, listening in.' Laura pointed to the door. 'And the best thing for Shane is to have his family – *all* his family – in his life. But I'm done pussyfooting around you. You either accept us as a unit or not at all.'

Laura was surprising herself with her steely calmness. There had once been a time when she would have let loose at her mother-in-law for what she'd just said. But all that did was cause rows. She'd grown up a lot lately. Her own mother's failures had made her realise that Esme deserved better from them both. And when it came to Shane . . . she loved him. The prospect of losing his wealth didn't faze her. She would never let him go. She only hoped that his parents would stop getting in their way.

'If that's the way you want it.' Her mother-in-law's words were razor-sharp as she picked up her handbag from the floor. She turned towards Shane. 'You've made your bed, now you can lie in it. You'll soon come knocking on our door.'

'The thing is, Mum, I won't.' Shane smiled. 'I have everything I want right here.' He seemed taller. More self-assured. It had been a hell of a long time coming, but he'd finally got there.

Mrs Taylor-Brown sniffed. 'Let's see how in love you both are when the money runs out!'

Laura blurted out a laugh. 'There's this thing called work, where they pay you for doing your job. We'll survive.'

Shane dropped his arm from Laura's shoulders and followed his mother out.

Oh God, Laura inwardly groaned as she waited for him to apologise. Instead, he held out his hand.

'Keys, please.'

Mrs Taylor-Brown glared at her son.

'Keys,' he repeated. 'My name is on the deeds. You want to visit, you ring the doorbell like everyone else.'

Laura watched as Mrs Taylor-Brown rooted in her designer bag and thrust the keys in Shane's hand. Then she quietly made her exit. Even in the heat of her anger, she took Esme's feelings into consideration.

This wouldn't be the end of it. She loved her granddaughter too much to let her go. If Laura was out of the picture, everything would have been perfect in her world.

Shane's cheeks puffed as he exhaled a breath. 'Mum excelled herself tonight.' A sudden bout of emotion came from nowhere and Shane opened his arms as Laura sobbed. 'Hey, are you OK? I'm so sorry, you shouldn't have had to hear that.'

'No . . .' She gulped, pressing her face into his chest. 'I'm glad I did. It's just . . .' A soft hiccup followed in a rush of emotion. 'I . . . I don't want to break your family up. Everything's been so shitty and I . . .'

'Shh.' Shane kissed the top of her head. 'You heard what I said – you're my family now.' He paused. 'You did mean what you said, didn't you?'

'Of course I did.' Laura sniffled.

'Then everything else will sort itself out. I promise. I won't let my parents come between us again.'

Laura nodded as her sobs subsided. She didn't want to talk about her mother-in-law, or what had happened at 1 Aspen Hollow for that matter. She was just glad to be home.

CHAPTER 41

'Sorry to bother you again,' Laura apologised to the PCSO for the second time as they both inspected the house the next day. Her name was Gina. She was close to retiring and had given Laura her card when she'd conducted house-to-house enquiries after the tyre incident.

'It's no trouble,' Gina said, taking everything in as she slowly climbed the stairs. 'If you hear an intruder in the future, best to call it in at the time.'

But Laura wasn't sure anymore and was beginning to doubt herself. She'd always had an active imagination. Some noises had been so faint, and the house was far from soundproof, as was the way with modern builds. The walls just weren't as thick as their older counterparts. A slam of a car door outside could be mistaken for a noise upstairs. Then there was a plethora of wildlife in the woodland, with the creepy screeching and screams every night, and the magpies that bounced around on the roof during the day. Things always seemed creepier in the evenings when she was in the house on her own. But then, she hadn't made up the sudden bout of destruction of the staged items in Cindy's old room.

Now it appeared as if nothing had happened there to begin with. She'd removed the torn books and toys. She hadn't been sure what to do with the doll so she'd thrown it into the back of her car.

She'd half expected to find the thing sitting on the bed when she made her return.

'There's no signs of disturbance,' Gina reassured her after checking each room. 'But there's been a lot of comings and goings here. Might be best to get the locks changed.'

'Thanks for your help,' Laura said with some relief as she showed the police community support officer out. 'I'll advise the agency.' She already knew what the answer would be to that. They wouldn't finance new locks when there was no evidence of an actual break-in. Whoever had trashed the room previously had clearly been allowed inside.

She gave a small wave as she watched Gina stride out to her car. The wind was picking up, and it came with a bite.

She closed the door behind her. The house was getting fresh interest from potential buyers, but someone had yet to offer the full asking price.

Laura walked to the bedroom window and stared out at the woodland. The slender aspen trees bowed back and forth, their loss of leaves signalling a sudden turn in the weather. Time was running out.

Last night she'd curled up beside Shane, their bodies warm beneath the duvet. But even in the quiet intimacy of the moment, she'd kept her worries concerning the house listing to herself. It just wasn't the right time. It had been so lovely to see Esme this morning and drive her to her Sunday-morning dance class. Things were going well, but it was still early days.

Soon she would sell No. 1 and be able to move on. There would always be a portion of potential buyers put off by murder. But then there were people who were more pragmatic – those who could appreciate No. 1 for the steal that it was. It was a place Laura would have dreamed about living in, had it not been for its history. That was the biggest obstacle.

The more she thought about Bruce Wilding, the more she pondered the possibility of his innocence. But if Bruce hadn't killed Ali and Cindy, then who had? And why? The fact he could have been having an affair was a huge red flag. What if his mistress had carried out the murders because Ali would never let Bruce leave? Was his mistress a woman scorned?

Laura turned over the thought in her mind. Had this woman framed Bruce for murder because of how he'd treated her? Maybe she'd thought that killing Ali and Cindy would pave the way for a longer-term relationship with Bruce. It was so messed up. Why hadn't Bruce mentioned any of this to the police? If he was as innocent as he said he was, he must have had his own suspicions as to who murdered his wife and child. Unless he thought his mistress wasn't capable of it. She would have been vilified in the press. Even so . . .

Laura sighed. Finding answers in this case was like trying to untie a knot in a bunch of Christmas lights and then finding a dozen more.

The morning went by quickly as Laura threw herself into her work. 'We have two other potential bidders in the running, and lots of interested viewers lined up,' she said as she showed the Conways, a family of five, out. 'So don't delay. You'd be perfect for this place. I'd hate for you to miss out.'

She closed the door behind them and leaned against the doorframe. The situation didn't sit well with her, because they'd seemed like nice people. Would they inherit the stalker who was making her life hell? The Conways had seemed sensible, wealthy, with no time for superstition. Their children were older, and mature for their age. It was the marina that had drawn them in, and No. 1 simply offered the biggest and closest home to it. But they had two more properties in other locations to view. Billie would wait to put her house on the market, given that No. 1

would be somewhat cheaper due to its history. A firm offer as soon as possible would benefit everyone. But God, she hated the idea of passing on so much potential grief.

Shaking off her thoughts, Laura entered the kitchen and recorded a quick Instagram post. 'Offers are coming in, the house will sell soon! But there's still time, so don't delay.' She added clips of the marina, and the woodland in autumn before the branches started losing their leaves. But all the while she was feigning excitement, and when she'd pressed publish, her smile faded.

She checked her emails. Nothing from Mags. Why wasn't she responding? She'd seemed so keen before. She recalled Mags's abrupt departure, the flush creeping up her face as Billie entered the room. How much of their conversation had Billie been privy to? Then following them out like that . . . Had the sudden intrusion scared Mags away? But Laura didn't have time to contemplate it more as the doorbell went. She marched out to the hallway to find Esme pushing open the door.

'Esme!' Laura exclaimed in surprise. She looked beyond her daughter, out at the drive. 'What are you doing here?'

Then Shane appeared, ashen-faced as he took Esme's bag from the car. 'It's Dad,' he said. 'He's been rushed into hospital. Can you look after her? Sorry . . . I know you're working, but it sounds serious.'

'Of course!' Laura took the bag from his outstretched hand. 'Go.'

'Is Grandad going to be alright, Mummy?' Esme's big blue eyes were filled with concern as she took her mother's hand.

'He's in the best place,' Laura said, because false hope was cruel. But equally she didn't want her daughter to be upset. 'The doctors and nurses will take good care of him.'

Guilt bloomed as she recalled her conversation with her mother-in-law. Had the stress of the fallout contributed to Shane's father's ill health? He was a keen walker and would be gone for hours at a time, most likely to get away from his wife. She could imagine Shane's mother ranting and raving over his decision to cut her out. She knew the pain of losing a much-loved father and hoped this wouldn't be the case for Shane. His dad wasn't the nicest of men, but she still hoped that he'd pull through.

She checked her watch. She had a two-hour gap before her next viewing. Enough time to settle Esme down with her colouring book and crayons.

'Can I look upstairs, Mummy?' Esme said, pausing at the stairs. The sound of her voice echoed eerily through the house, as if Cindy had somehow come back to life.

'No!' The word was sharp – too sharp given the situation. 'Sorry,' Laura said as Esme's face fell. 'It's against the rules. But I have cupcakes. Would you like one?'

Esme nodded enthusiastically, her hastily tied ponytail bobbing behind her as she went in search of the kitchen. But something about her daughter's presence in this house felt all wrong. She could stay; she'd be content watching TV until Laura finished her work. But Laura couldn't shake off the inner alarm bells telling her to get Esme out. Bruce's stalker could be watching them right now. The news that offers were coming in could have sent her into a spiral. If only she could speak to Mags.

Her head was so full of conflicting thoughts. She needed to sell the house as soon as she could.

Maybe Cally could take Esme out for lunch? Would she want to drive over from Louth on her day off to do it, though? Cally hadn't seen much of Esme lately. It was worth a shot. But it felt wrong to palm her daughter off when she enjoyed her company so much. Still, Laura brought up her sister's number on her phone. Waited in the hall as it rang out.

'Hi, sis,' she said, hating how she sounded on voicemail. 'It's me. Nothing to worry about, but I was just wondering if you had any free time today? Give me a dig out? Shane's dad has been rushed into hospital and he's had to drop Esme off with me, but I've got some viewings later on and I don't really want to leave her unattended in the house.' She emitted a soft chuckle. 'Not this house, anyway. Don't worry if you're busy, I'm sure she'll be fine. Hope the date went well. Love you!'

Then she sent a text to Shane asking him to update her about his dad. She might not get on with his parents, but she certainly wouldn't wish them ill.

She heard Esme's voice before she reached the kitchen. She was talking to someone.

'This is a nice house, isn't it? My mummy's going to sell it today.'

What the . . . ? Laura's maternal instincts went into overdrive. Who the hell was talking to her little girl?

CHAPTER 42

ALI

THEN

Cindy's off school with a miserable cold. I'm in bed too. It feels like someone's rubbed my throat with sandpaper and I'm so tired all the time. I don't have the inclination or the energy to update my socials anymore. I turn in my bed, tears prickling my eyes. It all feels so pointless. There's some toast on my bedside table and a cold cup of tea – for the morning sickness, according to Bruce. I rub the bruises on my wrists. I don't like who I become when we row.

He's gone to work as per usual, but he said he'll be home early to take care of us both. But his behaviour comes from guilt, not love. Too little, too late. He sleeps in the guest room now, the one with the spiral stairs that leads to its own back door downstairs. Ours is the only house with such a stairwell and it suits him perfectly. He can sneak out whenever he wants. His own private doorway to the outside world. When I look at what he's done to my family, it makes me wonder how I loved him in the first place. He's not apologised for his behaviour, but then again, neither have I. There's no going back for either of us now.

I used to believe that we could be the perfect family. But Bruce always had a way of catching other women's eyes. I thought I knew him, but I didn't have a clue. I got pregnant with Cindy for a reason. I thought she would fix us. That she would strengthen our marriage. That Bruce would never leave. I've worked so hard to keep our family unit together. Bruce's betrayal is a slap in the face. I got so many negative comments about how 'devastated' he looked when I broke the news in the first place. But all it did was strengthen my views. More comments equals a better algorithm; it doesn't matter if they're good or bad. If only it was enough to make me feel happy again.

I did some more digging. We are up to our eyes in debt. All those designer clothes we've bought. The holiday, the cars, the house. I think of our old home. So small and cramped, but less to worry about then. We've been in debt before, but nothing like this.

Bruce has been borrowing to pay back his gambling debts. The extent of his lies is staggering.

His credit score is down the pan. He has looming County Court judgements. There are loans all over the place. I dread to think how much he owes. What an idiot I've been. Yet things look fine on the surface. The perfect home, the perfect family. It's easier to pretend that I'm clueless than to confront him with the truth. I'm scared of what he might do. All those gambling apps on his iPad. Those nights he went out and played cards with his friends . . . He wasn't playing for matchsticks. I can only imagine the amount of money – my money – that must have changed hands.

And so I'm here, penniless and loveless, my life a sham. Cindy is all I have left. I can't live like this anymore. Bruce has taken everything. What is he capable of next? At least there's equity in our home. I'm too scared to do a credit check to see if he's taken out loans in my name. He wouldn't do that – would he? No. Even Bruce wouldn't stoop so low.

CHAPTER 43

Bruce blinked back his tears. DC Clayton sat across from him, her expression impassive. She was tall and slim, the cuffs of her white blouse too short for her arms as she leaned over the desk and took notes. Her features were sharp, her eyes filled with the cynicism of a woman who had spent too long in the force. Her colleague DC Gallagher sat next to her, his shirt bearing the hallmark of a tomato ketchup stain. He seemed distracted, as if he'd rather be anywhere else in the world than here. Bruce rubbed at the razor burn on his chin, watching DC Clayton write. Their expressions were impassive. It was hard to offer sympathy to a convicted child killer and wife murderer, Bruce supposed. Had he been in their shoes, he would have struggled to contain his contempt.

The designated interview room was contained within the walls of the prison. Grey, drab and instantly forgettable. It smelled of nothingness, as if it was a crime to allow the outside world in. Bruce inhaled a deep breath and caught the faintest stench of deodorant masking sweat on the man across from him. His senses had become attuned over the year inside.

'I still can't believe it,' Bruce said, his voice no longer sounding like his own. He had to make sense of this. Nothing felt real anymore. It was as if he was on some reality show and the audience were a bunch of sadists, seeing how far they could push him until he broke. According to the police, Mags had been found crumpled up in a ball on the floor of her living room. The heating had been on, full blast. There had been flies bumping against the inside of the windowpane and a puddle of congealed blood beneath her head. Rigor mortis had come and gone. She had been there for several days at least. Next to her body, a hardback yoga book had been found, its glossy pages left open on the crow pose. Bruce had tried yoga once, in an effort to achieve some inner peace. The crow pose needed balance and concentration, two things his sister had lacked.

He refused to believe that her death was a random occurrence. She hadn't done this to herself. Not when someone was out in the world, pretending to be her. Because it hadn't clicked until now. But he'd reflected on everything that Laura had told him. Her description of Mags, the details of her behaviour and the things that she'd said. Whoever had gone to see his old home in Lincoln wasn't his sister. He'd told the officers everything he knew.

'These letters . . .' he said, watching DC Gallagher shove them into a police evidence bag with little care. 'Do you think they could help? I was thinking, maybe they've written to me before, using their own name?'

He'd included the ones that sounded most like his stalker. There could be a link. Last night he'd gone through each one. There were letters from Kim, a mum of three; Sharon, who believed he was innocent and wanted to help; Paula, who didn't care what he'd done because 'society pushed people too far'. And, finally, letters from a woman named Cally, who wanted more out of life. She'd offered to come and visit. To be a shoulder to cry on. But these women had no idea who he really was.

'We'll include them in the investigation,' DC Clayton said, her features softening a little now that the paperwork was complete. 'Do you know if your sister had a flatmate? The neighbour that found her said they'd seen someone come and go. Had Mags any friends or visitors who liked to pop by?'

'I don't know anything about her friends,' Bruce was sad to say. 'She just said that she was happy enough.' He met the officer's eye. 'Why would anyone want to hurt her? She was the most inoffensive person I know.'

'There's no evidence to suggest that someone did – not yet,' DC Gallagher chipped in. His voice was gruff and low, and he checked his watch with some impatience. Unsaid words passed between him and his colleague as they got up to leave. Bruce caught the glint of DC Gallagher's wedding ring. He no doubt had a wife and children at home. He probably thought Bruce was a piece of shit.

'We'll be in touch,' DC Clayton added, gathering her paperwork as she stood. 'If you hear anything more, let us know.'

Bruce waited to be allowed out of the room.

It wasn't over. Not yet.

It was all he deserved.

CHAPTER 44

'Esme!' Laura called, her heart skittering with urgency. Like those moments when you lose sight of your child in the supermarket. The briefest of dread-filled seconds when you fear for their safety. Your breath trembles on your lips as you call out their name.

As her footsteps echoed down the hall, it seemed to stretch on forever.

'Esme! Who are you talking— Oh.'

Her daughter was sitting at the kitchen island, cupcakes on one side and doll on the other. She was talking to a doll. But it wasn't just any doll. It was Cindy's doll, or at least the one Laura had found in her room.

'What . . . what are you doing?' Laura slowed, catching her breath. She tried to suppress her panic as she took the scene in.

'I'm playing with my new dolly.'

'Oh yeah?' Laura's gaze darted around the room. 'Where did you find her?'

Esme gave her a look which suggested she had taken something that didn't belong to her. 'In the back of your car. This morning. I put her in my bag on the way to dance school.' She drew the doll close to her chest. 'Can I keep her, please?'

Of course. Laura had thrown it into the back of the car after finding it in Cindy's old room. Esme must have presumed it was for her. At least nobody had been here. That would have been far worse.

She sighed. 'For now. But it's not yours to keep. It came with the house.'

'OK,' Esme said, giving the toy an extra cuddle. Forbidden toys were much more endearing than the cupboard full of dolls she had at home. She'd soon get bored with it.

Laura took a glass from the cupboard and a carton of milk from the fridge.

'You can have one cupcake, OK?' She poured a glass of milk for her daughter and returned the carton to the fridge. A memory of a video arose: Ali pouring her daughter milk to go with her Oreo cookies. Cindy, sitting at the counter, playing with the same doll. It turned Laura's blood cold. Maybe she should leave. Go to the hospital with Esme. Reschedule the viewings for another day. She couldn't shake the feeling that everything felt off.

She groaned as her phone rang. *What now?*

The last person she expected to hear from was John, Bruce's priest.

'Sorry, is this a good time?' The lilting tone of his Irish accent sounded down the phone.

She glanced over at her little girl, who seemed content.

'Hang on a second,' she said to him, before turning to her daughter. 'Don't go anywhere, OK?' she told her, cupping her hand over the phone. 'I'm just going into the hall.' The doors were locked and nobody could walk in without Laura seeing them first.

Esme nodded dutifully, picking a cupcake from the box. Laura would clean up the crumbs later. She decided to take this conversation to the front of the house. She didn't want Esme hearing whatever the priest was going to say.

'Sorry,' she said, returning to her phone call. 'I can't talk long. We've had a bit of a family emergency. We need to get to the hospital to see my father-in-law.'

She had made up her mind. Shane wasn't answering his phone. Leaving this house was the right thing to do.

'It's probably a good idea for you to go.' The cadence in John's voice dropped. His tone was grim. It came with a warning.

Laura opened the front door and peered outside. The day was gloomy; the wind was whipping up dead leaves and driving them down the path. A slice of icy air played with wisps of her hair. There was nobody on the close. The place was eerily quiet.

'What's wrong?' She stood there at the front door, watching out for strangers. Nobody was crossing this threshold without her say-so.

'I've just been with Bruce. He asked me to pass on the news. It's Mags. She's dead.'

'Oh my God.' Laura closed the door as the bad feeling in the pit of her stomach grew. 'Sorry. I mean . . . It's a shock. She seemed like a nice lady. I've been trying to get in touch with her.'

She couldn't take it in. Mags was dead? How? Why?

'A friend called round to her address because she hadn't heard from her in a while. She was found dead in her living room.'

Laura shook her head. 'What did she die of? Do you know?'

'Head injury, as far as they're aware. The police broke the news to Bruce in prison. They'll probably be in touch as he's mentioned you to them, but he wanted me to pass on the message as soon as possible.'

Goosebumps rose on Laura's skin. 'I'll speak to the police tomorrow.' Laura remembered how scared Mags had been. 'I've got too much going on right now.'

She still couldn't comprehend the news. Head injury. At home. It couldn't have anything to do with Bruce, could it? How would he cope with this? She turned to make her way back down the hall, her mind racing ahead. She would pick up her things, tell the agency to reschedule the viewings, then leave for the hospital with Esme. The house could wait. Family came first.

'How awful.' She released a long breath. 'Poor Bruce. Losing his family, and now his sister. I only spoke to her a couple of days ago.'

'That's the thing . . .' John continued. 'The police said that Mags has been dead for some time. Whoever you've been talking to, it's not her.'

Laura couldn't believe what she was hearing. *That . . . that wasn't Mags?* The hairs prickled to attention on the back of her neck. She needed to get out of here – and fast.

CHAPTER 45

Today Scarlett was back with her therapist, sweating her way through waves of nausea and the compulsion to get a taxi to the first bar she could find. At that moment, if someone had offered her a bottle of cough medicine, she would have downed it in one. Scarlett's biggest challenge was accepting her nascent alcoholism. She'd been drinking to cope for over a year, but now it had grown into something more. Josie was helping her to see that acceptance of her situation was the first step towards recovery.

She was lucky that they'd caught it in time. Her addiction was relatively new and she had a lot of support. Josie was firm when it came to dealing with her problems and homed in on the issues with Aspen Hollow straight away. Scarlett had expected Josie to ask all about her childhood, but instead she'd encouraged Scarlett to open up about her present-day concerns. Scarlett took a deep breath before relaying what had happened the night Ali and Cindy died.

Scarlett told her how hearing David crying on the other side of the door had frightened her. The mention of them splitting up had made her feel like she was living in a snow globe that had been given a good shake. They'd made mistakes, big ones. They'd sought comfort with other people rather than working through their own issues. But that was all in the past now. Their mistakes had been buried, in more ways than one.

Scarlett wondered if some of the plants had been moved, or if her powers of observation were changing now that she was sober. Either way, the room looked different today. It felt warmer too, and the smell of the plants made her feel like she was somewhere tropical, rather than in a therapist's office on the outskirts of Lincoln. She was in the middle of her narrative about the dinner party she'd had with Bruce and Ali, but kept pausing for a break. The words were too difficult to say all at once, and Josie had to keep bringing her back.

'So where was Cindy?' she asked.

'In bed, asleep upstairs. She had a head cold, according to Ali. She hadn't been well. Not that I gave her a thought.'

'You were saying . . .' Josie urged. 'You were an hour into the meal.'

Scarlett raked her fingers through her hair, pulling it back from her face. Recalling this memory was like opening a door to somewhere monstrous and being pushed inside.

'I'd drunk way too much. David kept nudging me, telling me to eat more food. I'd try a tiny bit, make a face, then put my fork down. I asked Ali how she'd cooked it, and if she'd used much ghee. But she seemed too pissed off to play games. She said it was her own recipe and she hadn't had any complaints before.' Scarlett prickled, wishing she didn't turn into such a bitch when she was drunk. 'Bruce was uneasy. He kept looking at me. I could tell that he wanted to talk to me on my own. He could sense that things were escalating. At least, that's the vibe I was getting from him. The look on his face was almost pleading, but I was way past reason then.' She recalled sitting around the table. Ali's last night alive.

'David made up some excuse about getting back to the nanny and kept checking his watch. I told him she had nothing else on and that there was no rush. That's when I glared at Ali. I asked if she was alright. But it was the *way* that I said it that must have set her off.'

She recalled Bruce resting his cutlery on the table. The atmosphere turning brittle.

The warmth of David's skin as he touched her arm. She'd jerked away from him.

'What happened next?' Josie's voice dragged Scarlett from her thoughts. She had been back there in her mind's eye, shortly before setting a match to the powder keg that would blow up so many lives. Why had she opened her big hateful mouth? Ali had been the biggest victim in all of this. Scarlett hated herself even more for what she'd said.

'The poor girl was puce. I should have felt sorry for her, rather than having a go. That's when she said that she knew about Bruce's affair.'

Facing up to what she'd done that night left Scarlett feeling raw and exposed. She didn't want to shine such a bright light on her failings, especially when it had led to two deaths.

An air freshener in the corner of the room emitted a soft *pfft*. Scarlett closed her eyes and breathed in the scent of ferns.

'I remember Bruce's voice was shaking. Maybe I'm imagining it with the benefit of hindsight, but he had this darkness in his eyes. David said it was best if we left. I rounded on Ali, probably because I thought she was the weakest person in the room.' She looked at Josie in earnest. 'Do you hate me? Are you disgusted by what I've done?'

But Josie simply crossed her legs and smiled. 'I think you're brave. We've all done things we're not proud of. Nobody is exempt.'

Her words were like a soothing balm. 'Yes,' said Scarlett. 'You're right. What's done is done. I'm taking responsibility and moving on. I'll be better. There's still time.' But as she looked at her watch, she realised that time was in short supply. She had just five minutes left of her session.

'Don't worry about that. Keep going,' Josie urged, switching off her phone timer.

Scarlett nibbled her bottom lip. 'Maybe next time . . .'

'You're almost there.'

'I can't.' She clasped her fingers tightly together. This was too hard.

'You can and you will. Keep going. What happened next?' Her voice was suddenly commanding. It was the hardest Josie had pushed her so far. She couldn't stop now.

'I . . . was drunk. If you think I'm a bitch when I'm sober, multiply that tenfold when I'm under the influence. Ali . . .' Scarlett bowed her head, then clasped it in her hands and stared at the floor because she couldn't meet her therapist's eye. The memory was hazy and disjointed. Each word became forced. 'Ali accused Bruce of sneaking over to our house in the middle of the night. Then . . . I think she started screaming about him having it off in a hotel.' Scarlett heaved a sigh. 'I should have left when David suggested it. But then Ali turned on him. Her high-pitched voice was like a needle in my brain. So I screamed at her. Told her she hadn't a clue what had been going on.' She recalled Bruce, stony-faced as everything came out. 'I hadn't expected Ali to attack me. I didn't know she had it in her. She was quick, I'll give her that. She hit me, hard. Caught me square on the jaw with her fist. I was seeing stars. Bruce started shouting. I barely remember picking up my knife from the table. I wanted to kill her for that. David held me back.' She stared at the mossy-green carpet, groaning as she recalled how heated things had become.

'What happened next?' Josie's voice infiltrated the shameful memory.

'It was bedlam. David shouted something at Bruce. I laughed. I laughed so hard that tears rolled down my face. I tore her to shreds. I said she was a joke. That she hadn't a clue what her husband got up to behind her back. She was blaming it all on me . . . She didn't know him at all. He had been the instigator from day one. So I told her, all of it. Until Bruce called me something . . .' She tilted her head to one side, peering through the fuzzy edges of a memory she'd blotted out with alcohol. 'He called me something disrespectful . . . I can't remember now. Then he shouted at David to get me out.'

'And did you? Leave?'

'That's the surprising thing. David . . . He stood up for me. He planted his hands on Bruce's chest and pushed him hard. Said everything was his fault. Sent him sprawling backwards. Everyone was shouting and name-calling. That's when we left.'

Finally rid of the ugly words, Scarlett heaved a sigh. She felt like she'd just thrown up poison she'd been holding on to all year.

'You didn't go back there?'

Scarlett finally looked her therapist in the face. 'All I remember after that is waking up the next morning with a sense of impending doom and the hangover from hell. But Bruce . . . I'll always remember that look in his eyes. It was frightening. They were in so much debt. I called him out that night. Told Ali the whole truth. Backed him into a corner. If I hadn't done that . . . Cindy and Ali might still be here today.' The tears wouldn't stop flowing. She'd suppressed her emotions for so long. It was cathartic to cry. 'It's all my fault.'

'Listen to me.' Josie straightened in her chair. 'Do you feel like hurting your children when you're upset?'

'God no, not in a million years. I can't even comprehend . . .'

'No sane person can. You are light years away from being responsible for the deaths of Cindy and Ali Wilding. But there *are* two children that need their mummy back.' She nudged a box of tissues towards Scarlett. 'You've made real progress today. How are things now, with the home being put up for sale? Is the presence of an estate agent dragging everything up again?'

Scarlett talked about how she'd got drunk at the open house. Each word was thick with shame.

'It's not your fault,' Josie said softly. 'It can't be easy, now the place is up for sale. Don't worry. We'll find a way forward.'

'Thank you,' Scarlett's voice was a whisper. But she still had a nagging feeling of blame. She might not have killed Ali and Cindy, but her actions certainly hadn't helped. She hadn't told her therapist how panicked David had been when news of the murders got out. How he'd hidden her away from the world in an effort to protect her, but all it had done was make her feel worse. She leaned back in the comfortable cushions of her chair. Josie didn't have the full story, but it was as much as Scarlett could give.

CHAPTER 46

'Esme!' Laura called. 'Get your things, it's time to go!'

John had offered to stay on the line to make sure they safely left the house, but there was no need. All Laura had to do was get her daughter in the car and lock the door behind them. It would take five minutes, tops. She would let the office know when she got to the hospital. Appointments could be rescheduled, any offers fielded by Clio. This was a family emergency, after all.

She still couldn't believe Mags was dead. But she wasn't, was she? Not the Mags she knew. Bruce's sister could have died from some tragic mishap. Or maybe her heart had given out and she'd fallen over and hit her head. But then who was the woman who'd been visiting Laura all this time? She thought about how polite she'd been, and the gentle nature so at odds with the history of Bruce's old home. The Dundee cake they'd shared, along with stories of Bruce's childhood. Why had this fake Mags implied that Bruce was having an affair? Why had she got involved at all? They'd drunk tea together. Laughed. Talked about their love of books. Shared anecdotes about Bruce. She'd known so much about his life. The letter . . . She'd shown her Bruce's letter dated a month ago, which had carried the prison address. How was that possible? Surely the police had made a mistake.

'Esme!' Laura called again as she strode into the kitchen. Where was she?

She glanced at the uneaten cupcakes. At the empty glass, the remnants of milk still clinging to the inside. Was she hiding? Or had she gone to the toilet, perhaps? The hard knot that had formed in Laura's stomach tightened a little more.

'Mummy!' The sound of Esme's voice from upstairs made Laura's heart stall.

'Esme?' she called again, spinning around. Her breath quickened as she made it to the foot of the stairs, her panicked voice echoing in this space that had witnessed the worst of crimes. 'Esme? Where are you?'

She climbed the stairs, legs pumping. The landing felt cold and vacant as she called her daughter's name. The wind had picked up outside, and the house was cast in gloom.

'Mummy!' Esme called again. But was it her daughter?

With a dreadful sense of finality, she knew where to look. Cindy's bedroom. She took three steps forward, despite everything inside her screaming at her to leave the house immediately.

Not without my daughter, she thought. *Never.*

She'd rather die than leave Esme here. She could barely catch her breath as the bedroom door creaked open.

'Esme?'

But as it played one more time, she realised that it wasn't Esme's voice – it was Cindy's.

'Mummy!' it started again, but this time the recording continued.

Laura spun around two seconds too late, as she caught sight of a shadow looming from behind. The object in their hand slammed into Laura's temple. The force was enough to bring her to her knees.

CHAPTER 47

ALI

THEN

I stare at Scarlett from across our dining room table, hating every ounce of her being. It pains me to say it, but she looks amazing. She's nasty but naturally pretty, and dressed in a red jumpsuit that I could never get away with wearing.

My scalp itches from the hair clips digging in. I have raging indigestion from the curry I made and my feet ache from the high heels that are too small for my feet. I've gone along with the pregnancy lie for so long, it's like I've talked my body into believing it. But all of that fades as my anger grows. I've invited Scarlett and her husband here to have it out with them. Right now, Cindy's in bed, fast asleep after her nightly hot chocolate. My followers have left questions asking why my pregnancy isn't showing yet. It's not viable to keep up the pregnancy pretence. A part of me has enjoyed making Bruce sweat. But it's a dangerous game. He can cheat as much as he wants, but once he finds out *I've* lied, he'll kill me.

Scarlett downs a glass of wine while David and Bruce talk about golf. But their conversation is stilted. Bruce has been on edge since they got here. He didn't want the dinner party, but I went ahead with it anyway. Our argument got physical. Nothing serious this time, just some pushing and shoving. We've always been this way. It's passion, that's what I used to tell myself, but that's gone by the wayside now. I want to have it out with Scarlett, but I don't know where to start, so I sit here, fists clenched under the table, fingernails biting into my palms. Because I know it's her. Bruce has been complacent. I've watched him creep into her house when he thinks that I'm asleep. I imagine the two of them talking about me and I feel like a pressure cooker about to go off.

Scarlett picks at her food, then arches a perfectly shaped eyebrow. 'Are you alright, Ali? You look a bit flushed.'

I exhale a bitter laugh. 'Well, wouldn't you, if your husband was having an affair?'

Scarlett's eyes widen, but her silence speaks volumes.

Bruce's mouth drops open but he quickly composes himself. He glowers in my direction. 'This isn't the time or the place.' Perhaps he's guessed that I've known all along.

I push back my chair and stand, voice rising. 'Then when is? When you're sneaking over there in the middle of the night? Or when you're pretending to be in the golf club when you're getting your leg over at the Castle Hotel?' Fury burns inside me. I found the hotel booking in his emails just hours ago.

David stands, the blood draining from his face. 'I think we should go.'

Then the penny drops. 'You knew? Seriously? All this time and—'

'You haven't got a fucking clue about what's been going on behind your back!' Scarlett rises from the table. 'So don't start shouting the odds!'

I pull away from Bruce as he tries to grip my arm. Then I'm upon Scarlett, grabbing a fistful of her hair. Her scream echoes around the room as she manages to wriggle free. She takes two steps back, but I'm not stopping there. I clench my hand into a fist and connect with her jaw.

'Hey!' David shouts at Bruce. 'Call your nutter of a wife off!' I expect Bruce to grab me, but instead he turns on David, shouting at him to fuck off. I pant, breathless with emotion.

Everything has been building up to this point. All of Bruce's wrongdoings are closing in on him. I can barely breathe as they close in on me, too. In the last twelve months, Bruce has torn through my life like a tornado. His infidelity, his gambling – I can't take any more. Our argument erupts into chaos as we turn on each other. Scarlett has picked up her knife, hands shaking as she stands her ground. She's been humiliated by my assault. Then she proceeds to tell me what's really been going on. Tears stream down my face as everything comes to a head. Tomorrow, I'm leaving. I'm taking Cindy with me. We've reached the end of the road.

CHAPTER 48

Laura blinked as the world shifted around her. *Thump thump thump*, her temples pounded from the force of the blow.

'What? What happened?' The words barely made it past her lips.

A wave of nausea washed over her as she came up on to her hands and knees. It took seconds for her vision to clear and half a second more to tune in to the person at her side. She looked at the shoes and her spirits sank. Black Converse trainers.

Mags. But it wasn't Mags.

Laura's memory returned with a sudden sense of urgency. *Esme.* Where was her daughter? She winced as she tried but failed to stand. A trickle of warm blood ran down from her eyebrow, tainting her sight with a film of red. All of her maternal instincts hit her at once.

'Esme?' Laura groaned as Mags's face swam into view.

'Why, Laura?' Her face was blotchy and red, her words spoken on a furious breath. 'Why are you selling my home?' She spoke in a low tone, her Scottish accent falling away.

Laura touched her eyebrow, found blood on her fingers. She swiped it away.

'Esme. Where . . . where is she?' Her legs were weak, her words stumbling over each other as she tried to get her bearings. Hot white pain stole her breath. 'What . . . what have you done . . . with her?'

'This is my house. Mine and Bruce's.' Mags stood over her, ranting. Her voice was cold and hard, so different to before. Laura stiffened as she caught the glint of the knife in her hand. She looked for blood on the blade, her heart beating furiously as her body flooded with adrenaline.

Concussion, Laura thought. She must have a concussion because the ground felt like it was moving beneath her. She was on a weird merry-go-round that wouldn't stop.

'What have you done to me?' she managed to say. 'Who are you? Let me go.'

'I thought you understood that Bruce was innocent,' the woman said on the breath of a sigh. 'But no, all you wanted was to steal his home from underneath his feet.' She waved the knife in the air, her voice raising an octave. 'Your commission. That's all you care about. Not Bruce . . . the love of my life . . . rotting away in jail!'

The love of her life? So this was his stalker? The incessant letter-writer? Laura tried to get to her feet, but her limbs felt like rubber.

'Esme,' she tried to call, her surroundings blurred.

'Are you even listening?' the woman asked. 'After I've been so nice to you?'

'Who are you?' Laura blurted as she glared up at the woman before her. 'Because Mags is dead. The police are on their way!'

'But they're not, are they? You said you'd speak to them tomorrow. Family emergency, remember?'

Cold fear pricked Laura's skin as she recalled her conversation with John. This woman had been in the house, listening in all along. She had to appease her now, because she couldn't overpower her on her own.

'Please . . . Where's Esme?'

The woman observed Laura closely as she tried to get to her feet. The moment Laura wobbled on to her knees, she felt the firm nudge of the woman's shoe on her backside. It didn't take a lot to tip Laura over. Small white flashes burst before her eyes when she tried to exert herself. She was barely clinging on to consciousness. She breathed through the pain. She needed to find her little girl.

'It was the same with Mags,' her attacker sighed. 'She was trying to get me to move out, forever banging on about needing time alone.'

Mags? Laura thought, her face brushing against the carpet as she was shoved back on to the floor. Was this a confession?

The woman snorted, her brows knitting in a frown. 'She was doing some stupid balancing act on her hands when I walked in. All I did was give her fat bottom a little nudge with my foot.' She broke the confession with a sigh. 'How was I to know she'd hit her head? She was as good as my sister-in-law. Why would I want her dead?'

'Mags . . .' Laura began, pausing as she realised it wasn't her real name.

'Fiona,' the woman interrupted. 'It's Fiona. Bruce's soulmate. Soon to be Fiona Wilding. The person he found comfort with. All those letters I wrote him . . . He treasured every one.' She narrowed her eyes as Laura tried to pull herself up on the bed in an effort to get her legs to work. 'You can't sell our home. I won't let you. The universe won't let you. Because Bruce and I . . . We're meant to be.'

She's out of her mind, Laura thought, grabbing fistfuls of goose-down duvet and pulling herself up on to the bed. Her blood smeared the white material, making sticky red patterns in the cotton. A wave of nausea overcame her as she sat, trying to catch her breath. Fiona, if that was her real name . . . must have hit her with some force.

'Where's Esme? If you've hurt her . . .'

'Hurt her?' Fiona suddenly stopped pacing. 'What do you take me for?'

And then it struck Laura. Was Fiona responsible for Cindy and Ali's deaths? She'd already confessed to killing Bruce's sister. Had she murdered his wife and child too?

She had to find her daughter. She only prayed that she wasn't too late.

CHAPTER 49

'You alright?' Bruce's new cellmate spoke from the bottom bunk.

It was Gerald, the rotund investment banker who'd been imprisoned for fraud. Bruce had seen him during Laura's visit. Seen how his wife was falling apart. Both men were struggling to cope in an environment that felt utterly alien to them. Bruce had thought he was getting a handle on things – gaining the will to fight back. But now his sister was dead.

He and Mags had never been hugely close. There were times when Bruce had thought that Mags didn't like her family, never mind love them. It had comforted him to imagine her speaking with Laura, working in the background, trying to get him freed. Hearing of her visits to Laura had helped him to carry on. Yet a small part of him, the part that had grown up with his sister before she left, had known that Mags did not have such generosity of spirit. Mags had always put herself first. She was quiet and foreboding, only making use of people when they served a purpose.

'No,' Bruce replied miserably. 'I'll never be alright. Not after this. Life is too fucking hard. I don't want to be here anymore.'

A soft rustle, the jolt of movement as Gerald got out of bed and on to his feet. 'Do you need me to call a guard?' His grey hair stood in spikes, his watery eyes filled with concern.

Bruce shook his head. 'Don't worry. I don't have the balls to hurt myself.'

Gerald stared in the dim light. 'I lost a son to suicide. They don't think of the people they leave behind.'

Bruce could see the years of grief etched on the man's face. He didn't have anybody to worry about him.

'I did it to feel alive – the fraud, I mean. I wanted an adventure,' his cellmate continued. 'Not that it's any excuse. I just wanted to feel something apart from the pain of grief.'

Bruce could empathise with that. But he had enough to deal with today. At least John had been in touch with an update. He'd gone way beyond the prisoner/priest relationship, and Bruce was grateful to him. At least Laura was leaving the house and would speak to the police tomorrow. They didn't seem overly concerned. But Bruce was. Because whoever was writing to him in prison was also watching every move Laura made. His stalker knew all about his history. His childhood. His likes and dislikes. There was only one person who could have furnished her with the details. Mags. And now his sister was dead. What twisted game was this woman playing?

In the slate-grey evening light, Bruce turned in his rigid bunk bed and faced the wall. Whatever was happening, he had no control over it now. He stared at the cold brickwork, returning to that awful day.

It had been building up for months. Depression had hit him hard, and his self-destructive tendencies had come to the fore. Gambling had been the crutch that he'd leaned on. His affair was a result of loneliness. Ali's love for Cindy was boundless, but he was nothing more than a walk-on part in her reels. He had tried to keep the family together. He wanted to be a father to his child, but Ali had pushed him away. They had bought 1 Aspen Hollow with Ali's inheritance, but mortgaging the house behind her back had seemed like the way forward, to pay off his spiralling debts and start again. He'd sworn to himself that he'd stop gambling. He would go to the doctor, get antidepressants, see a therapist if he had to. But then Ali had announced that she was pregnant and his world came crashing down. Because that was the moment when he realised he'd been fooling himself. He didn't want to be with Ali. It didn't align with who he was. He didn't want another child. Their arguments scared him. It was a miracle no bones had been broken up until then. Raw panic had consumed him as Ali shoved the camera in his face – another tool of manipulation. He was battered and scarred from her endless outbursts. Burned from when she'd pressed a straightening iron to his arm. Scarred from when she'd smashed a mug over his head. Then there were the constant punches to his torso. He'd never laid a finger on his wife, apart from when he held her wrists in self-defence. But he was too proud to get help. It was easier to avoid Ali than admit to being a victim of domestic abuse. But news of the pregnancy had brought everything to a head. He couldn't face spending years with his violent wife. He needed an exit plan.

CHAPTER 50

As evening fell, David exhaled a weary sigh. He was dressed in his chinos, minus his tie, the top button of his shirt undone. His skin still carried traces of his last holiday tan, but a few extra worry lines creased his handsome face. The last year had not been kind to either of them. Scarlett moved around him, sitting down in the kitchen. The faint woody scent of his aftershave lingered in the room. It was a welcome change from the 'ocean breeze' or 'tropical fern' air fresheners that surrounded her therapist's office. The nanny was upstairs, their children in the bath.

'I feel like I've been pulled inside out.' Scarlett delivered a weak smile. 'But I've been sleeping better, and therapy is helping.'

'Good.' He looked quiet and thoughtful.

'Can I ask you something?'

'Anything.'

There were still things she couldn't remember and Scarlett needed to fill in the blanks. 'That day . . . after Ali and Cindy were murdered. Why didn't you tell the cops about the argument the night before?' It had bothered Scarlett like an itch that she couldn't quite scratch. 'I've raked over as much as I can remember. But that keeps coming up.'

'I panicked, I suppose.' David stared at his cup of coffee. 'I didn't want people to know about the affair.'

'Why?'

Several seconds passed before he replied. 'Because I was embarrassed. I felt less of a man. I don't like washing my dirty linen in public.'

'It might have helped with the case.'

'How?' He lowered his voice as he heard movement upstairs. 'It was open-and-shut.'

Scarlett waited until the movement stilled. 'We left them in an awful state . . .' She paused. She had to take responsibility. 'Sorry. *I* left them in a state. You tried to rein me in and I wouldn't listen.'

'We never should have gone there. That was all on me.'

'Would haves, should haves, could haves . . . What's done is done. I'm just trying to understand it, that's all.' She watched David sip his coffee. He'd got rid of all the booze in the house. He moved stiffly, staring but not seeing.

'Graham knows,' he said. 'I'm convinced of it. It's the way he looks at me. This smugness. Like he's keeping a secret. As if we're part of some special club.'

Scarlett didn't disagree. She had felt it from their neighbour too. 'For a long time I thought the police would come back and accuse us of lying. It was awful, waiting for that knock on the door.'

'The whole thing was horrific. I'm not surprised you turned to drink.'

'I'm more surprised that you didn't.' She smiled. A feeble attempt to lighten the mood. 'Where did you go, after we went home that night?'

David blinked twice before responding. 'Sorry, what?'

'That night. You weren't there when I woke up. Must have been around one. I went downstairs but you were gone.' She watched David leave his empty cup on the table and approach the window. The conversation was getting to him. He faced away from her, his muscles tense. 'I thought you didn't remember that night.'

'It's coming back now.' Scarlett stared at him, suddenly ill at ease. 'What is it? What are you not telling me?'

She was taken aback as he turned, a flash of anger streaking across his face. 'I can't believe you think I'd hurt that family. What do you take me for?'

Scarlett rose from her seat, a new-found calmness in her voice. The old Scarlett would have screamed. An argument would have ensued. One of them would have stormed out – probably her.

'Honey, I never said you hurt Ali or Cindy. I just asked where you went.'

'I would never . . .' he mumbled, his sudden bout of anger evaporating. 'Not in a million years . . .'

Scarlett touched his forearm. 'You know, it might do you good to talk about this with someone. My therapist might be able to fit you in.'

'I'm fine. I just . . . got the wrong end of the stick, that's all.' A sigh. 'I went for a walk around the close to clear my head that night.' He took her hands. 'Let's forget about all that now.'

But Scarlett hadn't forgotten about all the times David had locked her in the bedroom. What if she slipped back to her old ways?

'I want you to take the lock off the bedroom door,' she said, after he'd calmed down.

'But what if . . . ?'

'If I fall off the wagon I'll talk to my therapist.' Scarlett stared into his eyes, needing him to feel the sincerity of her words. 'It scares me, David. How close I was to throwing myself out of our window that day. I've talked to Josie about it and—'

'You told your therapist? Why?'

'Because I had to confide in someone. She understands your reasoning behind locking me in, but it's a bad idea. You can't possibly understand what it's like, seeing people go in and out of that house, knowing what happened there.'

'Alright.' His forehead furrowed. 'What else have you told her?'

'Nothing that should worry you.' She dropped her hands. 'I need patience and understanding, not locks on doors. This has been really, really hard for me. You need to meet me halfway.'

'I will. I'm proud of you. I'll do whatever it takes.'

'Good. Because from now on, we move forward. I need to be a proper mum to the kids.'

Letting go of her niggles about David was the only way to beat her demons. From now on, there was no looking back.

CHAPTER 51

'You should have walked away when you got the chance.' Fiona's voice thundered from above. What had once been so soft and gentle was now filled with venom. 'For Christ's sake, stop screaming, you stupid woman! Esme's asleep, not dead!'

Every time Laura tried to get to her feet, Fiona swished the knife before her. Laura wasn't strong enough to fight. Not yet. She wanted to believe that Esme was OK. She couldn't bear the alternative. But there was no way her little girl was asleep with all this going on. She swallowed, her mouth dry. She needed to tell Fiona what she wanted to hear.

'Listen to me. I know Bruce is innocent. It's not too late . . .'

'You're not interested in the truth . . .'

'Then check your emails. I was desperate to find out what really happened here.' She paused as her vision swam. *Stay with it*, she warned herself. Because history could be about to repeat itself. 'Tell me, Fiona. I've got thousands of followers online. They all want to know the truth.'

'But the house . . .' Fiona said. 'Why should Bruce lose his home?'

'I lied. It's a scarcity tactic, making out all these offers are coming in. In truth . . .' Laura sighed, her vision blurring as she tried to sound convincing. 'I've been putting them off. It's not too late for you to buy it yourself. We could run a fundraiser, enough for Bruce to buy it back. Oh God . . .' She touched her temple as a wave of nausea passed over her. 'My head.'

'Alright then,' Fiona said, her feet planted steadily on the floor as she held the knife. 'I'll tell you who killed them. But you won't want to believe it. The truth is ugly. You've got to keep your promise.'

'I will . . .' Laura said, breathing in through her nose and out through her mouth as she tried to stay conscious. 'And Esme?'

'Asleep, I told you!' Fiona snapped. 'Do you want to know or not?'

Laura nodded, each movement of her head delivering further flashes of pain.

'We'll work together,' she managed to say, because she saw the doubt on Fiona's face. Laura could almost read her thoughts and they were terrifying. *This house would never sell if a copycat murder took place under this roof.* 'Trust me,' Laura added. 'I wouldn't have gone to see Bruce if I didn't believe he was innocent.'

'I don't know . . .'

'Fiona. This is your only way out. I'll say that I was rushing to leave and fell over and hit my head.'

Fiona stood above her, her brow furrowed as she thought it over. Her eyes were like two black stones, her face troubled. She was wearing the same black dress as before, but now it was splattered with food. The stale smell of sweat emanated from her body. Wisps of her hair had loosened from her low ponytail. Her teeth were yellow from plaque. This was a woman on the edge. She took a breath and then spoke. 'Alright. But listen closely. I remember every second of that day. Because I was there, Laura.'

Laura closed her eyes as another wave of nausea took hold. She allowed Fiona's voice to wash over her.

'Cindy was asleep in bed. She had a cold, bless her. Such a delicate little thing . . . I was friends with Ali. We spoke often. I knew everything about her life. That night . . .'

Her words were followed by a dull thud as she crumpled to the floor. Laura stared at the person who had silenced Fiona as she'd prepared to tell all.

CHAPTER 52

'Are you OK?' Cally's voice filled the room. 'I've called an ambulance. The police are on their way.'

Fiona was lying face down, no sign of the knife she had brandished minutes before. The bronze ballerina ornament was on the floor next to her head. The same ornament that had probably brought Laura to her knees.

'But . . .' Laura frowned, clawing back her memory as she weaved in and out of consciousness. 'She was going to tell me what happened.' Another thought jolted her, becoming sharper now. 'Esme! Where is she?'

'Esme?' Cally's eyes widened. 'Oh God, I don't know!'

'Help me . . . get to my feet.' Laura breathed through the pain that held her temples in a vice. Cally lifted her up. She was stronger than she looked.

'I got your message. You sounded worried . . .' Cally explained. 'I came in . . . then I heard shouting upstairs.'

Laura could only imagine how it would have looked to her sister. Her, with blood running down her face; Fiona, holding a knife. But her main concern was her daughter. 'Esme? Where is she?' Her sister supported her as she instinctively made her way to the master bedroom. The room in the house she most hated spending time in. And it was there, as she stood in the doorway, legs shaking, that she saw her little girl lying, eyes closed, on the double bed. *Oh God*, she thought, the foundations of her world crumbling beneath her feet. Was Esme dead?

'Esme!' Laura called, breaking free of Cally's grip as she stumbled towards her child. She gave her a gentle shake. Hands trembling, she touched Esme's cold skin.

'Is she breathing?' Cally said, standing over them both.

The look on Esme's face made the air leave Laura's lungs. No . . . It couldn't be true. Laura sank to her knees next to the bed. Not again.

Another wave of nausea told hold before darkness closed in.

CHAPTER 53

It was a whole twenty-four hours before Bruce got to see John again. He lived for their meetings and updates about the outside world. It was harder, now he had a cellmate. Their private conversations wouldn't be private anymore. Yet John felt like the last thread of humanity woven into Bruce's days.

Today he had sat through daily Mass in the small prison chapel, waiting for a chance to speak to him. It was a small but peaceful place – as much as it could be in prison. The dedicated room was used for all faiths, which is why the decor was so bland. There was nothing to spark the imagination or offer hope. But the air in there felt different – a little warmer, less stale, and filled with the breath of uncountable prayers.

'I'm afraid I don't have long,' John said, as the remaining inmates filtered out of the room. Bruce knew the gamble he was taking. Any special treatment in prison was frowned upon.

'I need confession, Father.' Bruce spoke loud enough for the stocky female prison guard watching them to hear.

In prison, confession was inviolate. There wasn't much about Bruce that John didn't know. And yet here the priest was, still willing to offer him his time yet again.

Bruce stopped John as soon as he began the prayers leading into confession. 'I just need five minutes with you alone,' he said quietly. 'I'm going crazy in here.'

'I know.' John rested his fist on his hip. 'Sorry I've not been able to speak to you before now. But our time together has been noticed. The governor suggested that I spread myself out with the other inmates more evenly.'

'I see.' Bruce sighed, feeling like the door was being shut on the last glimmer of light.

'Come.' John gestured towards the confession box, his face creased in concern.

The confession box was a small, unassuming cubicle tucked into the corner of the prison chapel, its walls scuffed and faintly yellowed. The wooden partition between them was splintered in places, the worn lattice grille giving off a faint smell of varnish. The air inside was stifling, sharp with the undertones of sweat and despair that clung to every corner of the prison.

Bruce sat stiffly on the narrow bench, his knees brushing the chipped edge of the cubicle's divider. The cushion beneath him was threadbare, leaving hard wood beneath his weight. He coughed – and the sound was amplified in the tight space.

John's voice, calm and measured, drifted through like a balm, though Bruce could barely focus on his words. 'I've spoken to Laura. There was an incident at the house.'

A moment of dread passed over Bruce as he forced his lungs to expand. The confession box felt too dark. The walls seemed to be closing in He peered around the space, which grew more coffin-like by the second.

John didn't keep him waiting long. 'They've caught your stalker, Bruce. Her name is Fiona. She broke into the house. Not for the first time, by all accounts.'

He relayed how a woman called Fiona Litchfield had drugged Laura's daughter with chloroform, then carried her up to bed. How she'd taken a knife from the kitchen and waited for Laura to come looking for her daughter. How she'd been about to confess everything when Laura's sister had knocked her out.

Knocked her out? This is crazy, Bruce thought. 'Where's Fiona now?' He was stunned by the revelation. Was this the name of the woman who started her letters 'Hello sausage'?

'In custody. She's been treated for a head injury. The thing is . . . and I might be wrong here . . . but she told Laura that she lived with your sister, Mags.'

Bruce finished the thought. 'Which means she might be responsible for her death.' Time fell still, the outside world reduced to a distant hum, leaving nothing but his own thoughts.

He rubbed his face with his hands. The police had yet to enlighten him about any of this. He was used to a slow response. Without John, he'd still be in the dark. After two more breaths, Bruce spoke again.

'How's Laura? And her daughter? Are they OK?'

The words were gravelly and he cleared his throat. Because all the while he was wondering – what did this mean for him?

CHAPTER 54

Laura sat next to her daughter's bed in the private hospital room. It was decorated with elephants and giraffes, flamingos and pretty parrots. It smelled comfortingly of antiseptic, and in the background, staff moved through the hospital with quiet efficiency. Three days had passed since Laura's encounter with Fiona. It felt like a distant nightmare.

She turned to Shane as he entered the room. 'How's your dad?'

He looked weary from lack of sleep, but relieved. 'Better than he was.' He smiled, keeping his voice low so as not to disturb their sleeping daughter. 'How's our little poppet?'

'Good.' Laura's chin wobbled as she tried to contain the swell of emotion. 'This is all my fault. We could have lost her. We could have lost our little girl.' She stood, grateful for Shane's embrace. She breathed in his scent, her face buried in his thick woollen jumper as she allowed her tears to flow. 'I'm so sorry.'

'Hey, it's OK.' Shane shushed her fears away. 'I told you. Everything's going to be alright.'

And it would be. His father's brush with death had turned out to be a mild heart attack. As for Esme – the paramedics had acted quickly to bring their daughter around. Her stay in hospital was to monitor her health. She would soon be allowed home.

At first, Laura couldn't understand why her daughter hadn't screamed at the sight of Fiona standing there. She'd been warned about stranger danger. Why hadn't she run to her mother when Fiona had turned up at the house? But she wasn't a stranger to Esme. She'd been watching her for some time. Fiona had approached her at the park, pretending she was with another child. She'd introduced herself as 'Fi', taking the opportunity to familiarise herself with Laura's daughter at every possible turn. In the shopping centre, waving when her father's back was turned. Outside the school, pretending to wait with the other parents. Then, in the house, telling Esme she was a viewer, waiting to look around the house. That's when she'd drugged her, then carried her up the secret stairwell. Fiona had laid her on the bed in the master bedroom. Unmoving, eyes closed, Esme had appeared lifeless when Laura checked in on her. But then she'd felt the beat of a slow pulse and what a relief that had been.

A key had been found in Fiona's pocket, which gave her access to the small rear door tucked away at the back of the house. Had she made a copy of the original? Or did Mags have a spare key for when she came to stay? Fiona had known everything about Bruce's life. She'd learned it all from Mags, in the guise of a friend and lodger until she didn't need her anymore.

Fiona would recover from her head injury, but her actions would never be forgotten. Laura took the tissue that her husband offered, never more grateful for him than she was now. If it weren't for Cally . . . Laura couldn't bear to think about what would have happened next. And Shane . . . He was here, his strong arms providing comfort. He'd been so worried when she'd arrived at the same hospital that his father had been taken to just hours before.

Now Laura got to wondering. What was Fiona's end game? To stop the sale of the house at any cost? Or had she really been about to reveal the truth about the murders? Laura and Shane parted as Esme murmured softly.

They stood at her bedside, not hearing the soft click of the door. Just then, Shane's mother stepped into the room. Things were changing between them. Her mother-in-law's haughty look had been replaced with one of regret. She had already apologised for her behaviour. Laura wasn't sure how much she meant it. She hadn't thought the word 'sorry' was in her vocabulary until then.

'How is she?' her mother-in-law asked, smoothing down Esme's bed linen. She looked to Laura for the answer. Another first. Usually, she pretended she wasn't there.

'She's coming home today.' Laura offered a smile.

'Good. Well, I've got to pop into work to schedule some time off. Keep me updated.'

Laura nodded. It would take time to mend their fences, but they were willing to give it a try. As for her own mother – she hadn't spoken to her since she locked her out of her house. Sometimes you had to choose who to keep in your life and who to let go.

CHAPTER 55

'You can do this.' Scarlett's therapist offered a reassuring smile. 'You're nearly there.'

And she was. Scarlett had come so far in such a short space of time. She was taking responsibility for her actions instead of living life by default. But she felt like she was wearing the most beautiful pair of shoes with a thorn jammed between her toes. She needed to talk about what had happened that night. Because she and David had caused so much pain.

'We should never have gone to the dinner party,' Scarlett admitted, taking slow, soothing breaths. 'Ali should have handled it better . . .' She caught Josie's look and knew what she was thinking: 'should haves', 'ifs' and 'buts' didn't have any place here.

'But, yes . . .' Scarlett continued. 'Ultimately, it was my decision to go. I suppose Ali wanted to confront us. See our marriage torn apart just as hers had been.' She looked down at her hands. At her nails, which were slowly beginning to grow back. 'It was cold that night, but we didn't have far to go, so I wore my killer red jumpsuit.' Only then did she realise how petty she'd been.

She saw no malice in Josie's eyes, only patience and understanding.

'David looked good, but not as drop-dead gorgeous as Bruce. I never understood what he was doing with Ali. She seemed so frumpy in comparison, and she was hardly his type.' Her glance flickered over to Josie as she replayed the scene. 'And I'm not being a bitch here, I was genuinely puzzled. He should never have got married.' She stopped as she realised 'should' had crept back into her vocabulary. 'It was Indian food, and there was lots of it. Korma, biryani, samosas that she took out of the oven. I laid into the wine. Figured I'd need it to get through whatever was ahead. The atmosphere was so stilted. I knew something was up.'

'How was David?'

'Quiet. Awkward. He kept looking at me in the way he does when he's trying to read my thoughts. But it wasn't me that he needed to worry about, it was Ali. By the time she sat down to join us, her face was all flushed. I knew it wasn't from cooking. Something was up. She was glaring at Bruce, like she wanted to kill him with her bare hands. And then I thought . . .' She touched her mouth with her hand. 'God, I'd forgotten that until now . . .' She glanced at Josie. 'Ali looked so mad that I wondered if she'd spat in our food.' She shook her head. 'I had no idea that Ali and Cindy would end up dead that night. That poor little girl.'

'Keep moving forward,' Josie urged. Their hour was almost over and Scarlett needed to get everything out. This chapter was too painful to revisit another day.

'I drank more than I ate. We all did, even David, but not as much as me. He was half watching Bruce, half watching me. They still had to work together. We all needed to live as neighbours, and he wanted us to move on. But it was clear that Ali knew about the affair. David and I had come to terms with it. We were able to look at it pragmatically – at least, that's what I thought at the time. Something was wrong. We needed to fix it. Going to Ali's dinner party was a small step towards that. We'd both had minor indiscretions in the past, but we always came back to each other. I suppose our marriage has been more open than most.'

'We've already discussed the row,' said Josie. 'Let's move forward from that. What is it you're not telling me, Scarlett?'

Scarlett wrapped her arms around herself. She couldn't put this off any longer. 'Every time I tell this story, you make a presumption, don't you?' She looked at Josie intently. At least she wasn't having as much trouble meeting her eye. 'I talk about indiscretions and affairs. How Ali was the innocent party. How David and I were to blame. I bet a part of you secretly thinks that I deserved that punch in the face.' Josie opened her mouth to speak but Scarlett raised her hand. 'Honestly, there's no need to say anything, because I did deserve a smack. I'm glad she got it in before she . . . before she . . .' Scarlett released a shuddering sigh. Josie waited for her to continue. 'But here's the rub. It wasn't me having the affair.'

She watched as Josie raised an eyebrow. Her signal to continue.

'I didn't have a fling with Bruce Wilding. David did. I told Ali that night. I told her everything.' Scarlett inhaled a deep breath, held it for three seconds and let it go. There. She'd said it. Apart from David and Bruce, their neighbours Graham and Walter were the only other people who knew. Like they were in some big gay boys' club. But David wasn't gay. He'd been experimenting. Something he'd done at university and returned to one last time. She could almost understand, given she'd had a crush on Bruce herself. The truth had come as a shock, but Scarlett was done living in the past.

CHAPTER 56

Bruce was hunched over yet another letter. He couldn't believe how much things had changed in the last week. This copy had been given to him by his lawyer, the original seized by police. Fiona Litchfield, if that was her real name, was in custody, under investigation for his sister's murder. There were deeper suspicions that Fiona knew about Ali and Cindy's murders too.

Bruce was grateful that Gerald was sleeping. His cellmate was getting on in years and usually had an afternoon snooze. He stared at the page, taking in the name of the sender, who was now being detained without bail.

Hello sausage,

I owe you the truth. You'll want to know the details and I don't blame you for that. My letter is nothing to be afraid of. Give it to the police if you want. I've told them as much, anyway.

I've known you, Ali and Cindy for much longer than you realise. It started with you, Bruce. We were at the same convention in Birmingham, remember? We were late for the hotel breakfast buffet. It was due to close, but the woman behind the counter gave us a wink and told us to help ourselves. It felt like we were two naughty schoolchildren as we laughed together.

You gave me the last sausage and I joked, 'Who said chivalry was dead?' I confessed that I almost hadn't come because I was a bit of an introvert. You were so kind, Bruce. Sitting beside me for breakfast, and making sure I had someone to talk to during the day. I've had bad experiences with men in the past. But let's not talk about that now.

You want to know how it happened, don't you? And I want you to hear it from me first. I thought about you a lot after the convention. I never imagined we'd cross paths again. Work became too much. It's my nerves, you see. My therapist said it's down to my brain chemistry. I hate taking medication, so I let things get on top of me. I left my job. I had enough money to take some time off before I got another one. That's when I saw you again. I was watching YouTube at the time, when you and Ali popped up. At first, I wasn't sure. But the moment I heard your soft, velvety laughter, I knew it was you.

I spent the next two weeks binge-watching Ali's content. I felt like I'd been invited into your home. I didn't mind that you were married, because I grew to love Ali and Cindy too. I've never had a proper family. I was in foster care from an early age. But it didn't stop me getting an education. I felt a strange kinship when I found out that we'd graduated from the same university, although I was a few years ahead of you. But my dream of being an architect fell apart when I couldn't handle the pressure.

I got myself an easier job, something less demanding on my time, working down the local Co-op, stacking shelves. Then, one day, I watched one of Ali's videos and thought she looked a little stressed. I'm not one for posting publicly, so I created the username @Miss53 and sent her an anonymous DM. She was sweet, or at least that's what I thought, sending me details of the Samaritans and advice on what to do when I was feeling down. But it wasn't me who needed help. It was her. I saw it in her eyes. Everything she talked about online was a lie. I knew what it was like to wear a mask in public and put on a brave face. I kept messaging, telling her I was here if she needed to chat. One day, she did. We became online friends and she opened up about her life, quickly deleting each message after she'd sent it. She said she had to protect herself. I was happy to comply.

I didn't like how she talked about you, Bruce. Because the man I knew wouldn't be capable of those things. She said that you were having an affair. That you were neglectful, and that you didn't care. I didn't believe it and my feelings towards her hardened. I watched more of your videos, and only then could I see the exasperation on your face. And that pregnancy video . . . Oh my Lord. How could she do that to you? She wasn't even pregnant. Yes, she told me. It was just another stupid game. Her head was all over the place. I wanted to warn you to be careful, but I've been in such situations before. Meddling in family relationships never works well.

She stopped messaging for a while, but I told her I was there every day. I had to keep an eye on things, to know what was going on. Then her message came. I only got to read it once before it disappeared. She said that she'd had enough. That the whole pregnancy thing had backfired. That she'd found out that you'd never really loved her. She said you'd been having an affair with one of your neighbours. That there was no going back from there. She missed her parents. She couldn't cope without them anymore. She said that life was too hard, but she'd intended on leaving you with a parting gift. That soon the world would know just what kind of man you were. I wish I'd had time to screenshot it, but all I could think of was getting over there. Yes, I knew where you lived. I'd been there before.

I should have called the police. Had I known that Cindy was in danger, then of course I would have. I didn't think for a second that things had got that bad. Should I continue, Bruce? Do you really want to know exactly what happened? Because you don't have to read the next letter. Perhaps it's best if you remember little Cindy just as she was. Sometimes the truth is too hard to bear.

Yours, always,
Fiona

Bruce blinked three times, trying to ground himself. For a moment, he was back there, at home. He strained to remember the conference and meeting Fiona over breakfast, but the memory wouldn't come. This woman who was part of the devastation had been instantly forgettable.

CHAPTER 57

Scarlett sat on her front porch, recovering from her morning with the children. She'd vowed to give them at least four hours of quality time every day. It was the only way she could bond with them again. She had researched studying for a degree at Lincoln University. If someone had told her last year that she would consider becoming a therapist, she would have laughed in their face. But she thought about Josie and her forthright ways. All this time, she'd thought David had arranged for her therapist, but it was Josie who had approached him during a charity fundraising event. Apparently, she was well known in business circles, and had connected with the boss of his architect firm. She'd slipped him her card, saying if he ever needed a therapist that she would offer excellent rates. David had said that it had felt like a blessing at the time.

And now Scarlett had come through the other side. The locks were gone from her bedroom door. David had bought her a bench and outdoor heater so she could watch the world go by. She wouldn't be hidden away anymore. She was even ready to face Graham and his knowing looks. *Speak of the devil*, she thought, as her neighbour joined her.

'Come. Sit.' She patted the bench. She had found Graham's mobile number through the Aspen Hollow WhatsApp group and messaged him privately. David was at work, the children having a nap.

'I'm intrigued,' Graham said, standing there in his faded black jeans and worn biker jacket. As far as she was aware, he didn't drive a motorbike. It wasn't the weather for sunglasses either, but it didn't stop him wearing them.

'Isn't intrigued your default setting?' She gave him a wry grin. 'Want a drink? We have Ribena or coffee on the menu.'

'I'll pass.' He waved the offer away as he sat next to her. 'Had a heavy night last night.' He paused. 'Sorry.'

'It's not illegal to talk about booze in these parts.' An understanding seemed to pass between them.

'How are you doing?' he said. 'David said you had a great therapist. Funnily enough, she approached me last week. I was at a literary event. She mentioned she was treating you.'

Scarlett's mouth dropped open. 'She can't do that!'

'I know! That's what I thought. It was all a bit strange. Talk about an ambulance chaser.' He shook his head at the memory. 'Seemed she'd done her homework on us lot. She kept talking about number one, saying the place shouldn't be put up for sale.' He delivered a bemused smile. 'Don't be too hard on her. She was tiddly at the time.'

'That's bloody unprofessional!' Scarlett groaned. 'Our sessions were meant to be private.'

Graham raised an eyebrow. 'Relax, love, she didn't give me chapter and verse, only that you were on her books. She was very interested in our little neighbourhood, though.'

'I'm not surprised,' Scarlett replied. 'Never a dull moment, eh?'

Graham smiled. 'You don't know the half of it.'

Scarlett shifted position as a thorn of unease dug in. 'So go on, then, share the goss. What do you know?'

'My husband doesn't want me getting involved.'

'Ditto. But since when did we ever listen to them?'

Graham snickered. 'I like you, Scarlett. I always thought that we could be friends. But you became a complete lush, and that's not good for my image at all. Good entertainment value, though.'

He spoke with such amusement that Scarlett couldn't help but smile. 'Why didn't you tell the police about Bruce's affair?'

'Not my business.'

'Please. Like that's ever stopped you before.'

'It does when cops are involved. You might not know this, but you're not the only one with a past.'

The wind whistled by, though it wasn't as cold as before. Soft light filtered through white fluffy clouds above. Halloween had been and gone. Children had dressed up in Burton Waters. Orange-and-black garlands had been hung. Doors had been knocked upon. But not in Aspen Hollow. Word had spread about the latest incident and the families from Burton Waters had given them a wide berth.

Scarlett waited for more, but Graham remained tight-lipped. This was a story for another day. 'You must have been questioned by the police. I'm surprised Walter didn't tell the truth.'

'He didn't lie. He never does. He just kept out of it.' Graham slipped off his sunglasses. 'Which is what I'm meant to be doing too. It's been nice to chat. We should do this again. Just a different subject matter next time.'

He moved to leave. But Scarlett needed to get it out. To clear the air between them. 'He's not gay,' she blurted.

Graham relaxed back down into the seat. 'That's what the Davids of the world always say. And the Bruces . . . And see where that got him.'

'You think that's why he killed Ali? Because he was a closet homosexual?'

'I think all this BS about a stalker is very convenient. Most murderers are motivated by something. A whopping big debt, an unwanted pregnancy, a social-media-obsessed wife . . .' He shrugged. 'She was never off his back. I saw her once, through the window, punching him around the back of the head. They were having a belter of a row. I used to feel sorry for him.'

It didn't surprise Scarlett. She had experienced Ali's temper first-hand. 'So he snapped?'

Graham nodded. 'Seems plausible.'

'And Cindy?'

Graham crossed a long leg. 'That's the bit I'm struggling with. Now don't take offence but . . . Can I be brutally frank with you here?'

'It's why I invited you for a chat.'

'For a while, I thought that it was David. That maybe he was in love with Bruce and wanted his family out of the way. He's always out on his lone walks. He and Bruce . . . Well, they seemed happy together. They had chemistry.'

'As friends. The fling was a mistake.'

'First mistake or . . . ?' Graham delivered a cheeky smile.

'Always fishing, aren't you? Well, you can get your beady eyes off my husband, he's spoken for.'

Graham barked a laugh. 'Please . . . He's not my type. We don't *all* cheat on our spouses here in the Hollow.'

'It was one time!' Scarlett lied, both mortified and strangely enjoying the banter.

Her bi-curious husband had assured her that she was enough for him. She was no angel herself, but the children needed their parents. It was time she and David grew up. 'Thanks for not saying anything to the police. If that came out . . .' An involuntary shudder drove down her spine. 'It would have been the end of us.'

'Enough families have been hurt. Your little ones need you now.' They sat in comfortable silence, as if they'd been friends for years.

'So what about this stalker, then?' Scarlett finally said, unable to resist the gossip.

Graham smiled. 'We are definitely going to be good friends.'

CHAPTER 58

As soon as Bruce saw the familiar 'Hello sausage', his stomach muscles contracted and he couldn't read any further. He waited until Gerald went to work. His cellmate was doing a few hours down the laundry and settling in quite well. Perhaps he'd found the adventure that he was looking for. He'd told Bruce that he was writing a book. *Good luck to him*, Bruce thought. His own life could have made a feature film, it had been so bizarre. Now, finally, he held the answers in his hand.

The letter shook in his grip. Did he want to know what she was about to say? And could this delusional woman be relied upon to tell the truth? He sat on the top bunk, trying to find the best light. His eyesight wasn't as good as it used to be.

> *Hello sausage,*
> *So you've chosen to read on. I knew you would. You're that sort of a man. You'll push through the ugliness and pain, force yourself on because you won't look away. I won't keep you waiting to hear the rest.*
> *I got to your house that night, not knowing what to expect. Ali's message was a cry for help, for my ears only. The one person she trusted most in the world. But I didn't*

trust her. I didn't like what she was doing – tearing you apart. How right I was.

The front door wasn't locked. That in itself was strange. She'd always been so security-conscious. The place was so quiet and cold. I didn't know it then, but you were in bed, drugged into your last peaceful sleep. I called out for Ali as I went through each room. I half expected to bump into you, for you to ask me what the hell I was doing in your home. I didn't even have Ali's messages to show you. I shouldn't be there, I told myself. I was about to leave when I heard a howl. It was the most chilling sound I'd heard in my life. You read stories about the hairs prickling on people's necks. Mine stood to full attention that day. I didn't think twice as I bounded up the stairs, calling your names.

I found Ali in the bedroom. What a mess she was, with mascara stains streaked down her face. She was leaning over Cindy, mumbling and wailing as she made the bed. 'Soon,' she cried. 'I'll be with you soon.'

She was so lost in her world that she never heard me come in. I stood back, away from the door. I don't know why. I thought Cindy was asleep.

Ali ran out of the room, not even looking down the hall as she went to the master bedroom. That must have been when she scratched your face. You, my beautiful man, who wouldn't harm a fly. I went into Cindy's room to check up on her. I . . . I won't go into details. You've seen the photographs. You know. She'd been given drugs in her hot chocolate, sent into a forever sleep before Ali pressed the pillow over her face. It pains me to say it. How my heart hurts as I remember that awful night.

Next I went to the master bedroom. I saw you lying there, the scratches on your face. I thought that you were dead too. I was devastated. It felt like my world had ended. You and Cindy were the people I loved most in the world. So many times I'd watched Cindy, imagining the three of us together. I would have made a wonderful stepmum. And now Ali was before me, her face glistening with snot and tears as she turned on me. Her eyes were wild. 'Ali, it's me . . . Fiona – Miss Fifty-Three.' I remember saying those words. I was in shock too. I couldn't comprehend what had just taken place. I think she'd already guessed who I was before I opened my mouth to speak.

'You shouldn't be here,' she said. Her chest was heaving by then, and sweat had broken out on her brow. She eyed the flask on the dresser and I knew. Whatever drug was inside was her way out of this.

'You . . . you killed her,' I said, because I knew that it couldn't be my beautiful man. Never. Never in a million years.

'Go,' she said. 'Just go. This has nothing to do with you.' But we both knew that wasn't how things were going to end.

Anger built up inside me. She'd had everything I wanted and destroyed it. You, and poor little Cindy, lying lifeless . . . I was filled with rage. I dragged her into Cindy's bedroom, made her look at what she'd done. I was screaming at her by then, asking her about her plan. That's when she told me that she was following her down. She was going to overdose. Make it look like you poisoned her with whatever concoction was in her drink. I grabbed the pillow from the bed. If death was what she wanted, then I'd give her a helping hand. Had I known that you were alive, I never would have done it. I gave her what she wanted. I couldn't understand why she was punching and lashing out. I didn't feel her fists, I only felt burning anger, eating me up inside.

I went to your room and my heart nearly seized in my chest when I realised that you were breathing. I paused to kiss your lips. Such a fairy-tale moment. Then it hit me like a brick wall. Ali was setting you up for her murder. Hers, and Cindy's.

I couldn't function. I thought about the consequences of what I'd just done. I couldn't go to prison. But neither could I leave you to take the blame. So I pulled on your coat and hat, wrapped their bodies in a duvet, and carried them out to your car. I didn't know that there were cameras. I thought I could clean up the mess. I wanted to spare you the pain of finding them like that. I searched her drawers. Found a journal where she'd lied about being scared of you – all part of her plan to frame you for murder. I didn't want you to take the blame. I almost turned myself in. I thought the truth would come out eventually.

I found Mags at the funeral. I moved to Scotland to be near her. Your family was my family, or so I thought. I stayed in the area, got a menial job. Served her coffee in her local Costa. When she said she was looking for a flatmate, I jumped at the chance. How I loved her stories of your childhood. I fell in love with you all over again. Your sister loved you, Bruce. I know she didn't show it, but she always spoke fondly of you. She didn't know that I knew exactly who you were.

She was a bit of a hippy, wasn't she? Into yoga and chanting and all that weird stuff. I didn't mean to kill her. I just booted her up the bum because she was getting on my nerves. I read the letters that you'd written her. She should have responded. She should have done more.

She was doing yoga in front of the fireplace when I came home. She asked me what I was doing back so soon. I shouldn't have felt so unwelcome in my own home. One quick kick to the backside was all it took. I'd only meant to make her take a tumble. I wasn't to know that she'd hit her head. It was quick. There was blood everywhere. I texted her boss to say that she was going away for a few weeks.

Please don't hate me for that, Bruce. I didn't mean it. We all make mistakes. I've only ever wanted the best in life for you. Ours is a love story that is unfinished. Write to me. Please.

I hope that by making this confession I'm helping the police so that they can reopen your case and you can walk free. Ali smothered little Cindy. But I killed Ali. I was just giving her what she wanted.

Everything I've ever done has been for you. When the house went up for sale, it damn near broke my heart – but I've already told you that. My therapist helped me through it. She encouraged me to stop the sale. Said I should do whatever it took. It felt good to talk to someone who understood. I only hope that now you can be free to live in your home again. One day I might even join you.

With love, always,
Fiona

Bruce didn't think it was possible to cry any more tears, yet here he was, shoulders shaking, as he tried to hold them in. Fiona was a disease that had infiltrated every aspect of his life, but she had finally given him the truth. It all made sense now. How could Ali plot to frame him for their murders? Hurting him was one thing, but this? Had he really driven her that far? 'You drove me to it!' How many times had she screamed those words when he'd shown her his bruises the day after they fought?

Her propensity for violence had been a dark side of her. Bruce had made excuses when David commented on his bruises, saying that he was clumsy when he was drunk. His father's words still stung from his youth, when he'd called Bruce a 'sissy boy'. All his life, he'd tried to make up for it, by putting on a hard front. Drinking, gambling, working out . . . That was what real men did, wasn't it? But he would never hit Ali, even when she was coming at him.

Bruce had vowed to take his secrets to the grave. He'd never for a second imagined that Ali could have hurt her own daughter, never mind planned to set him up for killing them both. He should have been honest with the police. Now that he read the letter, it all made sense. Nobody had ever hated him more than Ali did that night. And Cindy had paid the price.

The letters were in the hands of the authorities. Maybe one day he could be granted his freedom, but at least now he knew the truth.

CHAPTER 59

It was with some satisfaction that Laura fixed the 'Sold' sticker on the sign outside 1 Aspen Hollow. There were times when she'd thought that she would never see this day. The solicitors were moving quickly. A cash buyer with no chain meant contracts could quickly be exchanged. But the identity of the buyer was yet to be revealed. Great care had been taken to ensure they'd kept their name out of the press. The only people who knew were the solicitors dealing with it. Laura looked forward to the day when she could hand over the keys. But who would be moving in?

She walked back to her car, flooded with a sense of relief. That house had tested her beyond her limits, but she was still standing. Soon, she'd have a healthy commission in her bank account too. She couldn't wait to finally move on with her life with Esme and Shane. Mrs Taylor-Brown might have called a truce, but Laura didn't trust her one iota.

Laura waited until three p.m. to meet her sister for coffee at Stokes. Now the lunchtime rush had passed, they almost had the place to themselves. November had brought a fine dusting of frost. The sun beamed from a cloudless sky. It was good to have something different than the constant drizzle and damp.

Cally clasped her hands around her mug. Her nails had just been done, and her hair was freshly highlighted. She was making a huge effort since meeting her new boyfriend. The pair seemed head over heels in love with each other and Laura couldn't be more pleased. But there was a dark cloud looming on the horizon, keeping her awake at night. She inhaled the smell of freshly brewed coffee before taking a sip from her mug.

'How's my favourite niece?' Cally smiled. 'I was hoping you'd bring her along.'

But this conversation was not for Esme's ears. 'She's doing better. The nightmares have all but stopped, thanks to the kitten we bought her.' Esme had found comfort in the little Persian cat that Graham had sourced for her. Turned out he wasn't such a bad guy after all.

She maintained eye contact with her sister. Cally was quick-tempered and Laura didn't want her to take what she was about to say the wrong way.

'There's something I need to ask, and I didn't want Esme here for that.'

Cally's smile faltered. 'Oh yeah? What's wrong? Everything OK?'

'We've not really talked about that day.' Laura ran a finger down the side of her mug to catch the foam that had spilled over the rim. She'd rehearsed the questions that she needed to ask but now her words were falling away.

'You've been busy with Esme, and I've been loved up with James.' Cally's smile returned at the mention of his name. 'I think he's the one.'

'As in *Peep Show* "the one" or actually "the one"?' Laura was referring to their favourite TV comedy.

'Real-life "the one". I've never felt this way about anyone before.'

'Are you sure about that?'

'Of course I'm—' Cally tilted her head. 'What are you getting at?'

Laura's heart beat a little faster. She'd never really challenged her big sister before. There were times when she'd wondered if she was better off letting sleeping dogs lie. But she couldn't move forward until the past was dealt with. She'd had enough nasty surprises to contend with.

'That day, when you sent Fiona into next week . . .' She could still see her sister's face after knocking out the woman who'd been about to tell all. 'You could have killed her.'

'She could have killed *you*,' Cally said firmly. 'That wasn't happening on my watch.'

Laura appreciated her protectiveness, but still, she had questions. 'She was about to tell me what happened to Cindy and Ali. She wasn't any threat.'

That wasn't the story that Laura had fed the police. She'd told them that she was confused. That Fiona had assaulted her once already, resulting in her head wound. Then she had ranted and raved, while waving a bread knife around. When asked if she had been in fear of her life, she'd answered a resounding 'yes'.

'I didn't hear what she was saying,' said Cally. 'All I saw was you, lying bleeding on the floor, while she stood over you, knife in hand.' Her features hardened. 'What did you want me to do, tap her on the shoulder and ask if everything was OK? She could have stabbed us both.'

'Don't be like that, I'm only asking . . .'

'Well, a thank you would be nice. The second I got your voicemail, I dropped everything and drove straight over. I knew by the tone of your voice that something was wrong.'

'I know, and I appreciate it. It could have been so much worse.' Laura offered a weary smile. She played with her wedding ring, trying to build up the courage to ask the next question. Cally was already riled up. How would she react to this?

'Whatever it is, just ask,' Cally sighed. 'Because I don't want to talk about this stuff anymore. You haven't even mentioned James—'

'Did you write to Bruce Wilding in prison?' Laura blurted out.

'Shh!' Cally instantly reddened, looking around the coffee shop. 'Bloody hell, Laura, what if someone hears?'

'So it's true, then?'

Because had it not been, Cally would have laughed. Time stretched out between them. Laura watched her sister fiddle with her necklace. Nibble her bottom lip. Touch her hair.

'Cally?'

'How did you find out?'

'Bruce told me about the letters. We kept in touch.' The last time they'd spoken on the phone, she'd mentioned Cally, and he'd said he'd had letters from a woman with the same name. She could see he thought nothing of it. There were lots of Callys in the world. But he didn't know how fascinated her sister had been with the Wilding case to begin with.

Cally inhaled a long breath. 'I had a crush, alright? It was stupid. I was lonely. I wasn't thinking straight.'

'Did he write back?'

Cally shook her head. 'No. It's mortifying. I feel so stupid . . . especially now that I know he's gay.'

'Bi,' Laura corrected. 'Seriously, though, what were you thinking, writing to a convicted killer?'

'Kettle, pot, black!' her sister retorted, nostrils flared. 'You visited him in prison. I could say the same to you.' They looked at each other in silence as a woman and her daughter walked past. 'Anyway, it's water under the bridge now. I have James and we're really happy—'

'And I couldn't be more pleased for you,' Laura interrupted. 'But are you sure you never had any contact with Bruce or Ali apart from those letters?'

'I swear down,' Cally said. 'What do you take me for?'

'OK, OK, I believe you. I just had to ask.'

Laura swallowed a mouthful of the coffee that was rapidly turning cold. She knew when her sister was lying, and she knew when she was telling the truth. Fiona had already confessed to murdering Ali Wilding. New evidence had been found which backed up her account. She had actually produced Bruce's clothes that she was seen wearing that night, when Ali and Cindy's bodies were hastily disposed of. Her fingerprints had matched those found at the scene, too.

'Then let's put all that stuff behind us,' Cally said. 'I'm done watching true crime.'

'Amen to that,' Laura said, clinking her mug against her sister's. She just hoped that true crime was done with them.

CHAPTER 60

Bruce stepped into the sunlight. The legalities had taken six long months. But, at last, they proved what he'd known all along – he was an innocent man. Everything felt so surreal. It was as if he'd been living in a nightmare and had finally woken up. He turned around and stared up at the walls of the prison that had changed him immeasurably. He had got help inside for his gambling addiction. He'd learned to take responsibility without wanting to end it all. But those were the only good things he would take from that place. It had left him with scars, both physical and mental. He wasn't sure he'd ever be able to sleep properly again. All that time lost. It felt like the world had moved on without him. He had no family, but he had one friend. Yes . . . The prison had given him that much too. Hopefully, he wouldn't fuck it up.

He'd always felt like he was living a lie. He'd tried to deny his true self. He'd grown up feeling at odds with the world and been desperate to fit in with his peers. Ali had felt like the answer. He'd obsessed over their perfect home . . . their perfect life. But he'd driven her to kill their child. Ali had always believed in the afterlife. Not in a fanatic religious way, just a strong belief that something better was waiting for her. Losing her parents had caused her such pain. He should have seen it coming. Her depression had returned. When their perfect life fell apart, there was nothing left for her anymore. But she'd taken Cindy with her. He couldn't forgive her for that.

When he thought of the texts he'd sent – the ones that Ali had discovered on his phone . . . David had texted something about blaming 'David', talking about himself in the third person, because Ali had never suspected him. She was too busy looking at Scarlett. It was only after their dinner, when Scarlett had drunkenly blurted it out, that the truth was finally revealed. Ali had punched Scarlett hard, unable to contain the violent streak that he'd learned to live with. That night, they'd had another argument and Bruce had finally come clean. He'd told her about the house being mortgaged and about David, who he'd slept with. It had taken him years to come to terms with his sexuality. But instead of being apologetic, he'd put the blame on Ali, because that was how it had always been between his mum and dad growing up. He'd learned a lot since then. He wished he could see Ali one last time. To ask her why she hadn't just walked out of his life.

Had Ali thought they would all be together again: her, Cindy, and her parents that she missed so much? Setting him up for the murders had been her final parting shot. But then Fiona had turned up at the house. If only she'd managed to stop Ali. Called an ambulance for Cindy. It might not have been too late. It was a small comfort to know that Cindy had passed away in her sleep, with no knowledge of what was going on. Bruce would never have another child. He didn't deserve one.

Fiona had written to him so many times. Confessed to her crimes in the end. The killer of his sister and wife had a conscience after all. He was grateful for her letters, if only to clear his name. He would never respond to that woman, but he hoped she got the help she needed. He had to let hate go. Fiona didn't know what love was. If she did, she would never have let him take the blame for murdering his wife and child.

He'd already signed on with a literary agent from Aspen Hollow. As Graham said, people needed to know the truth. Only then would Bruce be safe out in the world again.

He closed his eyes against the sun and took a deep breath. How fresh the air felt when you were a free man. His psyche was flooded with gratitude. He was getting a second chance and he'd better not mess this up. He turned as the car pulled up by the kerb, the unique thrumming of a lovingly restored engine by his side.

'They let you out early!' John said, killing the engine and jumping out of the car.

'Or a year too late.'

Bruce had never been so glad to see him. Gone was the dog collar. They didn't need to hide anymore. No more words were needed as they fell into an embrace. Bruce slapped him on the back. A gesture from his days of pretence.

'It's OK.' John grinned, stepping back. 'Nobody cares what we do now.'

He opened the car door and gestured for Bruce to get in. There was a basket of fresh flowers sitting on the back seat. Lilies for Cindy's graveside. John had asked him where he wanted to go first. They'd made many plans for the future. But first, Bruce needed to say goodbye to his little girl. The next hour wasn't going to be easy. He had a lot to atone for.

CHAPTER 61

The house felt so different now, as if the ghosts of the past had moved on. Laura hovered around the landing, touching the beautiful banisters one last time. She could barely believe that 1 Aspen Hollow had finally sold. There were times when her confidence had faltered. So much had happened here. When the news of her attack got out, her buyers had pulled out. She'd almost given up trying to sell the house herself. Six months was the longest it had ever taken for her to shift a property. During that time, all her energy had gone into launching her own estate agency. Soon she wouldn't need to answer to anyone but herself.

Her footsteps echoed in the hall. The overshoes had been packed away for another day, the sales brochures disposed of for recycling. Now it was time to reflect. Valuable lessons had been learned after dealing with Clio at Ridgeway Residential, who had been putting off buyers behind her back. Clio had a vested interest. She'd wanted to buy the property with her cousin at a knock-down price and flip it later on. Her cousin had even posed as a psychic, trying to throw Laura off her stride. No wonder Clio was never in the office when Laura turned up. She'd been sabotaging the sale of the house all along.

It was Shane who'd made Laura see the true beauty in the house. She credited him for the sale.

'Dress it like it's your own home,' he'd said. So she did. She returned the designer furniture and went for full-on cosy aesthetics, with Laura Ashley furnishings and soft touches of pink to break up the earth-toned palette. The soothing colours grounded the home, and she filled the children's rooms with sturdy, chunky furniture and beds made to be jumped on. She thought of Esme as she placed pictures of unicorns on the walls. The furniture rental price was low as the store was grateful for the promo, and it was amazing to see the house reinvented once more.

Laura's Instagram stats had trebled after she sold her story to a leading magazine. She didn't post as much online anymore but received double the number of views when she did. For the first time in a long time she had a decent amount of money in the bank. She was excited for the future. It felt like the old days, when Laura and Shane hadn't taken each other for granted. Now that Shane's parents had backed off, things felt . . . carefree. But still, there were times Laura wondered about her mother-in-law's sudden turnaround. Perhaps her husband's heart attack had been enough to make her see the futility of arguing, or maybe Esme's brush with death had made her see sense. Mrs Taylor-Brown still FaceTimed Shane most nights, but Laura could live with that.

There were voices outside. Laura was ready to hand over the keys. A sudden bout of nerves hit. *There's nothing to worry about*, she told herself. *This is a good thing . . . isn't it?*

Yet, strangely, she was going to miss Aspen Hollow. The neighbours had taken some getting used to, but they were OK.

Billie had decided to stay put after everything came to a head. She'd been more worried about the murders than she had let on – scared of her own neighbours, who she suspected of being involved. She'd always thought Bruce was gay, but believed there was some kind of love triangle going on with Graham in the mix. Who could blame her for being concerned when she thought her neighbours were responsible for the most horrendous of crimes? But now the truth had come out. It was a dreadful story – how Ali had been abusing Bruce all along. Pushed to the limits by his infidelity and gambling debts, she must have felt she had nothing left to live for. Finding out that her home had been mortgaged was the straw that broke the camel's back. She had aimed for the cruellest revenge, framing her husband for murder. It wasn't the first time that she'd hurt him. But then Fiona had turned up.

Laura opened the door, snapped out of her thoughts as Shane's voice rose from outside. He had dropped her off at the house that morning and now he'd arrived to take her home. But who was he talking to? She inhaled a sudden breath as she took in the other person standing there. So he was the mystery buyer? Laura hadn't been expecting that.

'Bruce,' she said, looking him up and down. 'You look . . . you look great!'

He was wearing a crisp white shirt and navy jeans with leather shoes. His teeth appeared whiter, his skin slightly tanned. Rumour had it that he'd sold his story in a seven-figure book deal.

He smiled in response. 'Thanks. I was just saying to Shane, it's the sunlight. That and eating proper food.'

Laura couldn't think of any reason for him to be here other than to pick up the keys. She slipped her hand into her pocket and they jingled as she pulled them out. Laura closed the front door so that he could have the satisfaction of opening it with his key in the lock.

She was more than a little surprised. Since his release from prison, she'd thought Bruce would want to move elsewhere. He'd made some big mistakes in his life. He needed a fresh start. And Laura had always fantasised about a family living in No. 1.

She painted on a smile. 'Congratulations.' She raised the keys. 'Am I right in saying that these are yours?'

But Bruce looked at her, bemused. 'I'm just here to say goodbye. I'm off to Thailand tomorrow. I wanted to wish the new owners luck.'

Laura wasn't convinced that this was the best of ideas, but she smiled regardless. 'Where are they, then?'

'They're here.' Shane touched Laura's shoulder, his smile widening. 'I bought the house. For you . . . and me. Our own place. This time, both our names are on the deeds.'

Laura blinked twice before the news sank in. 'What?'

'I said, I bought—'

'I heard you,' she interrupted, her heartbeat picking up pace. 'I just don't understand. You bought the house? Are you joking? Is this a joke?'

'It was a bargain. I managed to get an extra fifty K knocked off the price. They were desperate to get rid of it.'

'I know.' Laura laughed. 'So you were the mystery buyer. What about your mum and dad?'

'They'll get used to the idea.' He took her hand. 'We need a new start. Something we *both* own.'

'But . . . who paid for it?'

'Mum took our old place back. I get this house in return.' He raised a hand as Laura inhaled a breath to protest. 'It's part of my inheritance. Now this is ours alone. She won't turn up unannounced again.' That much was true. His parents had gone travelling halfway across the world.

'And let's face it,' Shane continued, 'despite everything . . . you've always loved this place.'

Laura forced a smile. That wasn't exactly true. There were times when the house had made her skin crawl. She'd never told her husband because she knew he'd make her pass the listing on to somebody else. Words wouldn't come. She didn't know how to feel.

'What about Esme?' she said at last.

'She's excited.' Shane smiled. Of course. He would have consulted her first.

'Congratulations, Laura.' Bruce smiled. 'I'm glad it's you.'

Bruce. She'd almost forgotten that he was here.

'Are you sure you're OK with this?' she said.

'Over the moon. I couldn't have asked for a better family to move in.' He rested his hands on his hips. 'But it's yours now. Fill it full of happy memories. That's what it was made for.'

After shaking their hands, he left. She watched a car pull up to the drive. Its occupant gave her a wave. John . . . The priest. Laura waved in return. He wasn't wearing a dog collar today. She watched their happy exchange as Bruce jumped into the car. Something told her that John wasn't a prison chaplain anymore.

'I can't believe you bought this place.' Hands shaking, Laura fumbled with the keys.

Shane's eyes were twinkling. He seemed a lot happier these days. 'It's my grand gesture. You know, like in the movies. You're always saying I should be more romantic. Unless you don't want it?'

'I do! Of course I do.' Laura smiled once more.

She was on a better footing this time. Financially independent. No more bullying from Shane's parents now they had backed off. Yet . . . All those nights when this place had given her the chills. The dark presence. The creepy feeling. The lingering fear. It would be OK . . . wouldn't it?

'Hang on, let me take a photo.' Shane was too excited to notice her concerns.

Laura dismissed her fears and shoved the key into the door.

CHAPTER 62

'Anything for me?' Fiona asked hopefully, as the prison guard walked past. A shake of the head was all she was granted. Fiona's shoulders slumped. She'd been so happy to hear that Bruce had been freed, but he'd long forgotten about her. She didn't even have an address to write to anymore.

He was angry, that's all. But he would come around. He must have heard about her confession and all the evidence that she'd come forward with. The clothes she'd worn the night she'd hefted Ali and Cindy's bodies out to Bruce's car. Her fingerprints, which matched the unexplained set they had found in the house that night. That evidence had set Bruce free.

She had burned Ali's journal too, and that was the most damning evidence against him. Those lying entries saying how scared she'd been that Bruce was going to hurt her, when all along she was plotting to kill herself and little Cindy and then frame him for their murders. Fiona had read and reread each page, trying to memorise every word. Setting Bruce up for the crime . . . What a nasty piece of work Ali had been.

Fiona paced her cell, as she often did these days. The door was open; she could go out on to the wing. She was afraid of nobody in here. Not now that she'd put a few of them straight. Fiona liked her privacy, but there was Debbie Wilson, a tough nut who had taken her under her wing. Debbie actually *liked* the thought of Fiona having killed Ali after what she had done. So she was safe. She was warm, and she was fed three times a day. She got plenty of alone time. Her cellmate liked to read. She didn't say much. Not a lot to complain about. Life on the outside was just too hard. Especially now her beautiful house was gone. The news of its new owner had floored her. Bouncy-haired Laura was living there now, according to Debbie.

Debbie was a long-standing prison inmate. She got away with a lot of things. She also had a phone and access to the internet. The Wilding murders fascinated her. Fiona had told her all about them, her exchange for a window into the outside world. Today, Debbie was allowing Fiona to use her secret mobile phone. She had questions, and they couldn't wait.

She'd already tried once before. Her therapist was on leave, according to a message on her office answering machine. Luckily for Fiona, she'd memorised her mobile phone number. She closed the door of her cell and dialled the number, but the ringtone sounded strange.

'Hello?' Josie's voice sounded guarded.

'It's Fiona. I'm—'

'I know who you are. Why are you ringing? The practice isn't open today.' Her voice was sharp and edgy – so different to her previous coaxing tones.

'Why did you tell me to stop the sale of the house?' Fiona's time was limited. If a prison guard caught her with the phone, she'd be in big trouble.

'I . . . I was trying to help you, Fiona.'

'Helping yourself, more like,' Fiona grumbled, head down, voice low. 'I know exactly who you are, Doctor Taylor-Brown.'

Their first meeting had felt so odd. She remembered how she'd thought that the game was up. She'd been spraying graffiti on the wall of 1 Aspen Hollow when she realised that she was being watched. It was before six a.m. – too early to be seen, or so Fiona had thought. But instead of reporting her to the police, Josie had handed her a business card.

'You need help, not criminalising,' she'd said. 'I won't report this as long as you come for therapy. The first session is free.'

'What were you doing there?' Fiona continued. 'You never said. You must have known Laura was taking on the listing. Were you there to sabotage it too?'

Josie's silence spoke volumes.

At last, she replied. 'A few smashed windows weren't going to do any real harm.' A door closed in the background. 'It was never meant to go so far.'

'Really?' Fiona sulked, twirling a strand of her long greying hair. She wasn't taking the blame for this. She'd come to like Laura after bringing her the Dundee cake. But her therapist twisted Fiona's thoughts all out of shape. Josie had never once said that she was doing anything wrong. 'You told me to stop the sale.'

'I never told you to kill her, you crazy bitch!'

Fiona gasped at Josie's sudden outburst, struggling to keep her voice low as a bell rang in the distance. 'You call *me* crazy? I'm not the one going after my daughter-in-law!'

Debbie's internet research had revealed their relationship. The revelation had sent Fiona into a spin. Mrs Josie Taylor-Brown, a woman with a doctorate in psychology and numerous awards, had been using Fiona all along. Why smash windows yourself when you could set someone else up to take the rap?

'Alright . . . alright . . .' Josie exhaled a long breath. 'Let's not do this, OK? What do you want, Fiona? Because I can't afford for any of this to get out. You're not on a prison phone, are you? Are we being recorded?' Panic rose in her well-spoken voice.

'Of course not. What do you take me for? I haven't mentioned you to anyone. Not yet.'

274

'Then what do you want?' Josie's voice grew more strained.

'You can pay for my legal fees. A fancy lawyer should be able to shave a few years off my time inside.' While Fiona didn't *hate* prison, she didn't want to spend the rest of her life locked away. She glanced at her poster of a cute kitten on a branch with the phrase 'Hang in there!'

'Alright.' Josie swallowed loudly down the line. 'I'll arrange it, anonymously. Are we done?'

'For now. But make sure you answer your phone when I ring. You don't want me getting twitchy, Josie, otherwise I'll tell Laura.'

'She won't believe you.'

'Want to take that chance?' Fiona smiled, feeling on top of things again.

By the time their phone call ended, Josie had promised to cover Fiona's legal bills and send her money for goodies in the prison shop. Fiona pocketed Debbie's mobile phone. Josie was utterly terrified. So scared that she'd gone abroad, her tail between her legs.

All the times that Josie had encouraged her to take action to ease her pain. 'Do what you have to do,' she'd said, agreeing with Fiona that Bruce's home shouldn't be put up for sale. 'If only there was a way of stopping the estate agent,' Josie had mused, when they'd met for a coffee one day.

Fiona had thought they were friends, meeting outside the office. But all along she was being used. What had Laura done to deserve that? Families were meant to protect and care for each other, weren't they? But Fiona had grown up in care. She didn't have a family of her own.

Her thoughts became occupied with Laura. She had an adoring husband, and a little girl, too. Her socials revealed a lot. Fiona liked what she'd done with the place. It was more natural, cosier. Laura didn't need to try so hard now; *she* was a good mum. Fiona had been wrong to threaten her. She could see that now. Her steps came to a halt as another thought filtered in. Maybe she could send her a message. Not as herself, not yet. Just a few words of support. She could get to know her husband, find out what made him tick. She could do a little more digging on her daughter. They had a new cat. Esme liked Taylor Swift and unicorns, too.

All thoughts of Bruce left her mind as she focused on the family of three. They could be friends. Laura could come and see her in prison. And one day, when she was free, Fiona could pay them a little visit. Because that's what friends were for.

ACKNOWLEDGEMENTS

I might have written the first draft of this manuscript alone, but it's taken so many amazing people to bring the book to fruition. I'm so grateful to my brilliant agent Madeleine Milburn, who I've been with for many happy years, along with the rest of her amazing team. They are always there when I need them. I'm also truly grateful to my publishers, Thomas & Mercer, with whom I have published so many books now. A special shout-out goes to my lovely (and very wise) editor, Maisie Lawrence, who genuinely cares for the authors in their care. Thanks also to genius editor Ian Pindar, whom I've been lucky enough to work with for several books now. He's got me out of a few tight spots with this particular book!

I'd also like to give a shout-out to the wonderful cover designer Lisa Brewster and copyeditors Gemma Wain and Silvia Crompton, who have helped breathe life into my work.

There are so many great authors that I'm fortunate enough to know, but a special hello to the fabulous Mel Sherratt, a brilliant author and true friend who is always there for me. Speaking of brilliant authors, I'd also like to mention Lisa Cutts, Angela Marsons and John Marrs – wonderful authors and friends who have been a huge inspiration during my writing career. There are so many more, but I can't fit them all in! You know who you are.

Thanks so much to all the readers, book clubbers, book bloggers, and anyone who has read my work. Words cannot cover my gratitude. I mean that from the bottom of my heart. I'd also like to give a shout-out to my ex-colleagues in the police. You have all shaped my writing and I often think of you. Last but certainly not least, to my lovely family. My sons, my daughters and my husband. Thank you for understanding when I'm tapping away on my laptop long into the night.

If your heart was in your mouth as Laura raced to uncover the secrets in the Wildings' house, then *The Village* by Caroline Mitchell will have you absolutely gripped!

Ten years ago, the Harper family disappeared. Their deserted cottage was left with the water running, the television playing cartoons, the oven ready for baking. Where did they go and what really happened?

Available now or read on for an exclusive extract!

PROLOGUE

MARY

1 October 2003

I'm going to drown today. My thoughts are morose as I fight a rising sense of dread. I think it every time we cross to the mainland, but tonight I *know*. *Éireann Rose*, our barnacled half-shell, has served us well, but the little boat will not make a safe crossing tonight. My cheeks burn from the wind, and my shoulders inch upwards as waves lap against our boat. I cradle the tightly swaddled newborn close to my chest. The eye of the lighthouse glares at us, and I stiffen beneath its beam. Gabriel, my husband, sits at the stern. His hand grips the tiller of the outboard motor as he negotiates the choppy Irish Sea. He is a handsome man, but not a good man, and I wish he hadn't roped me into this. Gabriel has the innate ability to take something from every person he meets. But life was a darkened room until he came to Selkie Island, which is why I will do anything to stop him from leaving me.

My nameless charge is a wee thing, no more than six pounds in weight. The rocking motion comforts her. But there are five of us in this boat and her twin fusses in Isla's papoose. Isla, with her almond eyes and trusting nature. She stares at me unblinking, the tip of her tongue in its usual resting place between her slightly parted lips. Shame washes over me because I do not deserve her trust.

The storm has come in quickly and we're stuck between the island and the mainland, bobbing to and fro. Gabriel raises his voice over the noise of the engine.

'It's rough, but we'll get there soon enough.'

So we hold on, because our cargo is precious, and the twinkling lights of the mainland are in view. I turn to Isla to reassure her, but I quickly drop my gaze because I cannot bear for my beloved daughter to see my guilty face. The strobe of the lighthouse reveals a boat in the distance, and it becomes hard to breathe. I think of the people I've left behind. Of the baby in my arms. Suddenly the waves sound like thunder in my ears. Each one crashes like an accusation – *traitor, traitor, traitor* – the spray of angry spittle hitting my face. I taste the salt on my tongue and my emotions rush upon me like the swell of the sea.

This is wrong. I cannot do this. This must end. I peer down at the baby, her little cherub nose barely visible beneath her cocoon.

'I'm sorry,' I whisper.

But the rising winds steal my platitudes. Soon I will come to realise that it's too little, too late.

I never make it to the mainland alive.

CHAPTER 1

CLAIRE

Friday 10 June 2022

The award lies against the wall of our London apartment, a fine layer of dust coating the once shiny glass. The words still burn on my memory: *For outstanding excellence in the field of paediatric research and achievement.* For months it has rested there, untouched since that day. So many times Daniel tried to hang it on the wall, and I barked at him to leave it be. Its presence is a constant reminder, not of my successes but of my failures. I do not deserve the award. It is a reminder of my vanity. How ironic that I was on-stage accepting it the night my patient succumbed to the illness that would claim her young life. An illness that could have been avoided if she hadn't been misdiagnosed. I can still see my sister Susan's waxy face, staring but not seeing as she tries to comprehend the news. I can still hear the screams – the animalistic howl that could come only from a mother who has lost her child. They'd rebounded in the hospital corridors that day, and now they play in a loop in my mind. For once I was powerless to make things right. Too wrapped up with my award, I'd let my family down in the worst possible way. It is my fault that little girl died.

A swirl of warm night air curls around the nape of my neck and plays with my hair. I lean forward from my vantage point on the window ledge of our fifteenth-storey flat, my shoe balancing on the tip of my toes as I sit. Somewhere from inside a hollow voice tells me to climb back inside. As always during times of stress, my husband's Irish accent has become more pronounced. Shaky with panic, he reaches out his hand.

'Please. You're not thinking straight. Come inside. I can't do this on my own. Not again. We can talk things through.'

He looks so handsome tonight, the scar from his cleft lip only adding to the character of his face. I should feel guilty. I know this is wrong. Daniel's life has been touched by tragedy. He lost both his parents at an early age. What sort of monster am I, leaving him like this? But my pain is insufferable and relief so close.

The warm breeze tickles the sole of my foot as my shoe dangles on my toe.

'Stay there,' I say in a level voice. 'Take one more step and I'll jump.'

I cannot unbreak the broken. There is no sliding back to normality. Such overwhelming guilt and loss are impossible to dismiss.

London looks beautiful tonight. The air feels thick and warm, and black cabs beep while pedestrians mill on the streets below. I inhale a deep breath, the smell of street food and petrol fumes enveloping my senses.

Daniel gestures at me. 'Please, darlin', just . . . just come back inside. I can help you. Please. Come in.' He is fighting hard to stay calm but a sheen of sweat glazes his forehead.

I edge forward on the thick ledge. We live high enough for me not to survive the fall. A familiar depressive blackness is closing in on me as a physical weight on my chest. I can't do this anymore.

'For Christ's sake, will you listen to me . . . ?' His gaze locks on to mine. 'Just . . . just come back inside and we can talk about this . . . OK? Are you listening? Because I love you, Claire. Do you hear me?'

His pleading is laced with urgency. He knows his words are having little effect. His eyes are wild with panic as he fights an internal battle. I can almost read his thoughts. If he lunges for me now, he will never reach me in time. My shoe slips from my foot on to the streets below. I kick off the second shoe and feel a sense of freedom as the breeze skims both my feet. Soon the pain will be over. But my husband edges closer, and I cannot risk him pulling me inside.

'Step back, or I'll chase them all the way down,' I threaten.

Below us, life goes on as normal, but our world is ripping apart at the seams. I watch him retreat, analysing him one last time. Deep down, he knows these moments are important, but everything is moving too quickly and he is powerless to stop it. I imagine his heart beating with the force of a steam train in his chest. If I ever doubted that he loved me before, I have my answer now. This man loves me more than anything in the world.

But my suffering is eating me from the inside out. This is not a cry for help. This is me, wanting out from this world. I'm not strong enough to shoulder the burden of my actions another day. Daniel had smiled at me tonight, not realising that I was brighter only because the end was in sight. But now he is home early, standing behind me as he tries to buy enough time for the emergency services to save my life.

'Please . . . I can't live without you.' My husband continues to plead.

'Then come with me,' I whisper, but he looks so horrified at the prospect that I quickly regret my words.

'I . . . I can't.'

I sigh. The wind that swirls around me whispers that the time for talking is over. I am drawing out the inevitable and the heavy stomp of boots in the hall means the emergency services are here. Daniel must have called them. By the way he is holding his phone, they are probably still on the line. I feel the sting of betrayal. This was a private, intimate moment, now being played to the outside world. Pedestrians have noticed and are being directed away. I whisper a silent thanks as I don't want to hurt anyone on the way down.

'Claire . . . look at me, will you?' Daniel steps forward and I move towards the edge.

'No!' he screams, his eyes brimming with tears. 'Please! Come back inside!'

'Sorry,' I whisper. 'I love you.' Tears blur the edges of my world. 'But I can't do this anymore.'

I must make this quick. I close my eyelids, having decided I do not wish to see the ground rushing up to greet me as I fly.

'No!' Arms outstretched, Daniel lunges, but we both know he'll never make it in time.

I push myself forward and jump.

CHAPTER 2

DANIEL

I thought my wife was getting better. I fooled myself into believing she had turned a corner. I should have seen the clues. Despite the smile she had painted on, her award still lay against our apartment wall. She had been unable to even think about returning to her job. I knew she loved me, but not enough to live through the pain she must have been feeling when she climbed on to the window ledge. I honestly believed she had managed to drag herself out of the black hole that had claimed her. She looked so beautiful tonight. The hollows beneath her eyes hadn't seemed quite so pronounced, and her smile had made a welcome return. But the second I stepped inside our apartment, I knew there was something wrong. Perhaps it was the kiss of the outside breeze, or the sense of despair which hung thick in the air. My heart flipped an extra beat, my senses heightened, my body taut. I stepped inside the living room, and my attention was drawn to our floor-length net curtains swirling in the breeze. I blinked at the sight of Claire sitting on our window ledge. My brain tried to comprehend the vision before me, trying but failing to reject the thought that she could fall to her death.

'Claire!' I called, the word a shriek on my lips. I was shocked into sobriety, gripping the back of our leather sofa. There was no point in asking what she was doing. It was plain to see. 'Please,' I said, my heart hammering in my chest. 'You're not thinking straight. Come inside, we can talk things through.'

She glared a warning. If I ran at her, she'd jump before I reached her on the window ledge. During the chaos that followed, I activated the emergency call feature on my iPhone. Cold dread rose inside me as I begged my wife to come in. There was nothing in her expression. No fear, just quiet acceptance. Tears rose in my eyes as I watched my wife give up on the life we shared. It was like speaking to a statue. Each time I tried to inch forward, she did too. It was a battle I was going to lose. I could feel her slipping away as she warned me off. For a fleeting second, her eyes brightened.

'Come with me,' she whispered, and the flicker of hope inside me died.

'I . . . I can't,' I instantly replied. What kind of madness was this?

She stood up on to the ledge, ignoring my screams to come inside. Then she closed her eyes and jumped. I lunged towards her, stumbling as I grasped the air. I was too late.

There was a sudden flurry of movement. A flash of fluorescent jacket as the firefighter abseiled from the apartment above. Then a scream, a firm voice. I clung to the window ledge as my legs became weak. Thank God.

Claire was safe.

ABOUT THE AUTHOR

A former police detective, Caroline Mitchell now writes full time.

She has worked in CID and specialised in roles dealing with vulnerable victims – high-risk victims of domestic abuse and serious sexual offences. The mental strength shown by the victims of these crimes is a constant source of inspiration to her, and Mitchell combines their tenacity with her knowledge of police procedure to create tense psychological thrillers.

Originally from Ireland, she now lives in a woodland village on the outskirts of Lincoln with her husband.

You can find out more about her at www.caroline-writes.com or follow her on X @caroline_writes, Instagram @Caroline_writes or at www.facebook.com/CMitchellAuthor.

Follow the Author on Amazon

If you enjoyed this book, follow Caroline Mitchell on Amazon to be notified when the author releases a new book!

To do this, please follow these instructions:

Desktop:

1) Search for the author's name on Amazon or in the Amazon App.

2) Click on the author's name to arrive on their Amazon page.

3) Click the 'Follow' button.

Mobile and Tablet:

1) Search for the author's name on Amazon or in the Amazon App.

2) Click on one of the author's books.

3) Click on the author's name to arrive on their Amazon page.

4) Click the 'Follow' button.

Kindle eReader and Kindle App:

If you enjoyed this book on a Kindle eReader or in the Kindle App, you will find the author 'Follow' button after the last page.

Printed in Dunstable, United Kingdom